RAVE REVIEWS FOR DAWN MACTAVISH

PRISON

"MacTavish melds the _____ *ne Opera* with the histori_____ *r* an enthralling, non-sto_____ and history? You'll clamor for more.

—*RT Book Reviews*

"The action-packed story line uses real persona and a period of dangerous unrest as a backdrop to this excellent love story. . . . One of the subgenre's top novels of the year."

—*Midwest Book Review*

"What a completely engrossing tale! . . . Ms. MacTavish once again [writes] a dynamic and vital story that captured my imagination from the first page to the last."

—*CK2S Kwips and Kritiques*

THE PRIVATEER

"Dawn MacTavish transports readers back in time with this enchanting tale. *The Privateer* is full of characters you'll either love or love to hate but I can guarantee you won't be bored as you immerse yourself in this Regency story line. Beautifully written Ms. MacTavish! This is Regency storytelling at its best!"

—*Romance Junkies*

"I readily recommend *The Privateer*. It's an exciting book with a fresh plot and likable, lifelike characters."

—*Romance Reviews Today*

"Adventure on the high seas, family drama, rescue from a fate worse than death, passionate love; what more can a romance reader ask for? Dawn MacTavish draws us right in and paints her absorbing story with authentic historical detail in *The Privateer*."

—*Single Titles*

THE FAST & THE FRAUDULENT

He came out of nowhere, his face hidden behind a feathered hawk mask. All that was visible were his piercing, glacier blue eyes. Alice was in his arms before she knew what was happening, and her breath caught in a strangled gasp. He whisked her onto the ballroom floor at such speed she feared her headdress would come flying off and she would be revealed as the imposter she was.

"And who is this lovely creature?" the man said. The burr of his deep, cultured voice sent shivers snaking down her spine. "Not someone I've seen before, that is certain."

Alice ignored the question. "And not someone you are likely to see again," she returned. "Do you always engage your dancing partners with the velocity of a cannonball, sir?"

"I beg your pardon, my lady," he said, inclining his hooded head in a bow. His masculine scent threaded through her nostrils, leather and lime, with traces of tobacco, and the ghost of recently drunk wine. She inhaled deeply. "I was so caught up in the moment, and so anxious to snatch you up before another bested me that I quite forgot myself. You looked so . . . vulnerable standing there alone. I couldn't help but come to your rescue."

Other *Leisure* books by Dawn MacTavish:

PRISONER OF THE FLAMES
THE PRIVATEER
THE MARSH HAWK

Writing as Dawn Thompson:

THE BRIDE OF TIME
THE RAVENING
THE BROTHERHOOD
BLOOD MOON
THE FALCON'S BRIDE
THE WATERLORD
THE RAVENCLIFF BRIDE

DAWN MACTAVISH

Counterfeit Lady

LEISURE BOOKS NEW YORK CITY

*This book is dedicated to DeborahAnne Macgillivray, for all the
things she did to help my sister for the final two years of her life.
And for giving Miss Fuzz a good home. Without her protecting
my sister's works when she became ill, these final novels would
have been lost, and that would have been too sad.*

Diane "Candy" Thompson

A LEISURE BOOK®

November 2009

Published by

Dorchester Publishing Co., Inc.
200 Madison Avenue
New York, NY 10016

ISBN 10: 0-8439-6321-2
ISBN 13: 978-0-8439-6321-2
E-ISBN: 978-1-4285-0724-1

Visit us online at www.dorchesterpub.com.

Counterfeit Lady

Chapter One

London, 1815

No, my lady, I couldn't!" Alice said to Lady Clara's reflection in the cheval glass. "Just think of the consequences if we were to be found out. We would both go down in disgrace for doing such a thing, and I would lose my position. Not to mention what I would face were my father to hear of it." Backing away from the mirror, she fumbled with the laces on the gown. She just wanted to see how she looked in it. How could she resist? It was so beautiful. Marie Antoinette. The fabric was silk, the color of butter and just as soft. The ivory side panniers sprigged with dainty roses hugged the cinched-in waist, and the daring bodice plunged so low along the décolleté, it barely covered her charms. One deep breath would surely render her indecent.

She only meant to slip the costume on for a moment. It was one thing to play dress-up in the privacy of her own chamber, but to attend a masked ball pretending to be someone she wasn't was to invite every kind of mischief. Such behavior from the daughter of an austere Methodist minister was unthinkable. She knew better.

"Nonsense!" Lady Clara insisted, her mouth pursed in an unattractive pucker. "You agreed the minute you put that frock on." Spinning Alice back toward the glass, she shoved Alice's hands away and began to do up the laces herself. "Where is the harm? No one knows me here as yet. Besides, you are my paid companion. You must do as I say."

"I must do as your lady aunt says," Alice corrected her. "And she would never approve of such a thing."

"Ahhh, but she isn't here, is she, Alice?" Lady Clara said. "And she'll never know, will she? Hold still! How can I get these laces right with you wiggling about like that? There's nothing for it. You're going. You may as well resign yourself."

"They will find me out the minute I open my mouth, my lady," said Alice.

"Twaddle! Your voice is just as cultured as mine."

"They'll know! Lady Pembroke will know. I'm not good at deception."

"How will they know?" Lady Clara asked, giving a ruthless tug on the laces that challenged Alice's breathing and balance, not to mention the décolleté. "We're close enough in age, both fair, and your deportment is without flaw. How are they going to know you aren't who you say you are?"

"They just will. My ineptitude will give me away. I lack the experience. I am not schooled in the ways of the upper classes. I know naught of the proper behavior for masques and fetes and grand parties. I lack the confidence to be convincing. Besides, you are supposed to have a chaperone, my lady. It's scandalous to attend without one. Think of the on-dits . . . your reputation!"

Lady Clara shrugged. "Say that Aunt Regina is detained at Greenbriar Grange due to a spring complaint, and dealing with damages to the grange caused by foul weather. No one will question it. Storms are always brewing in the North Country at this time of year, especially along the coast. You'll see soon enough. We always repair to the Yorkshire estate after the little season. Aunt Regina detests staying in town through the winter. She's bored with Mayfair once the social whirl winds down, and the cottage in Wiltshire is too small for a winter stay."

Alice disputed that. She'd been hired at the cottage, an impressive three-story Tudor tucked away in a parklike setting of rolling green and patchwork hills, not far from her father's church on the outskirts of Warminster. "But she isn't at the Yorkshire estate, my lady. She's at the cottage still," she pointed out.

"And who is going to know that, pray?" Lady Clara snapped, arms akimbo. "Nobody—unless you tell them. Just do as I say. You cannot say she's at the cottage. You know as well as I do that no one would believe a storm has delayed her from *Wiltshire*. The climate is much too temperate. And you don't dare tell the truth. If it ever got out that she suffers from rheumatism, I shudder to imagine the consequences."

"All well and good, but they're bound to know something is amiss when I arrive without a chaperone. It just isn't done. If we must do this, why can't we both go? That is what your aunt would expect.

Only, I could go as you and you as me. We would be above reproach in that case . . . at least on the surface, and you would be close enough to coach me if needs must."

"I cannot do that," Lady Clara snapped. "I have . . . other plans. Just say that your aunt did not want you to miss the masque on her account, since she has arranged an introduction for you, and insisted that you come. If there are repercussions, they will fall upon Aunt Regina, not upon me. It would serve her right for conspiring to shackle me to that coxcomb Nigel Farnham behind my back. If anyone persists, just say your companion is coming on shortly or something. I've attended these house affairs. Now, if it were Almack's, it would be out of the question. Those old peahens who call themselves patronesses are more like jailers. We could never pull it off. But a private house ball—a *masque* at that—why, all manner of shocking things go on at such affairs. They will be so castaway, so caught up in the festivities, no one will give your behindhand chaperone a second thought, believe me."

Alice fingered the sumptuous fabric. "I don't know," she hedged. "You actually believe they will just take me at my word that I am Lady Clara Langly when I arrive?" She couldn't imagine it.

"You'll announce yourself to the footmen, and show the invitation if you are questioned. We've been all round this, Alice. Now sit and let me help you with this wig and hat. The coach is waiting."

"The coachman!" Alice cried, with a start. "He will know me!"

"Your own father wouldn't know you in this outlandish headpiece and that feather mask."

"Don't be too sure, my lady," Alice despaired, watching her short-cropped curls disappear beneath the towering wig. "If you don't want to be introduced to the earl, why not send your excuses? Say you are indisposed, and just stay at home. Neither of us need go."

"I cannot do that," said Lady Clara. "Aunt Regina engineered the invitation to Lady Pembroke's masque to the sole purpose of negotiating a match for me with that foppish toady, Farnham. She will trounce me with that dreadful cane of hers if I do not attend. She'll want a full report. I am counting upon you to quash it!"

"How can you accuse the man, when you've never even met?"

"Hah! I have it on good authority that he has a nose like a hawk, he dresses like a pink of the ton, and he drools and spits on you when he talks! Why, he even pads his spindly legs to fill out his hose and wears a *corset*." Lady Clara shuddered. "Besides all that, he has a reputation—heaven above only knows how. If you think I'll settle for the likes of a hawk-nose toady who preys upon the affections of young ladies with no thought of marriage at the end of it, you can think again, even if he is Earl of Romney. Besides, I have a suitor—an earl of my own—and he doesn't have to pad *anything*."

"What authority, my lady? Who told you such things?"

"Isobel Rutledge, and I wish you would cease

with the *my lady* and simply call me Clara as I've repeatedly asked you, at least when we're alone."

"I have only met Isobel Rutledge once, but that
was enough to be wary of her judgments as ironclad, and as to the issue of addressing you as 'my
lady,' my lady, I prefer to keep things in their proper
perspective."

Lady Clara shrugged. "Very well, suit yourself. It
shan't matter for long in any case." The last was spoken in a dark mutter, and Alice pounced on it.

"What is that supposed to imply?" she asked.

"Oh, nothing," Lady Clara warbled, jabbing the
last hatpin in place. "There! You're done! Now, hurry.
You don't want to make a grand entrance do you?"
She raised Alice to her feet and propelled her toward
the chamber door.

"Why are you rushing me, my lady? What are
you up to?" Alice cried. She gasped, as realization
struck. "You mean to sneak out and meet that rap-
scallion tonight!" she cried. "You *do*! That's why you
won't trade places and go with me. Oh, my lady!"

"When will I ever get a better chance?" admitted
Lady Clara, primping before the mirror. "It's been a
challenge, what with Aunt Regina always underfoot.
She wouldn't approve of him, of course. He does have
a bit of a reputation, but that only makes him all the
more appealing."

"What have you threatened the servants with to
keep silent?"

"Nothing you need concern yourself about. Just
do as I've told you, and discourage Farnham. That
is the whole purpose of this little farce. I won't have

that coil hovering over my head like a dark cloud for the rest of the season. See that you put paid to it. Well, what are you waiting for? Go!"

Alice was well aware of Lady Clara's suitor, though she did not know his identity; Clara had used her enough in the past as a means to cover her assignations with the man. She wasn't supposed to know this, and Lady Clara wasn't aware that she did, but one would have had to be blind not to have seen, and Alice was hardly that. Six months in the Langly family's employ had opened her eyes to many things—far more than James Jessup, her minister father, could have anticipated, much less approved of, when he'd arranged for the position. He'd given her a choice: go into respectable service as a governess or companion, or marry one of the parish locals. Having no desire to settle into a loveless marriage with some simpleminded farm laborer or sheep farmer handpicked by her father, she had chosen what she considered the lesser of two evils. That is, she'd considered the job that way until now, as she approached the Langly carriage pretending to be someone she wasn't. Never was it more evident that she was out of her element.

Lady Clara was right about one thing, however: the coachman set the steps on the carriage without batting an eye. Alice climbed inside, mindful of her oversized headdress in close quarters, wondering how the women of Marie Antoinette's day ever managed so much weight on their heads. She decided that they must have had sturdier necks than she. Hers was already beginning to cramp, and she dreaded the prospect of dancing in such an encumbrance. Perhaps she could engineer an early introduction to the earl and bow out gracefully. That was the plan, and she leaned back against the tufted leather squabs and tried to muster composure.

There was no question that it was wrong, this scandalous gambit, but there was a certain air of irresistible excitement at the prospect nonetheless. Becoming a lady for a night—how many commoners had dreamed that dream, and here she was, about to have it come true. To see firsthand how the ton behaved at such functions as one of them was her secret fantasy since she'd cast off her leading strings. It was a delicious temptation, and she hadn't been equal to it. Her father would be ashamed of her participating in such a deception, but it was only for one night, and he would never know. Where was the harm? She had almost let Lady Clara entirely convince her. Still, there was that irksome little demon jabbing deep inside that refused to allow her to enjoy the situation completely.

Lady Pembroke's town house was in Hanover Square, and the coach tooled down George Street before she was ready to face it. The stately houses there were in the German style, built during the first George's reign. The lane broadened as they neared High Street, giving a panoramic view of the area, including the small, gated park in the center. Alice gasped in spite of herself. Narrow though the properties were, they were deep and well landscaped, with hedges and gardens and manicured walks. When the coach squeaked to a halt before a particularly fine one with an apron of rusticated stone on the facade, she gasped again. It was too late to turn back. The steps were set, and the door swung open in the coachman's gloved hand.

Alice stepped down. Lively music rode the evening breeze. Candles inside oiled parchment sleeves, like fairy lights, lined the walk. The door was open, flanked by footmen in wine-and-gold-colored livery, standing ramrod rigid, waiting. Somehow she managed to announce herself, and again Lady Clara was right. Neither questioned her. She didn't even have to present the invitation tucked safely away in her reticule.

Caught up in the thrill of the moment and emboldened by her success, Alice entered the ballroom, where a gallop was in progress. Dazzled by the spectacle, she kept to the fringes of the room, observing the gathering. Men—some in costume, some in flowing, hooded dominos sporting all manner of masks, from birds to devils—kept time to the music with ladies decked out in every garb and plumage imaginable. Alice was pleased that she seemed the only Marie Antoinette in attendance.

Absorbed in that observation, she scarcely saw the advance of a tall man in a billowing black hooded domino. He came out of nowhere, his face hidden behind a feathered hawk mask. All that was visible were his piercing, glacier blue eyes. She was in his arms before she knew what was happening.

Alice's breath caught in a strangled gasp. He whisked her onto the ballroom floor at such a speed, she feared her headdress would come flying off her head. It would have done, if the gallop were still in progress. Fortunately, it had ended. When had that happened? The musicians had begun one of the new French quadrilles. She was never more grateful than she was in that moment that her father had engaged a dancing master for her from amongst his congregation as part of the preparation for her new situation. Aside from the gift of her beloved sorrel mare, Treacle, when she was little more than a child, the dancing lessons were the only extravagance he had ever bestowed upon her.

"And who is this lovely creature?" the man said. The burr of his deep, cultured voice sent shivers snaking down her spine. "Not someone I've seen before, that is certain."

Alice ignored the question. "And not someone you are likely to see again," she returned. "Do you always engage your dancing partners with the velocity of a cannonball, sir?"

"I beg your pardon, my lady," he said, inclining his hooded head in a bow. His masculine scent threaded through her nostrils, leather and lime, with traces of tobacco and the ghost of recently drunk wine. She inhaled him deeply.

"I was so caught up in the moment and so anxious to snatch you up before another bested me that I quite forgot myself. You looked so . . . vulnerable standing there alone. I couldn't help but come to your rescue."

"Do you always prey upon vulnerable young ladies, sir? That doesn't speak well of your character, does it? It makes you out as one of those rakes one hears so much about." His hand was warm against her side as he turned her. The heat radiated through his glove as he caught her fingers and squeezed them familiarly, swinging her outward to complete the step. The caress was not part of the dance, and her heart leaped as his hand moved in hers. Perhaps it wasn't prudent that she'd likened him to a rake; she could very well have pegged him nicely. It was moments like this that made her wish she had more experience with men, and any at all with the enigmatic *aristocratic* male.

"I'm off on the wrong foot . . . again," he said, the words riding a sigh. "I beg you to forgive my want of conduct, dear lady. I am often too bold. It is my most grievous fault."

He sounded sincere, but Alice was wary. It was hard to be certain, when his elaborate feathered mask hid all but those penetrating eyes, and his closeness was doing such strange things to her equilibrium and her innermost regions as well. It was as though a flurry of butterflies had been set loose in her stomach. She had never felt like this in her dancing master's arms.

Yes, being a minister's daughter had definitely left her lacking when it came to dealings with members of the opposite sex. All such associations were strictly prohibited. She hadn't given it much thought until now. The sudden realization that she was no match for the advances of an obviously experienced gentleman caused her hands to perspire until her demigloves stuck to her palms. There was only one defense. She had to keep him at his distance. But how, when he had her so firmly in his clutches?

"You haven't answered my question," he said, bending close as he turned her again. "With whom am I having the pleasure of this dance?"

"Someone who is allowing it to avoid a scene," she responded. "If this were not a masque, and we danced without being properly introduced, there would be a scandal."

"I see," he mused. "You intend to wait until we unmask and I corner our gracious hostess to initiate a formal introduction, is that it?"

"Yes . . . if I'm still here, that is." Did her voice really quaver?

"But you've just arrived."

"Just so, and I can leave whenever I wish."

"You know, I could easily inquire of the footman who admitted you as to your identity, dear lady," he said. That rumbling baritone voice reverberated through her in a most alarming manner. His twinkling eyes blazed with recklessness. She didn't need to see the rest of his face to be certain he was in earnest.

"You could," she said, "but to what purpose? We shan't meet again."

He nearly misstepped. "And why is that?"

"Because I do not wish it, sir," she said.

The quadrille ended, and he bowed dutifully over her hand and kissed it. Her instinct was to pull away, but she didn't. She hadn't offered it. He had taken a bold liberty, sliding his hand down her arm until he'd captured it. To her relief, no one seemed to notice. Lady Clara had been right when she'd said such private balls were more relaxed and quite the scandal. All around her men and women, shockingly half-castaway already, though the night was young, were behaving in a manner her father would have deemed lewd and vulgar. The gentleman who had hold of her now was not the only male in the ballroom taking bold liberties. A dandy who had whisked his partner into a recessed alcove behind a potted fern had plunged his hand down inside the woman's bodice, and more than one couple was straying from the dance floor in search of other such intimate retreats.

It was a long moment before he released Alice's hand, and not before his fingers lightly caressed the tender flesh of her palm again through the lace. That they were both gloved, preventing them the intimacy of touching skin to skin, did not spare her. Hot blood surged to her temples. Thank divine Providence for feathered masks! She could only imagine the color of her cheeks, especially now, when those glacier blue eyes shot up and met hers so seductively.

"We shall see, my lady," he murmured, sketching a proper bow as he reeled away. "We . . . shall see."

The orchestra was striking up a scandalous *valse à deux temps*, and Alice wasted no time losing herself in the throng. Her father had drawn the line when it came to her dancing master's teaching her that dance, citing that it was much too familiar for a proper young lady to indulge in. Lady Clara had no such reservations, however, and was only too glad to instruct her one rainy afternoon. That notwithstanding, Alice made her way to an unoccupied secluded alcove, where she watched the couples step out on the ballroom floor from behind pillars and potted topiaries.

Her mysterious partner was nowhere in sight, but that gave her no comfort. He'd appeared out of nowhere before; he could do so again. There was something in the sound of that last *We shall see* that didn't bode well.

Tucking her voluminous skirts behind the pillars, she tried to put him out of her mind and concentrate upon the other men at the gathering in search of Lady Clara's spindly-legged and drooling toady, Nigel Farnham. Only one thing was certain. She had to settle that situation and take her leave before it came time to unmask.

There were several likely subjects. Two of them seemed rather old, but since Lady Clara hadn't addressed the subject of age, Alice couldn't dismiss them out of hand. The third seemed more likely. He was the right age, dressed as Henry VIII—padded legs and all, which were easy to detect through white hose that had become twisted from dancing. His abundant paunch, evidently left uncorseted in view of the costume, would certainly have been laced under ordinary circumstances. It was grotesque. All that remained was to meet and discourage the man. That shouldn't be too difficult. She'd already managed such a task once since she arrived. Hadn't she?

Glancing back toward the ballroom arch, she noticed a full-figured though graceful older woman in pastoral costume, whose head was inclined in conversation with one of the footmen who had admitted Alice earlier. Evidently, all the guests were accounted for, and the servants had moved inside. After a moment, the woman floated in her direction. Her mask was attached to a ribbon-wrapped wand, and she held it away from her face as she approached. Could this be her hostess? It must be. Amelia Armbrewster, Countess Pembroke, to be sure. Alice smoothed her gown and squared her posture.

"My poor Lady Clara," the woman gushed. "Can you ever forgive me for not being on hand to greet you and your dear aunt? There was a . . . domestic emergency that needed my attention." She craned her neck, observing the gathering through the eyeholes in the mask now. "Where is she—your aunt?"

"Au-Aunt Regina is detained at Greenbriar Grange, my lady," Alice said. "A spring complaint and concern over damages done by a dreadful storm that needed her immediate attention prevented her from making the journey with us. She sent us on ahead of another tempest that was threatening, else we be delayed and miss many of the events. She should be joining us soon now." She'd gotten past the first lie, but more were sure to follow, and she detested them.

"Surely, you haven't come *alone* tonight?"

Alice moistened dry lips. "I . . . m-my . . . Aunt Regina insisted that I come tonight in any case, and make my predicament known to you," she answered. "She has arranged an . . . an introduction to take place this evening, I believe?" The orchestra was taking a break between dances, and Alice glanced toward the spindly-legged King Henry

VIII. He was conversing with a devil, complete with pitchfork, and several domino-clad gentlemen over glasses of wine and ratafia at the refreshment table nearby. The quicker the introduction, the quicker she could leave and resume her proper identity. The experience thus far had taught her one thing, if nothing else: she hadn't lied when she'd said she had no talent for deception.

Her heart was hammering against her ribs. Perspiration was running in rivulets between her breasts. Her cheeks had to have turned scarlet, judging from the heat they generated beneath the feather mask, and she'd begun to tremble. How would she ever be able to extend her hand to the man while it was shaking so?

"Ahhh, yes, with Lord Romney," said the countess, following Alice's eyes toward the gentlemen across the way. "Well, this is most irregular. There would have been other opportunities for a proper introduction. I do not know what gets into Regina at times. I shall have a word with her about this, to be sure."

"Oh, please don't do that, my lady!" Alice panicked. "She has evidently presumed upon your friendship to keep watch of me in her absence. That was wrong of her. But the fault is still mine. I should have known better."

The countess clicked her tongue. "The very idea, sending you out unescorted, *unchaperoned*! What could she have been thinking? You have a companion do you not? Where, pray, is she, my dear? Why didn't she accompany you?"

"A sudden indisposition, my lady," Alice said. She dared not say she was coming on shortly, as Lady Clara had suggested. Lady Pembroke's guests might be foxed, but the hostess was not. The countess was far too proper for that, and far too clever to be duped by such a feeble excuse—which meant another detestable lie. "The sudden change of climate has rendered her prostrate, I fear," she murmured.

"Hmmm. Well, that is most unfortunate," said the countess. "She must indeed be fragile if a change in the climate from Yorkshire to London has taken her to her bed. I am surprised that Regina would employ such a person, but then, good help is impossible to find these days. Well, never mind. We shall salvage what we can of the situation. I shall serve in her stead, have no fear, and once the guests unmask, I shall introduce you to Lord Romney."

"W-when will that be, my lady?" Alice said in a small voice. "I have never attended a masque before."

"Well, of course you haven't, dear child. Such things vary, but tonight we shall unmask at midnight."

"But that's nearly three hours away!" Alice blurted. She was sorry the minute the words were out. Did it make her appear too anxious—too forward? The countess lowered her mask. By the look of her slack jaw and raised eyebrow, of course it did. Alice's heart sank. "It's just that I'm embarrassed now, having come without a chaperone," she recovered. "And I would really like to have the introduction over with, so I may leave before anyone else realizes that I've made such a glaring social blunder. Protocols are so much stricter here in town. I do not wish to become the topic of London gossip."

"Nonsense," said the countess. "I've just said I shall chaperone you, dear, and I did promise Regina that I would take you under my wing, as it were, this season."

"That is kind of you, my lady," said Alice. "But I fear this headdress is giving me a dreadful crick in my neck. I really must decline."

"Well, we shan't waste the opportunity, then," the countess said. She turned toward the gentlemen still gathered at the table. "Nigel," she called, steering Alice toward them. "This is the young lady I told you about. May I present Lady Clara Langly?" Then to Alice, "Nigel Farnham, Lord Romney, my dear."

All three men turned around. Alice's eyes were riveted to Henry VIII. The closer she came to the man, the more odious he seemed. Nonetheless, she steeled herself and extended her hand. Discouraging him wasn't going to be too difficult a chore. Even at an arm's length of distance, he reeked of strong drink, body odor, and onions. He was repulsive.

Alice squared her posture. The ruse was nearly over. Emboldened at that prospect, she even managed a smile. Henry VIII didn't smile back, however. He looked nonplussed, and her smile dissolved as the domino-clad gentleman on his left set his glass aside and stepped forward, taking her offered hand.

"My lady," he said, raising it to his lips. "We meet again."

"You?" Alice cried, her eyes oscillating between the man who had captured her hand and the one she was so certain she'd come to meet. "B-but . . . but . . ." she stammered. How could this be, when Henry VIII fitted Lady Clara's description so exactly?

The countess uttered a strangled sound. "You two have already met?" she said, her confusion plain.

The earl flashed a lopsided smile that weakened Alice's knees. Were those dimples, peeking out from behind the fearsome hawk mask? How bizarre.

"Not formally," he said in the husky baritone that resonated in the very marrow of her bones. "I had the pleasure of a dance with Lady Clara earlier," he said. "It was all quite anonymous, of course. This is a masque, after all." Did the man *wink*? Cheeky devil!

"M-my lord," Alice got out, reclaiming her hand, as though she'd pulled it out of a spring trap. All she could think of was that Isobel Rutledge must have a bizarre sense of humor to have painted him as such a toady. *I'd love to know the whys and wherefores of that!* she thought. Her embarrassment was profound, her cheeks positively on fire beneath the feathers. Her moist skin had begun to itch from those, and she resisted the urge to scratch, though her fingers worked to do just that.

"Lady Clara has expressed a wish to take her departure," said the countess.

"So she said to me earlier," the earl returned. "I do hope I can persuade her to change her mind."

"I'm sorry, but no," said Alice. "The headdress . . .
It's given me a wretched headache, my lord. I must
cry off."

"Poor child," the countess crooned. "Since she
won't be here at midnight, I thought it best to make
the introduction before she takes her leave, since I
did promise her aunt. Then, when next you meet,
that bothersome formality will be behind you."

"Am I not to have a glimpse of my lady's face
before she departs?" the earl said silkily.

Drat and blast! Alice regretted the mental outburst the minute the expletive entered her mind.
What was happening to her? First consenting to
take part in such a scandalous deception, and now
profanity. Fine behavior for a minister's daughter!
Worse still, she really didn't want to leave the
masque. She was bedazzled. It was wonderful. She'd
never imagined, much less experienced, the like,
and if truth were to be told, she was just as curious
to see his face as he seemed to be to see hers. She
dared not give in to that temptation.

"Another time, my lord," she said, sketching a
curtsy as she backed away. Henry VIII and the
devil had moved on, but several other gentlemen
were still staring with not a little interest. One was
costumed in the long black cassock of a vicar. That
set her feet in motion.

"At least let me see you to your carriage," the earl
called after her.

"No!" Alice cried, her quavering voice turning
heads. "Please do not trouble yourself. I can manage quite well on my own." She sketched another

curtsy. Was that even appropriate? She was so distressed, she'd forgotten the proper etiquette for such a situation. "My lord . . . my lady," she said, streaking toward the ballroom arch, and escape.

"May I call?" the earl asked, his voice raised over the strident party hubbub.

Alice stumbled to a halt. "*No!* I mean . . . That is . . . I think not, my lord," she called over her shoulder as she fled.

Chapter Two

Well, well," Nigel mused, watching Alice disappear through the ballroom arch, a swish of buttery silk challenging the woodwork. The air she stirred spread her scent. It threaded through his nostrils: sweet clover, with just a hint of violets. *Mmmm, wildflowers . . . How refreshing,* he thought as he drank her in and made a rapturous sound. "Fascinating creature."

"*Strange* creature," the countess amended. "I credit her aunt with that. I have it on good authority that Lady Clara Langly is a bold, mischievous gel in need of taking in hand. Evidently, my dear friend Regina, Countess Greenway, her aunt and guardian, isn't equal to the task."

"Oh, I don't know, my lady," Nigel observed. "She seemed more like a frightened doe to me. Why wouldn't she unmask, do you suppose?"

"She dismissed you out of hand, dear boy," said the countess. "There was no point to unmask. I hope she hasn't wounded your ego too severely."

Nigel laughed outright. "She boosted it, actually," he said. "I held her in my arms, my lady, albeit briefly. You can tell a good deal about a woman from a whirl around the dance floor. Dancing is nothing more than making love to music, after all."

"Nigel!" the countess cried, swatting his arm with her mask. "You are a scandal, but then I suppose you would know, wouldn't you?"

Again he smiled, but the smile was superficial. He felt silly all of a sudden in the elaborate hawk mask. Why hadn't he gone after the Langly chit, seen her to her carriage despite her protests? Outside there would have been no excuse not to remove their masks. There was no question that she was a beauty under all that hair and feathers. He'd seen the little wisps and tendrils of sun-painted gold peeking out from under the ridiculous wig. And her eyes! He had never seen eyes so green, like the translucent curl of a high-rising comber, backlit by the sun. He was intrigued, and he had lost his chance. If there was one thing Nigel Farnham hated, it was a missed opportunity. He wasn't going to rest until he'd created a new one. Only, next time he wouldn't let her slip right through his fingers.

"Is she invited to your fete on Thursday?" he inquired, hopeful.

"Of course, Nigel, but I doubt she'll attend, unless Regina has come on from Yorkshire by then; she was most embarrassed at having come without her tonight. She shan't make that faux pas again. She only came because your introduction had been arranged. One doesn't disappoint Regina Langly without consequences. Whatever did you do to put her off? Regina was counting upon a favorable introduction.

This won't set well. You haven't disgraced yourself, I hope? I leave the room for only a moment, and chaos reigns!"

"I had no idea who she was, and I engaged her for the quadrille somewhat . . . abruptly."

"Hmmm," the countess mused. "She is young, and she may be lacking in refinement and the social graces, but she is still a lady, my dear, hardly a lady-bird from down round the Garden. You need to take stock of yourself, Nigel. I promised your dear, sainted mother—"

"Yes, yes, I know, my lady, that you would save me from ruin and see me properly wed," Nigel chided, with not a little drama.

"And so I shall," the countess returned, "if I have to accomplish it with my last breath. Hereafter, re-member yourself! You're not carousing about with the Navy any longer, and you're not a lad, either. You're thirty-five, come winter. It's high time you settled down."

"Where is she staying?" Nigel asked, only half-listening.

"At Langly House, Regina's town house in May-fair, I imagine. Why?"

"I shall call upon her, of course."

"She did not give you leave, dear. If my hearing serves me correctly, the lady said no."

"When have you ever known that to stop me?" Nigel returned. Giving a wink and a grin, he left her and rejoined the dance.

* * *

The wheels had barely stopped rolling when Alice leaped from the carriage. She didn't unmask until she'd locked herself inside her chamber. It was over, and nothing too disastrous had occurred . . . unless one wanted to count her bizarre encounter with Nigel Farnham. She flushed just thinking about it. She'd behaved like an absolute ninnyhammer, but she'd accomplished her mission—or rather, Lady Clara's mission—to put paid to the matter of the Earl of Romney. And she hadn't had to show her face to do it.

She should have been ecstatic with relief. Instead, she was feeling something else. Something she didn't want to feel, had no right to feel. Deep down in the most private sanctum of her heart, she didn't want the masquerade to end. She didn't want her time with *him* to end.

Alice hugged herself, recalling the gaiety, the dashing men in their hooded dominos, and the ladies decked out in parti-color hues. How grand it was—how wonderful to dance! She had never danced with a man before, other than her dancing master. Thank the stars she'd taken her lessons to heart.

How tall and graceful the earl was, how easily he moved her to the rhythm of the music. His scent was still with her, leather and lime laced with wine, and his own distinctive male essence. She wondered what Lady Clara would say after learning how shockingly Isobel Rutledge had lied about the man's appearance. Why had the chit done such a thing? Alice couldn't help wondering if Lady Clara would have been so quick to cry off attending the masque if she'd known Isobel's description of Nigel Farnham was so false.

She shook her head as if to shake free those thoughts. None of it mattered anymore. Why couldn't she stop thinking about the man? She sank down on the edge of the bed, removed the elaborate headdress, and fluffed out her short-cropped curls. Rotating her head, she soothed her neck. It was still early. She doubted Lady Clara had returned as yet, but she decided to take the costume back to her suite. Perhaps that would put the stamp of finality on the matter. Something had to—and quickly. She had no right to her stolen moments as a fine lady. She was who she was: Alice Jessup, the daughter of a poor country minister from the southwest Midlands, the paid companion of a legitimate lady. She never should have pretended to be anything else. Yet, she had. She'd tasted something forbidden that she had no right to taste. How would she ever be able to cleanse her palate of that delicious flavor now?

As she suspected, Lady Clara hadn't returned. For that reason Alice left the gown, wig, and hat draped over the rolled-arm lounge in her dressing room and returned to her chamber down the hall. Exhausted, she slept. It was a deep, dreamless sleep that chased away all thoughts and nagging regrets until Agatha Avery, the housekeeper, woke her just after dawn.

At the sound of the shrill voice and frantic rap at the door, everything came back in a rush of heart-palpitating frenzy that catapulted Alice bolt upright in the mahogany sleigh bed. Something was wrong.

"C-come," Alice called, pulling the counterpane up to her chin.

"Beggin' your pardon, miss," the housekeeper said, bursting in, out of breath. "Lady Clara's not in her rooms and her bed's not been slept in."

"What do you mean, it hasn't been slept in? Of course it's been slept in."

"No, miss, it has not. Her costume's up there, where she left it on the lounge when she come back from the ball, but there's no sign of her anywhere, and none o' the servants have seen her neither, not since Simms the coachman handed her outta the carriage last night."

"Perhaps she rose early and made up the bed herself," Alice said. No one had seen her return the costume, and she dared not tell that she had done so now; they all thought that Lady Clara had gone to the masque. It was too much to hope for. They'd fooled them all! But where had the silly goose gone? She couldn't still be with the man she had stolen out to meet, could she? If she was, her reputation was ruined.

"Now, ya know not, miss," said the housekeeper. "Fie! The sun'll never rise on the day *that* one makes her own bed!"

"Do not overset yourself, Mrs. Avery," said Alice. "I'm sure there's a perfectly reasonable explanation. I shall dress and join you in the search. We shall find her walking in the garden . . . or something, you'll see."

But they did not find Lady Clara in the garden, or anywhere else. She had vanished without a trace, and Alice met with Mrs. Avery in the servants' hall belowstairs in the early afternoon to discuss what was to be done.

"I never should have said I'd look after the girl," the housekeeper lamented. "Her Ladyship never should have sent you two on ahead. You should have waited and come on together."

"You know why Her Ladyship did that," Alice defended. "She wasn't prepared to travel. She's recovering from megrims and a touch of rheumatism, though she'd die if that ever got out, and she insisted we come on ahead. She didn't want Lady Clara to miss all the important festivities in town on her account."

"Fie!" cried the housekeeper. "Lady Clara was afeared o' that young rake she's playin' with takin' up with another if she was behindhand, that's what. I've got eyes in my head, haven't I? Her Ladyship put the bug in my ear, too, she did. A body would have ta go ta some trouble ta put anything over on the countess." She gasped. "Oh, miss! You don't suppose—?"

"Now, let's not borrow trouble, Mrs. Avery," Alice said. So, the servants were aware. She was almost relieved. Almost. "I don't think we need alarm the others."

"Lizzie knows," said the housekeeper. "She's the one who told me Lady Clara wasn't in her rooms. She always gets her ready ta go ta breakfast. She come down all out straight, when she saw that bed without a cover mussed."

"I suppose she's told the rest by now, then?"

"You know how word travels in a small house,

miss. Her Ladyship will have ta be told—rheumatism or no. We'll have ta send word at once! I can't handle this on my own. Neither can you!"

"Wait now," said Alice. "It's too soon for that, I think. She's only been missing a few hours. We need to give this a little more time . . . and more thought. We shall only alarm Her Ladyship if we send word straightaway and Lady Clara turns up with a logical explanation. Besides, there is nothing Her Ladyship can do, indisposed as she is and at such a distance."

"What, then? We can't just ignore this. If she's gone off with some scoundrel, anything could happen."

"If she's gone off with the man, there is nothing we can do. But let's not be hasty. Just yesterday, Lady Clara made mention of wanting to go round to that new mantua maker on Bond Street. I shall inquire if Simms might have driven her or sent for a chair."

"When the sun was barely up, and none ta accompany her? Oh, fie, miss!"

"Have you asked him?"

"Well, no, miss. He brought her home, 'twas round ten last night. We heard her come in. She left word she didn't want Lizzie ta tend her after the ball. Ohhhh, miss! Now we know why!"

"Calm yourself, Mrs. Avery. There is nothing to be served by jumping to conclusions. I shall go and speak to Simms now. Do not alarm the others. Just shrug and say 'She'll turn up' if they inquire, and she will, I promise you. . . . You'll see."

"And if she doesn't, miss?" asked the housekeeper, her voice like gravel.

"Then we shall do what needs must."

Alice had barely exited through the green baize door that marked the servants' quarters belowstairs, when a knock at the front door brought Whitney, the butler, to answer. She hesitated at the sound of voices, then dove into the shadows under the stairs as she recognized the caller. That sensuous baritone voice had left an indelible mark upon her memory, and upon her senses. It was Nigel Farnham.

"I'm sorry, my lord, Lady Clara is not in this afternoon," said the butler.

"Not in, or not receiving callers?" the earl persisted.

Alice braved a look. Did Whitney just flinch? She stifled a giggle. The aging, straight-backed butler looked like a strutting rooster when he bristled.

"My lady is not in," Whitney repeated. "Were you expected, my lord?"

"Why, no . . . not exactly" said the earl. "We met at Countess Pembroke's masque last evening. I simply implied that I wished to call. I made no mention of when."

"I see. I shall inform my lady of your visit upon her return," said the butler, attempting to close the door. Was that the earl's foot in the way? Sure as check. His polished black Hessian was wedged between door and jamb.

"If you would just give her this?" he said, handing the butler a sealed missive.

"As you wish, my lord," said Whitney. "Good day, my lord."

The door banged shut. Alice stepped from the shadows before the butler saw from whence she'd come, and she approached him.

"For my lady, miss," he said, exhibiting the note.

Alice extended her hand, palm upward, hoping he wouldn't notice how it was shaking. "I'll take it up," she said with as much authority as she could muster. The letter was for her, after all. She was dying to know what it said.

"Has my lady returned?" the butler said, hopeful, handing it over.

Alice's fingers closed around the parchment. The earl's scent was on it. She didn't even have to lift it to her nose to inhale him.

"Not yet, Whitney," she said. "But I will be sure she gets this the minute she does."

"Very well, miss," the butler replied, shuffling back toward the servants' quarters.

Alice hurried to her chamber and slid the bolt before breaking the seal on the missive. How elegant his hand was. She fingered the bold script, smoothed out the parchment, and read:

My Lady Clara,
I beg you to forgive my rash behavior at the masque last evening. I did not mean to offend. I implore you to let me make amends by doing me the honor of allowing me to escort you to Countess Pembroke's fete for the debutantes on Thursday. I shall call for you at one.
Your servant,
Romney

Alice did raise the note to her nose then. Leather and lime teased her nostrils. She gave a lurch. *What am I doing? What am I thinking? The masquerade is over—he is over. It never should have happened, any of it!*

Alice stuffed the missive in the little lawn pocket she wore on a silk cord attached under the bodice of her sprigged-muslin frock. Then, running a hand through her cap of natural curls to order them, she went back downstairs. She would speak with Simms in the carriage house. Granted, it was farfetched that Lady Clara had gone to the mantua maker, but any shred of hope to cling to was welcome then.

She stepped out into the balmy afternoon sun, pattered down the steps—and pulled up short before Nigel Farnham, who had exited his carriage and stepped back inside the gate at the sight of her. Was he lying in wait? It certainly looked that way. The cheek of the man! He should have been long gone by now.

"So, m'lady was in after all?" he said. "I thought as much."

"I—I beg your pardon, sir?" Alice returned. She steeled herself against the butterflies that had invaded her stomach again in the man's presence. This was her moment, the ideal time to put things right, if only she were a match for his prowess. "I'm sure you have confused me with my mistress, Lady Clara Langly, sir," she said, "and I assure you, she is not at home this afternoon." There! That ought to settle it.

He strolled closer. "Come, come, my lady," he scoffed. "There could only be one pair of eyes that shade of green in all England, and nowhere have I ever seen a head of curls so fine that they appear to have been painted by the sun. You are caught out."

Alice stared up at him. As though they had a will of her own, her fingers traveled to the tendrils blowing against her cheek in the gentle breeze that spread his scent to haunt her. How could he have seen her hair beneath that ridiculous headdress?

"Some of those tendrils there were peeking out from under your wig," he explained, as though he'd read her thoughts. Could she be that transparent? No, she definitely had no talent for deception.

"I'm sure you have confused me with my mistress," she persisted. His eyes were even bluer in bright sunlight, and those lashes! How long and sweeping they were. He'd doffed his beaver hat, revealing a crop of wavy mahogany hair. His features were strong and angular, and yes, those were dimples just outside his laugh lines when he smiled. "I, sir, am Alice Jessup, my Lady Clara's companion these past six months, and she is *not* in residence. Please let me pass." It was the truth. Why wouldn't he believe her?

He shook his head. "You shan't convince me, my lady," he said with a smile. "You may as well give it over. You couldn't be so cruel as to refuse me the opportunity to redeem myself with a second chance on Thursday."

"I don't know what you mean, sir," she said in her haughtiest tone. "And I must ask you to leave, or I shall have to summon Whitney to assist you in your departure."

He gave a guffaw. "If you're referring to the butler who took that missive there just now, I doubt
he'll be effective in evicting me on his own, my lady.
Have you no one sturdier about who might come to
your rescue?"

"Missive, sir? What missive?"

"*That* one," he said, crooking his thumb toward
her thin lawn pocket—and toward the parchment
peeking out of it, broken seal and all. "Would you
have me believe that you read your mistress's messages? Shameful behavior for a companion, I daresay. But you aren't a companion, are you?"

"What I do and do not do is none of your concern, sir," Alice hurled at him. She was angry now.
He didn't believe her, and he was not going to take
no for an answer. "Now, if you will excuse me?"

"I'm off on the wrong foot again, so it seems," he
said dourly. "If you will allow, my lady . . . When
Countess Pembroke told me that you are presently
bereft of a chaperone until your aunt comes on
from Yorkshire, I volunteered to escort you to the
debutantes' fete in hopes of making amends for my
behavior at the masque, nothing more. Her Ladyship feared you mightn't come for lack of an escort,
and she did not want you to miss the festivities.
Perhaps, if she were to pay you a call, she might persuade you of my good intentions."

"I am not 'your lady,' my lord!" Alice insisted,
little he'd said beyond that having sunk in. "I told
you who I am. That you do not choose to believe
me is . . . unfortunate. Now then, I doubt Lady
Clara will have returned by Thursday, so please do

not come round. I shall deliver your missive. If she wishes to accept your invitation, she will send word. And now, you really must excuse me."

Head held high, she floated past, ignoring without a backward glance his bow and the gloved hand outstretched to capture hers as she continued on to the carriage house tucked behind in the adjoining mews.

Chapter Three

Cheeky upstart! Alice half expected to find Nigel Farnham still waiting when she returned from the carriage house. Thank the stars he had the good sense to have already driven off. The man was so full of himself, he wouldn't take no for an answer. But all at once a new terror struck. What if Lady Pembroke were to call, as he'd suggested? Would Alice be able to convince her that she wasn't who they thought she was? How could she even try, or continue the hoax before the servants? Everyone would know what she'd done.

There was nothing for it. If Lady Clara didn't return, she would have to go to the fete to appease them. They weren't going to let this go. But how could she? She certainly couldn't let him come and collect her—and how could she go on her own? This was different. There would be no costume, no mask to hide her true identity. What reason would Alice Jessup have to attend a debutantes' fete?

Those thoughts rattling around in her brain were more than she could absorb as she dragged herself back up the front steps and reentered the house.

There were still four days until Thursday, but if she was to thwart a visit from Lady Pembroke, she had to do it soon.

Mrs. Avery descended upon her before she'd closed the door. Alice breathed a sigh that brought her posture down and shook her head. Simms was just as nonplussed as everyone else.

"What are we ever goin' ta do, miss?" the house-keeper whined, wringing her pinafore.

"We shall carry on as if nothing untoward has occurred until this time tomorrow," said Alice. "If there is still no word by then, we shall have no choice but to send word to Wiltshire."

"Oh, miss, the countess is goin' ta sack us all!"

"Nothing of the kind—but I wouldn't want to be in Lady Clara's shoes when Her Ladyship gets hold of her."

Excusing herself, Alice repaired to her chamber. Terrible pangs of conscience were crashing over her soul. She'd told the earl the truth. Why didn't he believe her? If only he had, that would have been the end of it. As it was now, she was trapped in a deception, with nowhere to turn. She'd been hoisted with her own petard.

They were going to have to send word to the cottage and bring the countess; she just knew it. Perhaps she'd spoken too quickly when she'd told Mrs. Avery that being sacked wasn't imminent. She popped a bitter laugh. Maybe that was the only way she could get free of the coil she'd wound.

The earl would find out, in that case. Why did that thought tug at her heart so? The answer to that was simple. Because he wouldn't give her a second look if he knew she was only a minister's daughter instead of the fine lady she'd pretended to be.

More than anything else, she needed to confide in someone. It was no use trying to perpetrate the hoax all on her own—especially since she would soon be facing the countess's wrath. But in whom? The servants were all loyal to the countess, albeit out of fear, and Alice certainly couldn't confide in *her*. The woman was a termagant. Perhaps it would be best if she didn't wait for the ax to fall. Perhaps she should pack her portmanteau and leave on the first post chaise bound for the southwest Midlands. Better to face her father's disappointment and whatever that brought to bear than Countess Greenway's wrath . . . or Nigel Farnham's scorn. But if she did that, she would never see him again.

It was still a while before the evening meal, and Alice sank down on the sleigh bed and closed her misty eyes. But she could not sleep. There were too many thoughts rattling about in her brain: thoughts of the consequences that would surely come from her foolish actions; thoughts of Nigel Farnham, the dashing Earl of Romney; and thoughts of what might have been, if only she had been born a lady.

Nigel didn't return to his town house straightaway. Instead, he barked instructions to his coachman, and the carriage tooled down St. James Street to White's men's club. Glancing through the bay window as the coach pulled to a creaking halt in front, Nigel spied the friend he'd hoped to find there, Viscount

Alistair McGovern. Just the man he needed to part the fog a certain little slip of a girl with hair like spun gold and eyes the color of a high-curling wave of the sea had caused in his brain. Instructing the coachman to wait, he entered the club, where his friend sat with his nose buried in the latest issue of *Ackermann's Repository*, and sank down in a horsehair armchair alongside. It was stiff and unyielding. He scarcely noticed.

"Well, well," said McGovern. "What's eating you, old boy? You look like a thunderhead."

"I need to talk to someone sane—possessed of an open mind," Nigel said, drumming his fingers on his knee.

"Me?" the viscount blurted. "You know I'm mad as a brush—always have been, old boy. You must be desperate. Who is she?"

Nigel heaved a sigh. "You know me too well, Al," he said.

"That, too," said the other. "So tell me. Don't keep me on tenterhooks. What's her name? More to the point, who's her husband?"

"It isn't like that this time," said Nigel, speaking in a hushed whisper. "I met her at Lady Pembroke's masque last evening. I thought to see you there. Weren't you invited?"

"I was," said McGovern, with a telling wink. "But I had a better offer."

"I wish you had been, old boy. I'd like to have had your opinion of her."

"Who, man, *who*?"

"She was costumed as Marie Antoinette," Nigel

told him. "The most fascinating creature I have ever clapped eyes upon."

Before he knew what had happened, he'd told his friend everything that had occurred during the masque, and since. The viscount hung on every word, just as Nigel knew he would. They'd been fast friends since they served together on the *Monarch* at Copenhagen. Those steel gray eyes of McGovern's spoke with more eloquence than his voice. They were studying him now, and when he stopped speaking, the viscount set the *Repository* aside and arched his brow.

"Does this paragon of womanhood have a name?" he queried.

"Lady Clara Langly," Nigel said. "Her aunt, Countess Greenway, arranged our introduction with Lady Pembroke, only I didn't know that it was she when I swept her out on that dance floor. I think I may have ruined it."

McGovern raked fingers through his wheat-colored hair and blew his breath out in a whistle that attracted the attention of more than one of the patrons. He nodded an apology, and after a wave of bristling and black looks, the others went back to their tomes.

Nigel shifted in the uncomfortable horsehair armchair, studying his companion's pained expression. He'd seen that look many times before. This was not a good sign.

"What? You're acquainted?" he prompted. The silence was unbearable.

"Not . . . exactly," McGovern hedged. "Look here, old boy, this isn't the place to discuss it. We've got an audience."

"Do you have your carriage?" Nigel said.

McGovern shook his head that he did not. "I hopped a chair."

Nigel surged to his feet. "Come," he said. "Mine is outside."

Neither spoke of the issue at hand on the way to Nigel's town house in Grosvenor Square. Once the carriage had proceeded past the garden in the center and pulled up before the stately brown brick building, with its red dressings and stone cornices, they wasted no time gaining entrance. They made their way to the study. Bad news was best had quickly, and in private. Over brandy.

"All right, Al," said Nigel, handing him a poured snifter. "Speak your piece."

"How serious are you about this gel, Nigel?" McGovern queried.

"I told you, we've just met."

"You haven't committed yourself to . . . anything?"

"No, of course not. I'm intrigued and attracted though, I'll admit. I would like to pursue it. I haven't felt like this in a good long while. She's enchanting, Al."

McGovern frowned, taking a sip from the snifter. "Then I'm sorry to be the bearer of discouraging news," he said. "It might be best if you *have* 'ruined it,' as you say, now . . . before it's gone too far. If you're after a dalliance, that's one thing, but if you're looking for something more permanent . . . Well, you'd best not invest in Lady Clara Langly."

"Why?"

"Because, old boy, she's involved with someone else."

"With whom?" said Nigel. He hadn't heard of it. But then, he hadn't really heard of her until the masque.

"Percy Arborghast," McGovern said.

"Lord Chesterton?"

McGovern nodded over his snifter.

"I didn't know you had Chesterton's confidence."

"I don't—that is, not exactly. I haven't got it from the horse's mouth, if that's what you're asking, but he's bruited it about shamefully all over town, bragging how he's got the gel wrapped around his little finger. That's why I didn't want to say anything back at White's. Lady or ladybird, I shan't be part of any woman's public debasement."

"I'd heard Chesterton was betrothed to Lord Chartle's daughter," Nigel mused, his eyebrows knit in a frown.

"He is," said McGovern. "And he has a mistress."

"Ah," Nigel murmured. His heart sank. Chesterton had a reputation with the ladies. Lady Clara Langly wouldn't be the first girl he'd seduced and cast by the wayside. So that was why she'd put him off. Her affections were directed elsewhere. If her involvement with the bounder was being bandied about all over town, the girl's reputation was in tatters no matter how far they had taken it. That's what Alistair McGovern was trying to tell him: not to become involved with damaged goods. Good advice, but it was already too late.

"Sorry, old boy."

"Don't be ridiculous. I'm glad you've told me. It's a shame. The man's reprehensible."

"As I said, if all you're after is a dalliance . . . I've heard she's a looker, and evidently ripe for conquest."

Nigel shook his head and began to pace the carpet, his attention fixed upon the Greek-key border worked in a woodsy shade of green into the Persian wool. Traveling back and forth, he stared at it until it threatened to make him dizzy.

"What are you going to do?" said McGovern.

Nigel shrugged. "I've invited her to Lady Pembroke's fete on Thursday. She's refused, of course, but I wouldn't take no for an answer."

"Let it go," McGovern said. "You're well out of it, Nigel."

"I wonder if Lady Pembroke knew when she introduced us?" Nigel mused, only half listening. "No, I doubt it. She wouldn't be so quick to shackle me to a fallen woman. But this does explain some of Lady Clara's rather shocking behavior."

"How so?"

"For one thing, she came to the masque unchaperoned. Not exactly the conduct of a proper young lady. Our introduction was prearranged. I believe she came just to fulfill that obligation and reject me.

What bothers me is that she didn't give that impression. I'm not usually mistaken when it comes to reading a lady's demeanor. I could have sworn . . ."

"What are you going to do about the fete?"

"What can I do?" Nigel blurted. "I've already asked her. I can't very well withdraw the invitation, Al. I shall have to follow through."

"You ought to cry off, you know," said McGovern. "Say something unexpected has come up. I would."

"Yes, well, I'm not you, am I, my friend? Now then!" he said, shifting the subject, and his posture along with it. "Might I induce you to stay to dinner? We haven't dined together in quite some time, and I would like to hear more of this on-dit."

"You might," said McGovern. "But it's only fair to warn you, I shall use the time to try and persuade you to come to your senses."

Chapter Four

The following day dawned gray with cottony fog drifting in off the Thames. It matched Alice's mood as she dragged herself through the motions of the morning. When nuncheon passed without word from Lady Clara, she went up to her sitting room to compose a missive that would bring the countess. She was on her way downstairs to deliver it to one of the servants, who would see that it was dispatched to Wiltshire by special messenger, when Mrs. Avery rushed up the stairs, winded, and met her halfway.

"Oh, miss, oh, miss . . . !" she panted. "I don't know what ta do! Countess Pembroke is downstairs. Whitney told her my lady wasn't at home, and she barged right in! He put her in the parlor and come for me. I told her my lady was called away of a sudden yesterday, but she won't settle for that. Why, she all but called me a liar! She says the Earl o' Romney came by and spoke ta her himself yesterday. How could that be? The earl come by, all right, but Whitney sent him off. He left a message for my lady. Whitney says he give it ta you. . . ."

"Yes, he did," said Alice. "Calm yourself. I can barely understand you."

"C-Countess Pembroke says she's goin' ta wait for my lady ta return, because she's convinced, after what happened at the masque, that she needs lookin' after till Her Ladyship comes on from Greenbriar Grange. Why would she think Her Ladyship was up ta *Yorkshire?*"

"You didn't correct her, did you?" Alice blurted. "You didn't tell her she's at the cottage?"

"I did not. 'Tisn't my place ta correct my betters. What I want ta know is what could my lady have got up to at that ball? I shudder ta wonder, the scamp. I bit my tongue for want o' askin' outright about that. How could she just run off and leave us in such a stew?"

"You mustn't overset yourself, Mrs. Avery," Alice said. "Why, you look about to topple over."

Truth to be told, it was Alice who was about to topple over. It was plain that none of the servants was equal to the task of this deception. Neither was she, but someone had to take control.

"You don't understand," the housekeeper whined. "She's set herself up as just the one ta take my lady under her wing. She says Countess Greenway would never forgive her if anything happens ta the silly chit. She should only know, it's far too late for that! She's made herself comfortable in the parlor, bold as brass! Oh, please, miss, ya have ta come! She can't stay here now, with all this trouble goin' on, and I can't do nothin' with her."

"No! I—I can't," Alice cried, her voice so loud it backed the housekeeper down a step.

"Ya have ta, Miss Alice," Mrs. Avery pleaded. "You've got more experience in such matters, bein' educated, bein' a minister's daughter and all. You know how ta handle gentlefolk—what words ta say. I'm just a servant. She'll put no store in anything I tell her. You know how the ton are with staff. We're invisible. We have no say, and they don't take our word for nothin'."

Alice gripped the burled wood banister. "You don't understand. I cannot come down, Mrs. Avery," she said.

"Whyever not?"

"I—I just can't," said Alice. "We need to talk, I know, and I promise I'll explain . . . but not now. Not until Countess Pembroke leaves. You need to do just as I say. Go back down to the parlor and tell her that Lady Clara has gone to visit a cousin in High Street until tomorrow morning. If she asks what cousin, you do not know, but that she is properly chaperoned, as her companion has accompanied her. As soon as she's gone, come to my chamber . . . but do not tell the others."

"You're scarin' me now, miss! What's goin' on?"

"Just do as I've said. Oh, and give this to one of the footmen to take round to the livery." She handed over the missive she'd composed, totally forgotten until that moment. "Tell him to see it's sent by special messenger at once."

"Very well, miss," said the housekeeper, turning back down the staircase. "But I still think you're the one who needs ta tell the old peahen."

Alice dragged herself back up to her chamber

and waited. It was only minutes, but it seemed an eternity before the housekeeper joined her there. She didn't want to admit what she'd done to the woman, but there was nothing for it. She needed an ally. How had things gotten so far out of hand? If only the earl had respected her wishes. If only he'd let her go, no one would have been the wiser. Instead, she'd wound a coil that she couldn't unwind without disgracing herself.

"Is she gone?" she asked, as Mrs. Avery entered.

"She's gone, but she'll be back, miss, sure as check. You should have heard her down there. She didn't believe me for a minute."

"Sit down, Mrs. Avery," Alice said, motioning toward a Chippendale chair across from the chaise longue she occupied. "There's something I need to tell you."

The housekeeper sank into the chair, arranging her pinafore before resting her plump hands in her lap, her owlish eyes staring in rapt attention.

"I've done something terrible," Alice began.

"You, miss? Pshaw, I can't imagine you doin' anything terrible."

"Oh, but I have," said Alice, absently tracing the flower on the skirt of her sprigged-muslin frock with her forefinger—anything to avoid eye contact. "Much of this brouhaha is my fault. I let my lady talk me into going to the masque in her place."

The housekeeper stared, slack-jawed. "It was you, miss? Why would you do such a thing?"

"Lady Clara didn't want to be paired with the Earl of Romney. She thought him . . . a toady. She convinced me to go in her place. No, that isn't entirely true. It didn't take much convincing. I thought it would be grand to see how the aristocracy celebrated such affairs, as one of them. It was foolish, I know, but I doubted I'd ever get another chance to find out, and neither of us thought anyone would be hurt by it. I was just supposed to go, discourage the earl, then bow out early, and that would be the end of it. I didn't know until I was nearly out the door that my lady had an assignation with someone else, and now I fear she has run off with whoever that person was."

The housekeeper covered her mouth with her stubby fingers, her eyes wide as saucers. Something escaped her throat anyway, but it wasn't distinguishable, and Alice went on quickly.

"My lady was misinformed," she said. "The Earl of Romney is no toady, and now he thinks he's met Lady Clara, and he . . . expressed an interest in pursuing her—*me*—oh, dear! He asked if he might call, and I said no and fled the ball before we were scheduled to remove our masks. He never saw my face. I thought I'd put an end to it, but then he called yesterday, and—"

Mrs. Avery found her voice. "So Countess Pembroke wasn't mistaken," she interrupted. "It was *you* who spoke with the Earl o' Romney yesterday."

"I did, and believe me, I told him the truth. I told him who I am, and that Lady Clara wasn't in, just as Whitney told him, but he wouldn't believe me, Mrs. Avery. It was dreadful. I tried and tried, but he's convinced he recognized me by the color of my eyes."

"They are a most unusual color green, miss, now that I take notice," said the housekeeper.

"They were all that he could really see through that costume, except for a few tendrils that had come out from under the wig, and he cited them, too. Now he expects me to attend Countess Pembroke's fete for the debutantes on Thursday, and I don't know what to do. He wants to call for me himself! I cannot in good conscience continue the hoax, and I cannot make a clean breast of it, either, without scandalizing Lady Clara. If she has run off with this scoundrel, her reputation is ruined."

"No wonder ya didn't want ta go down and face Countess Pembroke," the housekeeper murmured. "What are ya ever goin' ta do?"

"I'm sure I don't know," Alice lamented. "I didn't want to involve anyone else, but the way things are going, someone in this house needs to know. Elsewise how am I ever going to carry on the deception until we have some word of Lady Clara? I don't know what else I can do. Neither Lord Romney nor Lady Pembroke will take no for an answer, and I couldn't prove my real identity to either of them without Lady Clara to back me up here now . . . even if I wanted to." The shocking thing that shot her through with riddling chills and palpitations as the last slipped out was that she really didn't *want* to prove her identity. Not yet. Not until she'd seen Nigel Farnham once more. Just once.

"Maybe if you confessed all this ta Lady Pembroke?"

"Oh, I couldn't! I'd be mortified."

"You can't be thinkin' o' goin' ta that fete?"

"I don't see how I could. Suppose there is someone there who knows Lady Clara. Why, I'd be found out and humiliated in front of . . . everyone."

"In front o' *him*, ya mean—the Earl o' Romney."

"He quite swept me off my feet. Literally. I . . . I know there's no hope of anything between us, but I would die if he found out . . . because it would embarrass him as well, and he would despise me for it."

"Sounds like he's brought that on himself ta me, miss."

"He did, and so did I, and I *did* tell him the truth. If only he'd believed me. Oh, there's no way out of this! Please, don't tell the others."

"Do you know who the scoundrel is that Lady Clara has run off with?"

"Oh, please don't say that! We don't know that! I said I feared it, but I'm not ready to credit it as fact. Countess Greenway would never forgive me!"

"Do ya know who he is, miss?" Mrs. Avery persisted. "Her Ladyship mentioned she suspected there was somethin' goin' on, like I said, but she never mentioned the rascal's name. And why would she? I'm only a lowly servant. Fie!"

"No, I do not. I only know that he is an earl, and that it began while she was at the cottage. Where they could have met, I have no idea, but I believe it happened before the countess took me on as my lady's companion. She was always attending some garden party or soiree. It could have happened anywhere."

"Well, he's no gentleman, that's for sure."

"Don't say that, either! We have to pray that he is, and that he'll do right by the silly goose. Anything else would be unthinkable."

The housekeeper wagged her head. "It's a fine mess; that I'll own," she said. "What on earth are ya goin' ta do?"

"At first I thought I might best just pack my bags and go home. I'm sure to be sacked when all is said and done. Why prolong the agony? But then . . . I made the mistake, and it's up to me to rectify it, if it can be rectified, or at the very least see it through to the bitter end. I've never been one to shirk my responsibilities or run from a challenge. But *this* . . . !" They were the right words, and true enough, but the real reason she decided to stay was because if she fled, she knew she'd never see Nigel Farnham again. That, however, she would not confess—not even to herself. Those shocking feelings would remain suppressed. She was doing her duty. That she could justify, with head held high. All else was vanity.

"The letter you sent just now will bring Her Ladyship on from Wiltshire in a trice, miss. What are we ever goin' ta tell her? Hah! What have ya told her already?"

"Only that she must come to town directly because Lady Clara had . . . gotten out of hand. I was afraid to tell her the whole truth. That much will bring her. The truth entire would likely kill her, gotten that way. A situation such as this? It needs telling face-to-face with plenty of help and smelling salts about."

"I don't know how ta advise ya, miss," the housekeeper said, wringing the corner of her pinafore. "It's quite beyond me."

"I don't want you to advise me, Mrs. Avery," said Alice. "I just want you to cover for me if needs must until I can figure a way out of all this."

"If 'tis loyalty ya want, that goes without sayin'."

"Thank the stars for that," said Alice. "I've been served in my own sauce, and that I can accept, but I don't believe I could have stood it if you turned against me." Tears flooded her eyes, and her lower lip began to quiver, despite her resolve.

"Ahhhh, miss, don't take on now," the housekeeper soothed, waddling to her side.

"I've never been a watering pot, and I don't intend to start over this," said Alice, blinking back the tears. She surged to her feet. "We can't just sit here wringing our hands. We must discover the identity of Lady Clara's earl. That's where we shall begin."

"And how do you propose ta do that?" the housekeeper said.

"By doing something shamefully unethical," Alice returned. "If they've been carrying on a secret relationship, there are bound to be letters. I shall go up to her rooms and see if I can find them."

"And, what will ya do if ya do find out who he is?"

"I'll cross that bridge when I come to it."

Chapter Five

Nigel called upon Lady Pembroke on Wednesday afternoon. There couldn't have been a worse time to visit, what with the fete a day away and all hands engaged in a frantic attempt to ready the town house and grounds. Nonetheless, the countess received him with her usual, albeit somewhat frenzied, charm and grace.

They were seated in the salon, and a pot of Her Ladyship's coveted house tea had been ordered: gunpowder and China black, kept under lock and key in the scullery and served only on special occasions. Nigel would have been more cognizant of her efforts at such a taxing time if he weren't so obsessed with a certain little blonde-haired, green-eyed wisp of a girl that had ignited his curiosity and stirred his passions.

"You are obsessing over this gel, Nigel," said the countess, offering a biscuit, which he refused. "I don't for the life of me know why, when there are so many other lovely candidates in the offing this season, dear."

"Credit it to my fascination with mysterious women," Nigel returned.

"Mankind's greatest folly: questing after the unattainable."

"If you must put it that way, my lady. But in this case I fear it's rather . . . more."

"Something is not right in that house," the countess observed. "I don't believe Lady Clara was out at all when I called. That housekeeper of Regina's is a dimwitted sort. I could see right through the little performance she gave me. Visiting a cousin in High Street, indeed! I know of no such cousin, and I've been acquainted with the Langlys for twenty years. Why, one would think I meant harm to the gel, for the reception I received. Don't think I won't have a word with Regina about it, either."

"You're sure about Chesterton, then?"

"Nigel, I told you, I've heard no such on-dits—not that that makes them false, dear. You know how involved I am in trying to relieve some of the burdens weighing down the patronesses this season. Lady Jersey is inundated with come-out madness. Hosting a few parties here for the debutantes is the least I can do to relieve some of the pressure, considering our line's involvement with Almack's since its inception. But I will say one thing. If Lady Clara Langly is aligned with Chesterton in the way that you describe, she is ruined, Nigel, and you should have no part of her. The man is betrothed, and he has a mistress besides. He's been branded a rake of the first order. What could he want of her but bed sport, dear? Your sainted mother would spin in her grave if you were to settle for spoiled goods."

"I didn't think you'd have a hand in introducing me to, as you say, spoiled goods, my lady, but I had to be sure. Alistair McGovern has it on good authority that the on-dits are true, but I shan't settle for that. Gossip spreads like wildfire through the ton, in season and out. I would be lacking as a gentleman if I knew a lady's virtue was in danger and took no action in defense of it. I mean to have the truth of the matter before I condemn the gel."

"Before you pursue her, you mean?"

"I'm already doing that," said Nigel dourly, accepting a biscuit this time as the countess offered. "And being thwarted at every pass."

"Perhaps that is for the best, dear. Whatever happened with Baron Rutledge's daughter? Isobel Rutledge. Yes, of course. You remember Lady Jersey introduced you to her at Almack's last season? She was so certain to make a match there."

"She didn't suit, my lady. Let us leave it at that."

The countess's eyebrow lifted. "You drop such a bomb and expect me to leave it at that? How little you know me, Nigel. Out with it! Besides, I need to know. She's invited to the fete, dear. Her name was added late to the list. This is her second season with no takers. We do try to put forth our best for all the girls, you know."

Nigel mumbled an expletive disguised as a sigh. "We . . . weren't compatible, my lady," he said, brushing biscuit crumbs off his new indigo pantaloons, which only made the castor sugar that had sifted down more noticeable.

"In what way?"

"In every way."

"*Every way*, dear?"

"Not *that* way. It never went as far as that. We had no understanding. If you must know, the gel pursued me with all the aplomb of a juggernaut—stalked me all over town. A gentleman should do the courting, not allow himself to be manipulated by a fortune huntress. That's what it amounted to. The baron's badly dipped. His fortune has gone to the gambling hells, and Isobel thought to get her hooks into mine. I finally had to put a stop to it. I let her down gently— at least I thought I did—but she vowed to ruin me for it, and the curse might have worked, for all the luck I'm having with the ladies since."

Lady Pembroke suppressed a smile. "We make our own luck, Nigel," she said. "And as to curses . . . I do not believe in them, and neither do you. You will find your soul mate, dear."

"Yes, well, I'd hoped to do that without enduring another parade of desperate Almack's picks of the season. I've had a bellyful of choking down the tepid lemonade, dreadful orgeat, and stale cakes they serve along with the parade of insipid hopefuls, and of pretending to like it. They may as well be on the block at Tattersall's. And we call this a civilized society! Is it any wonder that so many men take mistresses?"

"Now, that is another topic altogether, my revolutionary young protégé, and, while my interest is piqued, I shan't have time to addresses it this visit, dear. The 'insipid hopefuls' are arriving in less than twenty-four hours, and unless you want to have me perpetuate tradition and serve them tepid lemonade and stale cakes, I fear you must excuse me soon."

"Of course," said Nigel rising. "Forgive my want of conduct, my lady. I have detained you. I shall go round once more and see if I can persuade Lady Clara to accompany me to your fete, and—"

The appearance of a liveried footman in the archway bearing a missive on a silver salver interrupted.

"Yes, Fredericks?" said the countess.

"Begging your pardon, my lady," said the footman. "The bearer said it was urgent."

Lady Pembroke took the letter and dismissed the footman. Breaking the seal, she lifted her pince-nez and scanned the script. "Well, well," she said at last, setting the note aside. "You needn't waste the trip. Lady Clara has cried off. What will you do now, dear?"

Nigel snatched up his beaver and gloves from the drop-leaf table. "Chesterton keeps a town house in George Street, so says Alistair. I think I shall go round and have a little talk with him."

"To what purpose, Nigel?"

"To my purpose, my lady—mine, and Lady Clara's . . . if it isn't too late."

Alice entered Lady Clara's chamber as though it were a sacrosanct cloister, and closed the door behind her. It went against all her principles to do what she was about to do, but these were extraordinary circumstances.

A stubborn fog hung over the house like a pall, casting shadows in every corner, and she lit the candles on the candle branch and carried it with her as she began her search in the sitting room. The writing desk seemed the most logical place, but she found no letters in any of the compartments, and moved on to the gaming table. Except for tallies, cards, and gaming pieces, those drawers were empty as well. There were several other chests, but she found nothing there like correspondence, either, and she soon moved on to the bedchamber.

The light had begun to fail by the time she'd searched the wardrobe and the Duncan Phyfe chiffonier. Bending over the middle drawer, Alice didn't hear Mrs. Avery enter through the open sitting-room door behind. At the sound of the housekeeper's voice, she spun around, dripping tallow on the polished wood.

"Did ya find anything?" Mrs. Avery asked, shuffling nearer.

"You scared me half to death!" Alice gushed, setting the candle branch down. "No, I haven't yet, but I haven't given up. There has to be something here to give us a clue."

"Where haven't ya looked? I'll help ya."

"I haven't done the dressing room yet."

The housekeeper nodded, and with no more said she moved on through the dressing-room door.

Alice's hands were trembling as she finished

probing the middle drawer in the chiffonier, being careful not to disturb the slips and shifts, night-gowns, and chemises neatly folded there. Nothing. Her heart sank. There were only two drawers left at the top, one left and one right. She began with the right-hand one, laid with neatly folded hose, hand-kerchiefs, and a silk-satin lingerie case containing fine lace chemisettes and hair ribbons. It was while rummaging through these that her hand closed around something stiff and unyielding. Her heart leaped as she snaked out a packet of folded missives neatly tied with a red silk ribbon.

"Mrs. Avery!" she called. "I think I've found something."

The housekeeper waddled through the open door-way from the dressing room, and Alice sat down on the edge of the bed and untied the wrinkled silk. It had been tied and retied a number of times in the past from the look of it, and it took a moment to work it loose. Once free of the knots, she began opening the parchments one by one.

"I feel like a thief," she said, hesitating.

"Nonsense, miss," the housekeeper returned. "How else have we any hope of finding the silly chit?"

"You're right, of course. It's just that I seem to keep digging myself deeper into deeds and deceptions so contrary to my nature that I fear I will never be my-self again. First, the pretense of the masque . . . and now this!"

"Don't fret, miss. If we find her, it'll all be worth it."

Alice doubted that, but she'd come this far, and there was nothing for it but to follow through. Spreading the parchment in her hand open, she scanned the bold script and the printer's embossed crest on the letterhead. Checking the others, she found that they were all written on the same stationary.

"The device reads 'Chesterton,'" Alice mused. "That must be his title. All these are signed 'Percy.'"

"Is there an address, miss?" the housekeeper queried.

"No . . . Wait, *yes*—here, on this one. He has a town house in George Street. She must have met him there. Here's the address, see?"

"I can't read, miss—not fine script like that, leastwise. I'll take your word for it."

Embarrassed, Alice tucked the letter away. "It should be easy enough to find. I shall go straightaway."

"Oh, fie, miss! Ya can't go round there on your own! Whatever are ya thinkin'?"

"I haven't got a choice, Mrs. Avery," said Alice, tying the missives back as she'd found them. Surging to her feet, she tucked them away inside the lingerie case again and bolted toward the door.

"Here, miss!" cried the housekeeper. "You aren't going there now, are ya? In the dark, with no chaperone?"

"I shouldn't want to break tradition," Alice said ruefully. "Besides, there'll be the coachman. Every second counts, Mrs. Avery. Why, anything might be happening to her. I only hope and pray we haven't found her out too late."

Nigel plodded back down Percy Arborghast's George Street town-house steps, muttering a string of blue expletives. The bounder wasn't in, and the butler had all but slammed the door in his face. Toplofty churl! Now what to do? Things weren't progressing at all well; he was being thwarted at every pass. Perhaps this wasn't meant to be. Still, something deep inside would not let him yield to defeat.

He hadn't lied when he told Lady Pembroke he would not permit a lady's virtue to be compromised, and it wasn't just the lady in question he was referring to in that statement, although she made the task more urgent. It was a point of honor with him. He'd fought more than one duel in his career defending the honor of a lady who was no more than a nodding acquaintance, and had come to the aid of many who were total strangers. What went on between two consenting adults was one thing. An innocent being seduced by an experienced rake was something else again, something he could neither conscience nor tolerate.

He climbed inside his carriage, leaned back against the plush, tufted squabs, and gave the carriage roof a glancing blow with his walking stick.

"Drive on!" he barked.

"Home, m'lord?" the coachman called.

"No!" said Nigel. "Just drive. I've not decided."

Set in motion, the coach left the curb, listing over the slick wet street. Here and there, the cobblestones shone like gold under the streetlamps through the stubborn fog that hadn't lifted with the turn of the tide. Drifting mist softened the shadows and bathed the darkness with an ethereal glow. Ordinarily, the sight would have pleased him, as he had an eye for the aesthetic beauty in nature, but not tonight. Chesterton's butler hadn't offered any information as to where the man had gone or when he was expected to return. Thinking on that, Nigel nearly didn't notice another carriage moving past into the lane from the opposite direction until it rolled to a creaking halt in front of Chesterton's town house. Then his cane beat a quick rat-a-tat-tat on the roof of the carriage.

"Carter, turn round!" he called. "Go back! That carriage . . . It could well be the man I've come to see."

The coachman did as Nigel bade him. By the time the vehicle maneuvered the turn, a figure had emerged from the parked coach and mounted the front steps. But it wasn't Percy Arborghast banging the knocker. Chesterton would have used his key. It was a woman garbed in a long indigo cloak, her face hidden from his vantage by a hood.

"Stop here!" Nigel charged, when they were several yards off. He leaped from the carriage. "Wait. I'll be back directly."

With that, he crossed the street in time to see the town-house door come open, throwing down a wan shaft of candlelight at the woman's feet. It was brief, and then the door banged shut, but not before Nigel caught a glimpse of sun-painted ringlets beneath the woman's hood. He reached her as she exited the gate and took hold of her arm, paying no mind to the startled cry that greeted him.

"Well, well, my lady," he said. "Fancy meeting you here, of all unlikely places."

Chapter Six

*L*et go of me, you great lout!" Alice cried, struggling against the hand clamped around her upper arm and steering her toward a carriage on the opposite side of the lane. "Simms! Help!" she shrilled at the dozing coachman.

"Stay where you are, Simms," Nigel called. "I shall have a word with my lady and return her to you safe and sound forthwith."

He was too strong for her, and before she could protest further, he'd handed her into the waiting carriage and sat her down.

"Let me out of this carriage!" Alice snapped, struggling with the rock-hard muscles flexing in the arm barring her way.

"Gladly," he replied. "But not before I speak my piece."

"I shall scream, my lord, and bring all of Hanover Square down upon you!"

He clamped his free hand over her lips. "You little fool!" he whispered. "Do you know what you're courting here? Sure and certain ruin at the hands of the rake that lives in that town house there."

He was so close, his lips only inches from her face. His hot breath puffed against her cheek. It smelled sweet, of peppermint and wine. His hold on her was firm but not threatening. Dazed by the strange sensations physical contact with the man was unleashing upon her most private regions, Alice felt her heart nearly stumble to a halt. His eyes, hooded with rage—and with something else she couldn't identify, though it thrilled her—bore down upon her relentlessly.

All at once he lifted his hand from her mouth and gave her a gentle shake. It jarred her back to the reality of the moment, and she began to struggle afresh.

"Stop that!" he snapped. "I'm not going to hurt you. I'm trying to *help* you. Stop it, I say! You shan't leave this carriage until you hear me out."

He moved across the span, slid onto the seat alongside her with ease, and took her in his arms. She was trembling—not from the cold the stubborn fog had inflicted upon the city, but from something deep inside that flagged danger. What could he think? That she had come to the town house for an assignation with Chesterton? Her heart took another tumble, and it was a moment before she remembered that he wasn't lecturing *her*, but Lady Clara Langly.

"That's better," he said, relaxing his grip, though he didn't let her go. "What can you be thinking? Arriving at the masque unchaperoned was one thing, but it should have taught you better. A lady does not go gadding about town after dark—or in full daylight, for that matter—unescorted. Surely, you know this. What's to become of your reputation if you keep this sort of thing up—or don't you care?"

"Who has made you custodian of my reputation, sir?" Alice retorted. Anger was her only defense against the pumping spurts of liquid fire his closeness ignited deep inside her. "I insist that you unhand me at once and let me out of this carriage!"

"When I've finished," he said. "The man you came here to meet is a notorious rakehell. He is betrothed to the daughter of the Earl of Chartle, and he keeps a mistress—"

Alice gasped, interrupting him. *Pop!* went her hope of Chesterton's honorable intentions. *I wonder if Lady Clara knows she's run off with a betrothed man who keeps a mistress?* she thought to herself.

"Yes, you've heard me correctly," he resumed. "I am simply trying to warn you away from the heartache you are courting before . . . it's too late."

Alice gasped again. Was he asking if it was already too late? The subtle inflection in his voice—ever so slight—that lifted his tone to almost a question proved the theory.

Cheeky rascal! The audacity of the man. How does he dare?

Why was the blood pounding in her ears like that? Why was she just sitting there? Why wasn't she awarding his indigo-clad shins a fine drubbing with the toe of her morocco-leather slipper?

She twisted against his grip on her, but his hold was firm. "What I do and do not do, where I go and do not go—chaperoned or not—are none of your affair, sir," she sallied. "Is your memory impaired? I have told you this before. Did you follow me here?" It was either that, or he'd come on his own to say the stars alone knew what to Chesterton. She had to know which.

"Of course I haven't followed you here," he returned. "If I had, you never would have gotten out of that carriage, let alone reached the front door, my lady. Someone has to look out for you, traipsing about town alone in the dead of night."

"It's hardly the dead of night, my lord. It's the dinner hour, and you are keeping me from mine. Kindly let me out of this carriage. You've made your point."

"Not . . . quite . . . yet," he said, his voice becoming suddenly seductive, dripping honey, resonating through her body just as it had done at the masque. "You need a little lesson, my lady," he continued, drawing her closer still.

"Here! What do you think you're doing?" Alice shrilled, both hands braced against his broad chest and the heart pounding beneath as he drew her to him.

All at once her hood fell away, and his long fingers cupping the back of her head burrowed deep in her curls as he lowered his warm mouth over her protests. The silken advance of his tongue parting her lips sent waves of gooseflesh racing down her spine, while achy heat invaded her very core. The effect was paralyzing.

Why wasn't she fighting? She should be pummeling his brocade-vested breast with both her hands balled into scathing, tiny but deadly fists. Instead she melted against him, until his hand began to roam over her body beneath the cape as if it had a will of its own.

All at once, he pulled sharply back. "This is what you can expect if you continue on your current course . . . my lady," he panted against her lips.

Come to her senses, Alice brought the flat of her hand across his face with all the strength she could muster. It dislodged his fine beaver hat. The carriage was parked beneath a streetlamp that illuminated the mark her blow had made, a perfect handprint blooming on the side of his cheek above the stiff muscles that had begun to tick along his jawline. The roughened texture of his skin where a new growth of stubble was forming stung the tender flesh of her palm. And there was something more. The contrast in textures, his angular male roughness against her feminine softness, fueled the runaway fire burning inside her in a manner that took her breath away.

Shock, desire, and anger in fierce competition roiled in a torrent of emotion that rose up and starred her vision. Again, it was the anger that spoke.

"And that is what taking bold liberties without a lady's permission will get *you*, my lord!" she seethed. Wrenching free, she scrambled out of the coach.

"Does this mean you aren't going to allow me to

escort you to the fete?" he called after her, meanwhile soothing his face, a maddening lopsided grin bringing out the dimples in his laugh lines.

Glancing over her shoulder, Alice uttered a strangled gasp, then an exasperated exclamation, and reeled through the fog to her waiting carriage as fast as her trembling legs would carry her.

Once the Langly carriage had disappeared in the mist, Nigel banged his walking stick on the carriage roof.

"Home now, m'lord?" called the coachman.

"Yes. *Now*," Nigel barked back.

"Wise choice," the coachman said in a low mutter.

"I heard that! Just stubble it, Carter, and on the way, pass by the Langly town house."

"*On the way*, m'lord?"

"Let's not spar over details. Damn it, man, just do it!"

"Yes, m'lord."

A snap of the whip set the carriage in motion, with a complaint from the nervous right leader. The coach shuddered as Carter got the animal in line, and Nigel snatched his beaver off the floor. After giving it a ruthless dusting with his coat sleeve and the back of his hand, he set it on the seat alongside him and ran his fingers through the hair that had fallen in his eyes during the assault.

He sank back against the squabs and drew a ragged breath. What had he done? Something he'd been aching to do since the masque, and it was sweeter than he'd dared to dream. She tasted golden, of clover and bee nectar, food of the gods—once eaten, forever craved. He shut his eyes and inhaled her: delicate wildflowers kissed by the sun, no heavy Parisian distillation that annoyed a man's nostrils. A soft moan escaped him. Her intoxicating scent was all over him. His head reeled from it as though he were foxed.

How soft and malleable she was in his arms; he could still feel her. How ripe for his embrace—for conquest. That thought gave way to another, more disturbing one. He frowned, trying to recall Chesterton's face. He could not. He wished he knew the man better. Drat, and blast! He was jealous of a phantom. *Jealous.* A gentleman should have no truck with jealousy. It was undignified. But there it was.

He leaned his head out the window and glowered at the earl's town house as the carriage tooled past it over the slippery, wet cobblestones, the hollow clopping of the horses' hooves, amplified by the fog, ringing in his ears. What could have possessed her to come to the man's home under cover of darkness? What, indeed, lest it be an assignation, some prearranged clandestine meeting. Why wasn't he there to greet her? He'd been detained with his betrothed or his mistress, more than likely. If Nigel himself had been in the bounder's place, he'd have been home, bet your blunt on that! But then, if he'd been in the bounder's place, he would never have put her in such a shocking, dubious position. He would never put her honor in jeopardy.

His hair was wet with the fog, which soon turned

to rain, before Chesterton's town house disappeared from sight. He leaned his head back against the cushions again and shut his eyes. No. The Langly town house was not on the way home, but he wouldn't rest until he knew she was safe inside, the horses unhitched for the night.

The argument he'd presented probably sounded like a cheap attack upon Chesterton, but he'd spoken nothing but the truth. He'd said what had to be said. He'd given her food for thought, planted a seed of doubt. At least he hoped he had, because it wasn't likely he'd get a second chance. He'd done his duty. He should be proud of himself, but he wasn't. He'd tasted Heaven. How could he ever again be content with the mere offerings of Earth?

Alice was too overset to go down to dinner. Instead, she opted for a tray in her room, and hardly even touched that. She hadn't told Mrs. Avery that their worst fears were realized. She couldn't bring herself to say the words, only that the Earl of Chesterton was not in. Afterward, she prepared for bed, but she couldn't sleep. How could she, while her body still tingled from Nigel Farnham's urgent kiss, from the familiar touch of his warm, caressing fingers buried in her hair, roaming over her breasts, tracing the outline of her curves beneath the bombazine cloak?

She had to keep reminding herself that he wasn't making love to her, but to Lady Clara Langly, who he thought had gone to Chesterton's town house to meet in secret with the bounder. Had he taken such liberties because her behavior suggested she was a loose woman? A surge of adrenaline crippled her momentarily. Well, of course he had. What else would he think?

How could things have gotten so out of hand? How could a silly ruse to switch identities with Lady Clara and attend a masked ball have caused such havoc? Alice wished she'd never set eyes upon her jingle-brained chit of an employer. She wished she'd never set eyes upon Nigel Farnham. She wished she never left her father's vicarage on the outskirts of Warminster in the quiet southwest Midlands. The last was wished in sheer desperation, considering the hellish existence she'd suffered under the yoke of her father's austerity. She wished all these things, while pummeling her feather pillow with clenched fists until some burst through the ticking.

She could still taste peppermint and wine, could still smell his essence, heightened in the heat of passion—but she hadn't aroused those passions. He didn't even know her. It was Lady Clara who had won his heart, and he was trying to save her from herself. If he ever knew who she really was, he wouldn't even give her a second glance. She wouldn't see him again, *couldn't* see him again. How could she face him after this?

Her bedchamber faced the street. The mournful sound of a carriage rolling through the mews, then passing in front called her to her feet. She blew out the candles and peeked through the mullioned panes. The street was deserted now, the sounds grown distant. Cold splinters of rain had swallowed the fog. It seemed more like September than June. She shuddered, and climbed into bed. *I know what I must do,* she thought. *I just pray I've got the strength to do it.*

Chapter Seven

*N*igel wasn't about to attend the fete alone, with Isobel Rutledge on the menu. He wouldn't give the little fortune huntress an opportunity to resume the pursuit. He was up at the crack of dawn, composing a heartfelt letter to a certain lady who had come between him and his slumber since Lady Pembroke's masque. He had to see her again.

"My dear Lady Clara," it began. "I humbly beg your forgiveness for my inexcusable behavior last evening—" No, scratch *inexcusable*. How could she forgive inexcusable? Another parchment letterhead landed in a crumpled wad on the floor amongst a dozen others.

He dipped his quill back in the inkwell and began again. "My dear Lady Clara, I humbly beg your forgiveness for my shameful behavior last evening." Yes! *Shameful* was good. It showed contrition, which was much easier to forgive.

I shan't try to defend my actions. They were intolerable. I do defend my intentions, which indeed were honorable, my lady. I meant only to demonstrate

how your behavior is certain to be viewed by gen-
tlemen and rogues alike, and show you the conse-
quences of such, in hopes of warning you sufficiently
away from unmindful conduct that might threaten
your virtue.

That was it. He certainly didn't want to undo all
the good he might have done in the demonstration,
but he didn't want her to view him as a monster,
either, or to fear for herself in his company in future. That is, if there was any hope of a future after
last night. It didn't bode well. He dipped his quill
again.

I have never permitted a lady to bear insult or
come to harm when I could prevent it. It is a
point of honor with me as a gentleman. Know-
ing what I know of Chesterton, it seemed to me
that drastic measures were in order. I assure you,
the lesson is over. I vow that no such tactics will
be repeated. I implore you, my lady, let me make
amends by allowing me to escort you to Lady
Pembroke's fete this afternoon, if only to give you
safe conduct there as someone who is mindful
and respectful of your sterling reputation. You
have but to reply with your acquiescence, and I
will call for you at one o'clock.
Your servant,
Nigel Farnham, Earl of Romney.

Should that be just *Nigel*? No, too familiar. Just
Romney, perhaps, as he'd done before? No, no—too

formal now. It was fine as it was, formal enough to show respect, while not presuming anything.

Folding the parchment in thirds to form an envelope, he sealed it with red wax and gave it to a footman to dispatch at once. No, he would not go himself this time. That was another sound tactic. He must be contrite, humble enough to let her decide without pressure. Satisfied, he indulged in a shuddering sigh. It was done, in the hands of fate . . . if he hadn't ruined it.

Alice went to the library after breakfast in search of a tome to take her mind off Nigel Farnham's bold advances. But that was impossible while she still felt his burning kiss on her lips and his strong hands exploring her person. His scent was still with her. It was as if it had become part of her. It was so wrong to dwell on the man. Soon now, the deception would end, and she would never see him again. The bitter sweetness of their brief embrace would live only in her memory, haunting her for all time.

She lifted down one of Byron's recent works, *Childe Harold's Pilgrimage*. What had she heard about this book? She leafed through several pages before she remembered, and quickly shoved it back on the shelf as if it were a glowing cinder. The last thing she needed then was a dissertation on the finite disparities between romantic idealism and cold reality. She was struggling with both. She needed no reminders.

She was just about to choose another tome when Mrs. Avery burst into the room, waving a sealed missive in her hand, her black skirts dusting the woodwork.

"It's from *him*," she said, short of breath. "His man give it ta Whitney, but I snatched it, since he don't know the way o' things."

Alice's posture collapsed. "I'm sure I don't care to read anything he's put on paper," she replied.

"Ya have ta read it, miss, or we'll have him back round here again."

"Not after last night, we won't, Mrs. Avery."

"Beggin' your pardon, but what *did* happen last night, Miss Alice, if ya don't mind my askin'? Ya come in like a whirlwind. I knew somethin' was wrong. Ya seen him, didn't ya, the earl? I could see it in your face."

"I did," said Alice. "He went to Chesterton's, too. The stars alone know why, and I shudder to wonder." Should she tell the housekeeper what occurred? It was the last thing she wanted to do, but Mrs. Avery was her only ally, and she did so need to confide at least part of the whole affair to someone.

"What happened, miss?"

"There was a terrible scene. He thinks I—I mean, he thinks *Lady Clara* went to that town house for an assignation with Chesterton. He said dreadful things about the man. There's no way to know for certain, but I do believe she really has run off with the bounder. I didn't want to worry you, but now I think you'd best be prepared for the worst. Lord Chesterton is betrothed. What's more, he has a mistress. That is all I could find out before . . . before the earl decided to teach me a lesson for venturing out on my own."

The housekeeper gasped. "He didn't hurt ya? Ya was so flushed when ya come in."

"No, but he made his point. It isn't safe for me to go abroad unescorted, no matter how noble the cause. I just wish I knew more about Lord Chesterton—where he's gone, where he might have taken Lady Clara. I'm sure he must have other properties. I just wish there were something we could do. I'm sinking deeper and deeper into this deception as though it were quicksand, and Lady Greenway is due to descend upon us at any moment. That letter I sent will bring her in a trice. How will I ever face her? What on earth will I tell her? I'd hoped to have some word of Lady Clara before she arrived, but now . . ."

"Don't ya think ya better read this, miss?" said the housekeeper, waving the missive. "It could be somethin' important."

Alice breathed a ragged sigh that brought her posture down again, and took the letter. Romney's all-too-familiar scent wafted toward her as she broke the seal and unfolded it.

"What does he say?" the housekeeper urged.

"It's an apology," said Alice, scanning the page. "He wants to escort me to the fete as an act of contrition." She went to the writing desk and snaked out a piece of vellum from the cubbyhole.

"Ya aren't going ta go?" the housekeeper cried, incredulous. "Ya already cried off. Ya was well out of it."

"Oh, yes I am," said Alice. "This might be just the opportunity I need to find out more about

Chesterton. I certainly shan't accomplish that entombed here, pacing the carpet in a taking till I've worn it threadbare."

"But ya can't, miss! It's too risky. Suppose somebody there knows Lady Clara. You'd be caught out, and shamed right then and there."

"I shall just have to take that chance," Alice answered, writing a hasty reply. "And now I must commit another crime to add to the rest. I have nothing fine enough to wear to a fete. I shall have to borrow something of Lady Clara's. So now we shall add thievery to deception."

"You're only borrowin', miss, not stealin'," said the housekeeper. "But are ya sure ya want ta do this? I won't draw an easy breath till you're back in this house safe and sound."

"I'm sure," said Alice, sealing the note. She handed it over. "Now, see that this is dispatched at once. Send one of the footmen round. Then meet me in my chamber with a suitable frock as soon as it's on its way. Lord Romney arrives at one o'clock. I shall need you to help me make ready."

Alice ranged herself as far from her companion in the coach as was possible. Ordering Lady Clara's pink muslin frock, whose neckline exposed more décolleté than she was accustomed to, she clung to the hand strap and focused upon the London streets zipping past the isinglass window as the carriage raced toward Lady Pembroke's town house in Hanover Square. She shuddered, finding herself so close to the incident of the night before. Even though

Lady Pembroke lived at the opposite end of the community, Alice wouldn't soon forget what had happened there in the very carriage they now occupied. Hot blood rushed to her temples.

Nigel Farnham, Earl of Romney, hadn't forgotten either, judging from what she'd gathered during the fleeting sidelong glances she managed to cast in his direction. When he spoke, she lurched as though she'd been struck.

"Thank you, my lady, for allowing me to make amends," he said. "Why did you?"

Alice hesitated. She opened her mouth to speak, then closed it again. She couldn't tell him the truth—that she meant to pump him dry of information about the Earl of Chesterton—and risk another of his lessons. She didn't want to seem like an empty-headed ninnyhammer, either. She gave a mental shrug. What did it matter what he thought of her? He didn't have the faintest idea who she was. He wasn't speaking to her. He was speaking to Lady Clara Langly, who was in Alice's estimation a ninnyhammer of the first order.

"I've never been to a fete before," she said. That raised his eyebrow. "And since I will be leaving London soon, I thought to embrace the experience."

"Is that what you were doing last evening, my lady? Embracing the experience?"

"I do not wish to discuss last evening, my lord," she said frostily. "It was not what it appeared, and that is all I have to say of the matter."

"So, you do know how it appeared?"

Alice glowered at him in reply. "What were *you* doing there, my lord?" she queried.

"I went round to have a word with the bounder on your behalf," he said. "Fortunate for him, he wasn't in."

"What made you think I needed your intervention?" she snapped.

"I had it on good authority that he was playing you false, and I wanted to warn him of the consequences of his behavior."

"And what good authority might that be, sir?"

"A very good and trusted friend of mine put me wise to him just the other evening."

"Oh, so my name is being bandied about in the gambling hells and public houses, is it?"

"Probably," he pronounced. "But I heard it within the cloistered walls of my town-house study. My friend refused to speak it when we met at White's— wouldn't say a word until we were safely locked away." The last was delivered with not a little drama, and it spiked Alice's anger. That was happening a lot of late, and only when she was in this man's company—shameful behavior for a minister's daughter.

But she wasn't a minister's daughter now; Lady Clara Langly was the one to answer. "I would like to meet your . . . friend," she said. "He sounds a proper gentleman."

"Oh, he is in ordinary circumstances, but I couldn't vouch for him in your case, since your reputation has been rather besmirched. I, on the other hand, am a different breed of animal."

"Animal, indeed!" Alice said in a low mutter, which caused him to raise his eyebrow again.

"So . . . where did Chesterton's butler say he'd gone?" she probed, avoiding his eyes. She had never seen irises so crystalline blue, so striking against sweeping dark lashes. They were riveting. She couldn't stand to meet his gaze for more than a second or two, else she risk another swarm of butterflies invading her stomach. Her hands had already begun to tremble from his closeness, though she'd clasped them so tightly, she'd wrinkled her lace-edged demigloves.

"He didn't," he replied. "I gather he didn't tell you, either."

"No, he did not," she said. "I didn't ask where he'd gone, only when he was expected."

"Hmmm. Rather shoddy behavior: inviting a lady to his home, then not being there to receive her."

"I wasn't invited. Look here, I do not wish to discuss this further," she snapped. It wasn't going well, and the conversation needed changing before it went beyond the pale. Perhaps someone at the fete could enlighten her about Chesterton. That seemed her last hope now. "I *was* invited to the fete, however," she said. "And since I have no idea what to expect, why don't you spend your energies addressing that, before I change my mind and instruct your coachman to turn this carriage round straightaway and take me home."

"It's nothing but a glorified garden party for debutantes," he said. "It shall begin out of doors, if the weather holds, with a veritable feast of viands and dainties to choose from. At dusk, the festivities will move indoors for more food, dancing, and socializing in the ballroom—you were there at the masque. It's three rooms actually, with hinged breakaway walls that open to create one ballroom, enormous by town-house standards. It's the largest in the square, which is why Lady Pembroke is so often called upon to host such gatherings. The dancing will go on until dawn."

"Until dawn?" Alice cried. "I couldn't possibly stay that long. Why, it wouldn't be proper, considering . . ." She was thinking out loud and was sorry the instant the words left her lips, watching his tight-lipped scowl blossom into a wolfish grin. No man should have dimples like that! They were far too distracting, framed by his shirt points like a work of art. Not to mention that shadowy cleft in his chin and those teeth, so straight and white.

He suppressed a chuckle. "She ventures forth in the dead of night to tryst with her lover, but she cannot dance until dawn with a bevy of her sister hopefuls? What a delightful little hypocrite you are. How charming, my dear."

"He is *not* my lover!" Alice shrilled. "All right, enough! I am not who you think I am, sir. I am not Lady Clara Langly, I am her companion, Alice Jessup, just as I told you when you called. And, if you must know, I went to Lord Chesterton's town house to demand an explanation as to what he has done with my lady, because she disappeared after *her* assignation with the bounder on the night of the masque."

"Nice try, but if that were the case, the ton would be buzzing with it. However, I can see how you might want to save face and spare yourself embarrassment by concocting such a story. Most imaginative. I applaud your creativity, my lady. You could have a future in Drury Lane."

You'll see creativity, my lord, if someone at the fete is acquainted with the real Lady Clara Langly, she thought. *The mortification would almost be worth it to watch that handsome jaw of yours drop down and challenge that perfectly tied neckcloth!*

They had nearly reached Lady Pembroke's town house opposite the park, and Alice returned her gaze to the scenery. It wasn't any use. She had told him the truth; it certainly wasn't her fault that he refused to believe her. Her conscience was clear. Well, almost.

"Might we call a truce, my lady?" he murmured, his voice mellowed somewhat. "I wanted to show you a pleasant time today, whilst atoning for my sins. I don't want to spar with you. We keep getting off on the wrong foot, and—"

"We are not 'getting off' at all," she snapped. "Right foot, wrong foot makes no difference. Just so you understand that."

"As you wish, my lady," he murmured in that seductive baritone voice of his. "But we are getting out. We have arrived."

So they had. How was it that the man always managed to have the last word? Cheeky devil! Still, there was something very admirable in the makeup of a man who took a lady's virtue so to heart. She strongly suspected that she wasn't the first to bring out such noble intentions in him. What had he said—it was a point of honor? Yes. Rare, for these were times when decadence brought out the worst in men, or at least those men she'd seen since she began her situation. The pinks of the ton came to mind, sporting outlandish clothes in garish hues. She'd seen them passing by the town house and parading in the parks like displaced tropical birds, with wits to match.

The Earl of Romney presented no such image, handing her down once the coachman set the steps. He was striking in his coat of gunmetal gray superfine, white embroidered waistcoat, and black pantaloons tucked inside polished Hessians. Oddly, he didn't seem to know it. Plainly, vanity wasn't his long suit. She'd noticed that from the first. The man exuded self-confidence. There was no pretense. He was what he was, plain and simple. But what impressed her most was that the gentleman *was* a gentleman, despite their shocking little set-to, and her heart sank with the realization that it wasn't likely she would ever again meet his equal as long as she lived.

The touch of his gloved hand in hers was a shock to the system, undermining her footing as she negotiated the crushed blue stone drive. His body heat penetrated the soft, dove gray fabric, and it was almost a relief when he looped her arm through his, allowing her to rest her hand upon his less provocative sleeve instead of those caressing fingers.

"Shall we join the gathering?" he asked, steering her through the garden arbor.

"Um," she groaned, in a small voice.

He popped a guffaw. "Bear up, my lady!" he said. "What a face. One would think you were headed for the gibbet, instead of a grand fete. Come, we shall find Lady Pembroke and let her have a look at you without your wig and feathers, hmm?"

Alice let him lead her through the walled garden, which was hung with colorful festoons of flowers attached with bouffant ribbon bows. It was breathtaking. Guests were still arriving. A liveried footman ahead was announcing them, and she dug in her heels.

"Please, I do not wish to be put on display," she said. "I do not wish my name announced."

"Whyever not?" he said, frowning. "That's the whole point of these affairs, isn't it?"

"I've told you, I am not who you think I am," she said. "Can we not just . . . blend in, my lord? I am a staunch advocate of anonymity."

"All right," he said, waving the footman off as they passed him by. "I'll play along. I like a lady of mystery."

"Thank you."

"I suppose this is my fault," he said, the words riding a sigh. "I've made you self-conscious, telling you of my conversation with Alistair."

"Alistair?"

"The friend I spoke of last night. You needn't be—self-conscious, that is. The on-dits haven't gotten this far, elsewise Lady Pembroke would have been the first to bring the matter to my attention. She's taken me under her wing until I've made a match—something she promised my mother before she died. Relax, my lady. If I would go to such lengths to protect your honor, why would I contrive to humiliate you in public? The real reason I wanted you to accompany me this afternoon is to make mock at the gossip. That you are here with me should put paid to any tales that do spread through the ton. I know you don't believe me, but there it is."

But she did believe him. That was the hellish part. What she couldn't bear was the deception, despite her having told him the truth. Why wouldn't he believe her? Because what she had done simply wasn't done. There was no precedent for such a thing. How could he believe her?

"You could help me, you know," he said, jarring her back to the moment.

"Sir?"

"You could begin by calling me Nigel. I know it isn't done on such short acquaintance, or any acquaintance, come down to it, amongst the upper classes. But I have never been one to bow to convention. That we are on a first-name basis couldn't hurt. It would certainly raise eyebrows in a different direction and give the masses something else to think about."

"Familiarity breeds contempt, my lord."

He popped another guffaw. "I thought we'd already achieved that plateau in our relationship," he said.

"We have no relationship, my lord."

"Then what does it matter?" he persisted. "It's

hardly a commitment, only a name. What harm to call me Nigel? And I shall call you—"

"My lady!" she warned him.

"What say we reach a compromise? You shall call me Nigel," he suggested, "and I shall simply address you as 'my dear'—just as I often address Lady Pembroke. Who is old enough to be my mother," he hastened to add. "A little more familiar than *my lady*, but not so intimate as *Clara*. That will leave just the right impression, without going beyond the beyond. It would be a help, considering the image I am trying to create for you. I cannot do it all on my own, you know."

"Oh, have it as you will!" Alice snapped. The man was smooth as silk, with a penchant for making the impossible seem perfectly normal. People were staring; it was concede or cause a scene. Well, two could play at that game. If she must address him by his first name, she would use it sparingly.

"Nigel, then?" he coaxed.

"Yes, yes. Anything to end this pointless banter."

"Good!" he said. "Now, my dear, we shall put it to the test. There is Lady Pembroke by the sundial."

He steered her there with firm but gentle pressure on the arm he'd captured, meanwhile casting surreptitious glances about the gathering, as if he were looking for someone—someone he wasn't anxious to see, judging from his odd expression. The playful sparkle had left his glacier blue eyes, and they'd darkened to a cold steely blue. The man had many facets, all of them intriguing. She could no longer deny her attraction to him, though she fought it like a Trojan. She had to. There was no hope for anything developing between them.

Of course, there had been matches between titled aristocrats and ladies of her station. The prince regent himself was a prime example, but he was the prince. Rich and handsome men like Nigel Farnham, who joined the marriage mart with getting an heir in mind, did not choose commoners for their wives, only for their mistresses—and that was not an option. She was what she was, after all: a minister's daughter, and a *lady* in every sense that mattered, at least to her.

"I am so pleased that you had a change of heart and decided to come after all, Clara," said the countess. "Your lady aunt will be pleased that I haven't shirked my responsibility in your regard."

"His Lordship is most persuasive, my lady," Alice returned, earning herself a disapproving look from Nigel. What? Did he think his given name would just roll off her tongue? She would more likely choke on it. She was scandalized just thinking it. A young lady of her class would never address a titled gentleman by his given name—never, *ever*. How many more social sins must she commit to see the hoax through to the bitter end? And it would be a bitter end. That was inevitable.

"We've been fast friends for ages, your aunt and I," the countess went on. "We were practically inseparable until that dreadful accident took your parents, and she moved to Greenbriar Grange to care for you. Though we've kept up a correspondence, you were only a child when I last saw her, dear. Perhaps, once you're settled"—she cast a meaningful glance in Nigel's direction—"I might be able to persuade her to move back to town. Why, even the Wiltshire cottage is too great a distance from us."

"I don't plan upon being settled anytime soon, my lady," said Alice, casting daggerlike glares in Nigel's direction.

Lady Pembroke didn't seem to hear. She was distracted by the new arrivals being announced by the footman. All at once, she inclined her head toward Nigel and whispered something behind her fan. Nigel glanced toward the footman, and at the young lady who was approaching the liveried servant for her introduction: a dark-haired beauty gowned in peach raw silk. There was something vaguely familiar about her.

"Who is that?" Alice asked, curiosity having gotten the better of common sense.

"A thorn in my side," Nigel said.

"Lady Isobel Rutledge," the footman intoned, admitting the lass to the fete.

Chapter Eight

Hot blood rushed to Alice's temples, and her heart leaped with such a shuddering thud that she was certain both the countess and Nigel Farnham heard. A strangled sound left her throat that turned them both around to face her. Isobel Rutledge and an older woman who had come in with her were headed in their direction, but hadn't seen them yet. Isobel was engaged with several other young hopefuls beside the bower, while her older companion moved on to the refreshment tables beneath an elaborate tent.

"Why, what is it, child?" Lady Pembroke asked. "You've gone all peaked of a sudden."

"I—I'm afraid I'm not feeling well," Alice said, turning to Nigel. "Please," she said. "Please take me home."

"Nonsense!" Lady Pembroke said. "You've only just arrived. You simply cannot keep running off like this, dear. Fetch her a lemonade, Nigel, or something stronger. Ratafia perhaps? Come, child, sit," she charged, leading Alice toward a carved stone bench amid the festoons. It looked like a throne framed that way, and Alice strained against the countess's grip on her arm. It was right in Isobel Rutledge's path.

"No! No lemonade, or . . . or anything. I must go. I never should have come. I haven't been myself for days." That was certainly no lie. "Nigel . . . please?"

He beamed. The churl actually *beamed*, dimples and all! Here she was about to swoon in a fit of apoplexy, and all he could do was stand there and grin like a satyr because she'd called him by name. She had half a mind to throw caution to the winds and let them find her out. That would wipe that silly smile off his face. It would serve him right. Hadn't she tried to tell him the truth twice?

"Pay her no mind, dear," said the countess. "Fetch her the lemonade."

"My lady, please, I am not in need of lemonade," said Alice. "The truth is that there is a person in attendance whom I do not wish to meet. I would take it as a kindness if you would just allow me to leave."

"Who?" Nigel demanded, a frown darkening his eyes.

Alice inclined her head toward Isobel Rutledge.

Nigel ground out a guttural chuckle. "What? Did she curse you too?" he asked.

"I beg your pardon?"

"It isn't important," he said. "You're acquainted with Isobel Rutledge?"

"We . . . had a dustup," said Alice, her mind racing to construct a believable lie. The truth of it was, they'd met, and Isobel knew Lady Clara. She would know Alice was an impostor. Would the deceptions never end? "I just do not wish to include myself in her society," she said.

"I would like to hear more of this," said Nigel, taking her arm. "Walk with me." Then, to the countess, "See that we aren't . . . disturbed."

Countess Pembroke floated off in Isobel Rutledge's direction, and Nigel steered Alice through a second bower onto a narrow, crushed blue stone walk walled with privet. None of the others had ventured back that far; they were all gathered about the refreshment tables at the other end of the garden.

Trapped alone with Nigel in that secluded setting was the last place Alice wanted to be, but better that than facing Isobel Rutledge and being exposed as an imposter before everyone.

"So, tell me about your little dustup with Isobel," said Nigel.

Alice swallowed drily. "Please," she said. "I just want to leave. I shan't enjoy the fete now in any case. Everything is spoiled. I would take it as a kindness if you would see me home."

"In due course," he replied. "You're trembling. What was the squabble about—a suitor, perhaps?"

"That is none of your affair," Alice snapped, wrenching free of his arm. "I have asked you to take me home. If you do not wish to do that, I shall find someone who will."

He recaptured her arm. "I haven't said I wouldn't take you," he pointed out. "You've aroused my curiosity, since the gel has injured me as well. I merely wish to know how she has injured you."

In such a panic over being found out, Alice had nearly forgotten how Isobel Rutledge had falsely painted Nigel as a toady. Her own curiosity was piqued, and she ceased struggling.

"I do not carry tales," she said. "I have heard something rather . . . unflattering that she's said about you, however, and I cannot help but wonder about that."

"What did she say?"

"Amongst other things, she called you a toady— a hawk-nosed toady, to be precise. She said that you wear leg pads and corsets, and prey upon innocent young ladies with no honorable intentions toward them, sir."

Nigel erupted in a fit of guffaws. "Well, if that's the best she could do, I'm safe enough," he said as the laughter faded to chuckles. "Leg pads, and corsets, eh?" He burst into laughter again.

"I see nothing humorous in it, my lord," Alice snapped. "I nearly made a fool of myself mistaking you for another at the masque because of her malicious lies."

"Ahhh!" he flashed. "So that was it! I wondered why you nearly gave your hand to Lord Wickham when we were being introduced. Wickham! You thought—!" He broke into a knee-slapping fit of laughter again, and Alice resisted the urge to stamp her foot.

"Please!" she cried. "I must insist that you stop braying like an ass and lower your voice. You'll bring the whole fete down upon us."

Nigel straightened up, holding his sides. "There's

nothing to fear," he said, through a chuckle. "Do you see that arbor over there? It leads to the rear entrance of the town house. We can easily duck inside, if needs must."

"I find no cause for levity in any of this, especially my humiliation, my lord!" Alice retorted.

"No, you wouldn't," he said, still laughing. Was the man addled? "And I am not laughing at your humiliation. I may as well make a clean breast of it. I don't mean to speak ill of the gel, but I do have to defend myself. Last season, Lady Jersey introduced me to Isobel Rutledge, hoping to make a match between us. The Rutledges are badly dipped, and Isobel made it all too plain that her interest in me was financial. Many matches are made on such conditions, which is why so many men take mistresses. Truth to be told, we had nothing in common, plain and simple. And there was never a relationship, but she made a spectacle of herself pursuing me all over town in expectance of one. It went beyond the pale, and I finally had to put a stop to it. I did so as kindly as I could under the circumstances, but she vowed vengeance—for what is still unclear, unless she assumed Lady Jersey's introduction represented an ironclad commitment. I laughed, because leg pads and corsets were the best she could do by way of retaliation, which in itself ought to exonerate me, I should think. So you see, my dear, I am no more anxious to court her society than you are."

Outstanding! Now we have something in common! thought Alice. Yet the last thing she wanted was any kind of bond with the man. As shocking as the realization was, it was clear that he was interested in Lady Clara Langly. In her secret heart of hearts, if she were the fine lady she pretended, Alice would have welcomed his courtship in a trice. If he knew he was courting Alice Jessup, a plain little country minister's daughter in disguise, he would avoid her like the plague, just as he had avoided Isobel Rutledge. But at least that mystery was solved.

"Am I forgiven?" She was silent. "For laughing, of course," he prompted her.

"On one condition," said Alice.

"And that is . . . ?"

"That you tell me where you think Chesterton has gone." It was a bold gamble, and he was sure to think her a doxy for it, but she had to know. She had to come away from the fete with something to justify her going. What did it matter anymore? After this, they were never going to see each other again. Besides, he wouldn't really be thinking *she* was a tart, but rather Lady Clara, and at this point, as far as Alice was concerned, that was almost justified.

She was proud of herself until she met his gaze. There was no trace of the handsome laughter now. A frown wrinkled his brow, and it cast his eyes deep in shadow. He sobered so quickly and looked so wounded, she nearly regretted her words.

"So you haven't given that over," he said, his voice as abrasive as the crunch of their feet on the blue stone walk. It shot her through with cold chills.

"There is nothing to 'give over,' my lord," she returned. "I simply wish to know. You evidently know more than I do about the man. It's little enough to ask that you assuage my curiosity."

He hesitated. "I cannot presume to know his whereabouts," he said. "We are not formally acquainted. I simply know of him, and wish to know no more. He's another whose society I would not court. I've heard that he has a cottage near Bath, and another property somewhere in the north. If I knew for certain how to answer you, you can bet your bonnet I wouldn't be standing here with you now."

"Who is it we're challenging this time?" said a stoical voice from behind that spun them both around to face a fair-haired gentleman decked out in impeccable afternoon attire of indigo superfine and faun-colored silk. "Am I to serve as second again? A body needs to know these things, old boy."

Nigel's demeanor softened. "Lady Clara Langly, may I present a good friend of mine, Viscount Alistair McGovern."

"Charmed," said McGovern, taking Alice's hand.

"Ah! So this is the gentleman," said Alice. "The pleasure is mine."

Both men raised their eyebrows at that—and for the first time since she'd set foot in Nigel Farnham's carriage, Alice began enjoying herself.

"So, who is the walking corpse this time, as if I need ask?" said McGovern. "Chesterton, I gather."

"Al . . . ," Nigel warned.

"You're a bit late, if he's your target, old boy."

"And why is that?" Nigel queried. There was no denying his discomfort. Stiff jaw muscles had begun to tick along his angular jawline, his color had heightened, and his eyes narrowed on McGovern.

"He was last seen speeding toward Gretna Green with nobody knows whom, except that it wasn't his betrothed . . . or his mistress!" McGovern drawled.

The words struck Alice like cannon fire. It was too much. A soft moan escaped her throat. The ground rose up to meet her as the filtered sunlight disappeared, and she spiraled into Nigel's arms, unconscious.

Chapter Nine

Well, I hope you're satisfied," Nigel barked, carrying Alice through the rear entrance of the town house with Alistair McGovern on his heels. The halls were empty, and he burst into a rear sitting room and laid her on a chaise longue.

"Sorry, old boy," said McGovern. "Who knew she'd keel over like that?"

"She was obviously expecting to be the one in that carriage bound for Gretna Green," said Nigel, rubbing her wrists. "What better opportunity? Her aunt has been detained in Yorkshire. She was probably intending to take advantage of her absence to run off with the bounder and tie the knot in Scotland while she had the chance. No doubt that's why she went round to his town house unescorted after dark last night, and he'd already gone off, the jackanapes."

"You've lost me, old boy."

"That's right! We haven't talked since all that occurred. Well, I haven't time to fill you in now. We've got to get her out of here."

"I shall fetch Lady Pembroke at once."

"No, don't! You'll bring the whole gathering in here upon us. Isobel Rutledge is here. That's something else I'll need to fill you in on, but not here. Suffice it to say that neither one of us is anxious to court her company."

"How do you propose to get her out of here?" asked McGovern, nodding toward the chaise longue. "You can't just hoist her over your shoulder and march her through that crowd out there in the garden. Think what the ton would make of that, not to mention Isobel Rutledge. You'll cause a riot."

"If you would be of help, find Carter and have him bring the carriage round back by the servants' entrance. Say nothing to anyone."

"Not even Lady Pembroke?"

"Especially not Lady Pembroke," said Nigel. "I'll explain later. Right now I need to see Lady Clara safely to the town house."

"*Your* town house? In broad daylight? Are you mad, Nigel? What if someone sees you carrying her into your house unconscious? Are you deliberately trying to ruin your reputation, not to mention hers? Not that there's much left to ruin at this point."

"It isn't far. Perhaps she will have come round by then. I can't very well take her home as she is. After the tales Isobel has been spreading . . . they'd probably have me hauled off by the guards from the watch. At least at my house Mrs. Davies can brew her an herbal cordial or something. Besides, I've not gotten to the bottom of all this yet, and I mean to do so before I let her out of my sight again."

"She's really gotten under your skin, hasn't she,

old boy? She's a looker, I'll own, but is that wise, considering?"

"Stubble it, Al! Just do as I've said and fetch the coach. Then later, when you're through mixing with the masses, come round and we'll talk."

Alice groaned awake to the aroma of smelling salts and chamomile, and the wavy image of a strange woman standing over her. Vertigo starred her vision. It was a moment before it all came rushing back: the fete, Isobel Rutledge, her vague recollection of having been introduced to someone—Alistair something or other, Nigel's friend. He'd announced that Lord Chesterton was on his way to Gretna Green. That could mean only one thing. Her worst fears were realized. Lady Clara Langly had eloped with the bounder. She remembered nothing more, and almost swooned again, recalling that.

She gave a start and glanced around the room. Was she still at Lady Pembroke's town house? She couldn't tell. The only room she was familiar with in that place was the enormous ballroom. This certainly wasn't that. It was smaller, a well-appointed parlor of sorts, and she was reclining on a lounge beneath a blanket that smelled of leather and lime. It certainly wasn't her parlor at the Langly town house in Mayfair.

She threw back the blanket and attempted to rise, but a woman's hand restrained her. At the same time, a terrible throbbing in her head drew her hand to her brow.

"Who are you? What is this place?" Alice demanded.

"Here, now, my lady," the woman replied. "You've had a bit of an upset, but you're better now." She placed a bottle of smelling salts on a nearby table and took up a steaming cup waiting there. "I'm Mrs. Davies, Lord Romney's housekeeper. This is his home, in Grosvenor Square. You're quite safe, my lady. I've brewed ya a cup o' chamomile tea, ta settle your giddiness."

"He's brought me to his home?" Alice shrilled, struggling to rise. "I—I can't be here! I can't stay here! I demand to be taken to my own home at once!"

"It's all quite proper, my lady," said the housekeeper. "I'm here ta see that all the proprieties are met. His Lordship couldn't see ya home unconscious like that, now could he? What a fine stir that would have caused! Here, drink your tea. He'll be down directly."

Alice swung her feet to the floor. She was still dizzy. Her hand was shaking as she took the cup, and she tried to keep it from rattling against the saucer.

"That's it, my lady," said the housekeeper. "There's a touch o' rue in it. That's what's hangin' round your neck there—rue."

Alice groped her throat. A twisted garland of small, spatulate leaves was draped there.

"Ta cure the dizziness," the housekeeper explained.

Alice tore it off. "I am quite cured," she said, "and I do not believe in Gypsy charms or witch magic."

The housekeeper bristled. "It ain't witch magic," she defended. "Why, everybody knows since time out of mind, the old folks have put great store in rue for curin' the headaches and dizzy spells."

"Well, I do not!" Alice informed her.

"You're sittin' up, ain't ya?" said the housekeeper, folding her hands in front of her starched white apron. She was a strange-looking woman, tall and thin, with eyes like a hawk's, dark and piercing, her graying hair all but invisible beneath a white lawn cap. It was impossible to tell her age.

"I don't want this," Alice said, handing back the cup. "I want to go home. I want to go home at once!"

"And so you shall," said Nigel's familiar baritone voice from the doorway. "As soon as you can stand without your knees buckling." Striding into the room, he turned to the housekeeper. "That will be all, Mrs. Davies," he added.

"No, it will not!" Alice cried. "Mrs. Davies will remain. You had no right to bring me here, my lord. I will not be compromised."

"Of course not," Nigel said. Then, to the housekeeper, "Leave the door open, and wait on the settle in the hall."

"Yes, m'lord," she replied. Sketching a curtsy, she did as she'd been told.

"You had a shock, and you swooned right in front of Alistair and myself in Lady Pembroke's garden," Nigel said, staring down at Alice, his arms akimbo.

"Nothing of the kind," she snapped in reply. "I repeatedly told you, I haven't been myself of late. I—I wasn't feeling well enough to attend that fete. That's why I cried off. I never should have let you persuade me otherwise. You are mistaken in your assumptions, and you have taken unfair advantage bringing me here, sir." She snatched the rue necklace up from the lounge beside her and waved it in front of him. "That woman put this around my neck. What sort of heathen creatures do you have in your employ here?"

"Mrs. Davies is a skilled herbalist, my lady," he replied, suppressing a smile. "She has doctored the inmates of this house with her herbal remedies since before I was born. We all rely upon her. So do the doctors hereabouts. They swear by her medicines and appreciate that her doctoring spares them coming round for every bellyache and splinter."

Alice wanted to vault off the lounge and slap that silly smirk off his face, but her hands were shaking too much, and her knees wouldn't support her yet. That wasn't due to the vertigo, however. It was due to his closeness, and his intoxicating scent threading through her nostrils. It was even on the blanket they'd wrapped her in.

"I've done nothing but try to protect you," Nigel said. "I knew you wouldn't have wanted to become a spectacle, and I got you out of there with no one the wiser and had you here in a trice. What did you expect I'd do with you? I couldn't very well carry you prostrate up your front walk in broad daylight, as Alistair pointed out, without alarming half of

Mayfair. I couldn't let you remain at Lady Pembroke's, either, else the whole gathering be made privy to your . . . indisposition. What other choice did I have, but to bring you here? Tell me."

He was probably right, but she wouldn't give him the satisfaction. What would her father say about garlands of rue and herbal medicines? She shuddered to wonder.

"I want to go home," she pronounced.

"And I will be happy to escort you there once I'm convinced you aren't going to faint on me again . . . or do something foolish. Meanwhile, I would appreciate it if you would drink Mrs. Davies's herbal tea. It will relax you."

"I would much prefer to relax in my own parlor at home, sir," Alice retorted.

"You were planning to run away with him, weren't you?" Nigel said, straightening a mussed bit of fringe on the Aubusson carpet with the toe of his polished black Hessian.

"That is none of your business," Alice snapped. "And what if I was? Who has appointed you my guardian?"

"Someone has to take on the task. Why not me? The bounder nearly ruined you. What have I ever done to cause you harm?"

Alice jutted her chin and cast him a meaningful glower, recalling his bold embrace in the carriage.

"That was not meant to hurt you, my lady, only to enlighten you."

"Yes, well, since I am now duly enlightened, and it is a moot point, considering current events, you may wash your hands of me in all good conscience, sir. I no longer have need of your services. Now, take me home."

She surged to her feet, trying not to waver. This was no mean task, considering traces of the vertigo still remained and surfaced each time her thoughts returned to Lady Clara on her way to Gretna Green, and what she herself would tell Countess Greenway when the woman arrived.

He reached her in two strides and took hold of her upper arms, drawing her closer than she deemed proper. The thrill of that did little to relieve her dizziness.

"You don't believe all of that nonsense Isobel Rutledge is spreading about me, do you?" he said.

"I neither believe nor disbelieve, nor do I care, sir," said Alice. Those were the hardest words she'd ever had to speak, considering that it couldn't be further from the truth. She did care, or at least she would if she let herself. That, however, she could not do. "I am not inclined toward pursuing or encouraging any sort of association with you, Lord Romney. I do not know how much plainer I can make it."

"Why? We've gotten off on the wrong foot, I'll own, but could we not begin again . . . as though we've never met? I would like to get to know you better. I would like to prove to you that all men aren't creatures of Chesterton's stamp."

"I think not, my lord," she murmured. "I shall be leaving London soon. . . . There is no point."

"So you've said. But, surely not until the season is over?"

"I'm afraid so. My plans have changed."

"Yes, I expect that they have," said Nigel, the words riding a sigh.

He relaxed his grip, his strong hands inching up and down her arms. "It's only fair to warn you that I shan't give up, you know," he said. "There is nothing more enticing to a man than a lady of mystery."

"Are you so vanity driven that you imagine every woman you meet will just fall into your arms, sir? Have I ever given you the slightest encouragement?"

"No. That is part of your charm."

"Just what do you imagine you see in me, my lord?"

"I see a very beautiful, misguided young lady who very nearly made a tragic mistake, and I feel duty bound to prevent history from repeating itself. She might not be so fortunate a second time. You cannot deny that there is a mutual attraction here. I see it in those incredible green eyes of yours. I hear it in the voice you dare not trust. I feel the heat of it radiating from those rosy cheeks, despite your supposed love for Chesterton, and on such short acquaintance, I'll be bound. Don't you think such an attraction deserves a chance to see where it might lead? Don't you think we owe it that much?"

She was clearly no match for him. He was suave and polished, a man-about-town. He was her first affair of the heart, and she lacked the experience to match his prowess. Deception had thrown them together, and it was the very same deception that would separate them for all time the minute he realized the truth. Their whole association was a lie.

Even if by some miracle he could forgive that lie, she was still beneath him socially, and she couldn't imagine him ever forgiving the fool she'd made of him by continuing the hoax, or the mockery she'd made of his noble aspirations attempting to save her from herself from the start. But that wasn't entirely her fault. Hadn't she tried to tell him the truth? He was so full of himself that he couldn't see it.

"I do not know where you have gotten such notions, but I assure you, you are mistaken," she said, as levelly as she could, while his hands were roaming up and down her arms—and at that, she couldn't meet his eyes. Were she to lose herself in their glacier blue depths in that moment, she would have come undone.

As if he'd read her mind, he tilted her chin up with his finger and forced eye contact. Was the man a sorcerer? Her heart tumbled in her breast, and she stifled a gasp. His lips parted. They were so close. How did that happen? When did he range himself close enough to . . .

Oh, my stars! He's going to kiss me!

He let her go instead. The sudden separation was a total shock, and she fought to recapture her composure, praying she didn't look as ridiculous as she felt.

"I shall make a bargain with you," he said, that seductive baritone voice even more riveting in close proximity. "If you can reach that door there on your own—unwavering, mind—I shall have Carter bring the coach round, and I shall see you home forthwith."

Everything depended upon her winning that

bargain. She didn't trust herself alone with him for another second.

"Very well," she said. Clearing her throat, she squared her posture and floated toward the parlor door as if flanked by invisible winged beings. Once out of range of his scent and the blatant seduction in those eyes, she began to regain control of her runaway emotions. He wasn't important, she told herself. Dealing with Lady Clara's debacle was. And it had to be done at once. She'd known all along what she must do, but she'd lacked the courage until now. Her error had to be faced, and dealt with. With that resolved in her mind, if not in her heart, she turned on the threshold to face him.

"Please send for your carriage, my lord," she said. "I believe I have won the bargain."

"I bow to a worthy opponent," he replied, bending from the waist. Moving past her into the corridor, he addressed the housekeeper, who rose from the settle at sight of him. "Have Carter bring the carriage round," he charged. "I shall see my lady home. Oh, and, when Viscount McGovern arrives, make him comfortable. He'll be staying to dinner. Inform Cook."

"Thank you, my lord," said Alice.

"What happened to *Nigel*?" he asked, tongue firmly in cheek.

"I left him behind at the fete," she returned. "It's where he belongs, after all."

"Ahhh, you think so, do you?"

"I do."

"Well, that just goes to show you how little you know me, my lady."

"I shall wait outside," said Alice. "You needn't accompany me, my lord. I'm sure Carter can find his way to Mayfair."

"Ohhhh, no," he replied. "I will see you home, my dear. You may have won the bargain, but you haven't won the war—if that's what we're waging here. I had something else entirely in mind. I shall concede defeat for today, but as I told you, I shan't give up. I never back down from a challenge, and you are, if nothing else, certainly that." He extended his crooked elbow. "Shall we go?"

Alice threaded her hand through his proffered arm and said no more. There wasn't any point. She hadn't convinced him, but that didn't matter. After today, she would never see him again.

No words passed between them on the drive to Mayfair. Once they reached the Langly town house and Carter set the steps, Nigel handed her out of the carriage and up the front walk. Taking her hand in his, he raised it to his lips.

His mouth was warm as he kissed her, lingering longer on her flesh than she deemed proper. Yet, though her fingers tightened, she did not resist. This was the last time, after all. What harm to savor it? When he caressed her palm as he had done at the masque, however, she did break away. What that intimate touch did to her most private regions was scandalous!

"Good-bye, my lord," she murmured, inclining her head as she grasped the door handle.

"Never good-bye," he returned. "I shall call again on Sunday. If the weather is fine, we shall have a drive through Hyde Park."

"I will not be here."

"You will," he called, bounding down the steps. "Oh, yes, my lady . . . you will."

He disappeared inside the carriage then, and the rat-a-tat-tat of his walking stick addressing the carriage roof shot her through like cannon fire. She didn't watch him drive out of sight. She slipped inside, slumped against the door, and shut her eyes.

Her reprieve was short-lived. A voice echoing down the staircase made her jump as though she'd been shot, and her eyes came open wide. It was Lady Clara.

"Well, well!" she said. "I see you've been enjoying yourself in my absence, Alice Jessup. I think we need to talk."

Chapter Ten

Alice was glad of the door at her back. Her knees threatened to buckle. Where were her winged supporters now? Gooseflesh puckered her scalp, and the blood rushed from her face. It descended like a lowered shade and made her lightheaded, threatening her balance. She could scarcely believe her eyes. Lady Clara bore an unearthly look—almost wraithlike—bathed in fractured sunlight filtering in through the window above the landing, her eyes filled with scorn.

"Is that my frock you're wearing?" she asked. "Of course it is. Who was that gentleman fawning all over you on the doorstep just now? This is not what we arranged. Well? Speak up!"

"Where have you been, my lady?" Alice breathed, avoiding the questions dripping such venom, in an attempt to beat back the inevitable. "We have been half out of our minds with worry!"

"Yes, I can certainly see that," Lady Clara returned, her cold gaze raking Alice cruelly. She made no move to descend from the landing, but stood her ground, her hand poised on the newel post.

"You left no word, no clue as to where you'd gone," Alice continued, having decided that admonishment was her most effective defense. "We were frantic here! Mrs. Avery nearly took a fit of apoplexy when you went missing, not to mention the fright you've given the rest of the staff, and myself. You put me in an impossible position."

"You don't look any the worse for wear."

"We've sent for your aunt," Alice went on. "We had no choice. I know where you've been, and with whom. What ever possessed you?"

"How would you know where I've been?"

"I know, because I made it my business to know. Somebody had to, and I've tarnished my own reputation doing it. Have you any idea what you've done? Regardless of the circumstances, you are ruined, my lady!"

Lady Clara's posture collapsed. "Come to my chamber," she said, turning away. "*Now*, Alice."

It was a moment before Alice was able to push herself off from the door at her back and climb the stairs. When she reached her employer's chamber, Lady Clara was standing before the window. It overlooked the street below where the low-sliding sun was casting tall shadows across the lane.

"You haven't answered my question," she said without turning when the door clicked shut. "Who was he?"

"That is all that concerns you, when the world as we knew it has caved in around us?"

"We shall start with that, and where you've been this afternoon in my best pink pongee-silk frock!"

"I am wearing your best pink pongee-silk frock because Lady Pembroke, believing I was you, came round here insisting I attend her fete for the debutantes. I tried to cry off, but I . . . could not, and I do not own a suitable frock of my own. Our little deception was only supposed to be for one night. When you didn't return, that changed matters, and you have no one to blame for that but yourself. I could hardly go about in costume until you decided to come home, my lady."

"Do not hedge with me! Who was that on the doorstep just now?"

"The gentleman who escorted me home was the very cause of this whole unfortunate deception—Nigel Farnham, Lord Romney."

Lady Clara did spin around then, her eyes wide as saucers. "Impossible!" she cried. "Farnham is a toady—an insufferable toady! Do not lie to me, Alice. Who was that man?"

Alice shook her head. "You were misinformed, my lady," she said. "It seems that he rejected the advances of Isobel Rutledge, and she retaliated by spreading vicious lies about him."

"So, you've got your hooks into him, clever girl. Does he know you are merely working-class—a nobody? Aunt Regina arranged that introduction for *me*!"

"You were the one who insisted that I go in your place in order to discourage him, my lady. It certainly wasn't my idea."

"But you did go, and it doesn't appear that you've discouraged anything, to me. You saw I was in error, that I have misjudged the man, and you've taken him for yourself!"

"I haven't taken anything," Alice defended. "Thanks to this ridiculous ruse of yours, he thinks that I am you, my lady. But it doesn't matter. There is nothing between us. As soon as your lady aunt arrives, I shall give my notice. I've had my fill of the ton and everything connected with aristocratic life. I'm going home, where I belong."

"You are just going to leave me—just like *that*— now that I need you most?"

"How can I possibly remain? You do not need me, my lady. It would be impossible for me to stay now. Surely you can see that?"

Lady Clara burst into tears. "You don't care a whit about what's happened to me!" she sobbed.

"Forgive me," said Alice. "But what has happened to you, you have brought upon yourself, my lady. You knew the risk you were taking when you ran off with the likes of Chesterton. How could you have been so blind? Did you know he was betrothed when you eloped with him to Gretna Green, and that he has a mistress as well? Yes, a mistress, my lady! Did you reach your destination? Did he marry you? Or did he hoodwink you into giving up your virtue and then cast you by the wayside?"

Lady Clara flung herself across the bed and burst into wracking sobs. Alice stole closer, reaching out, then retracting her hand. No. She would not comfort the spoiled chit. There was nothing to be done. If only she could turn back time. If only the deception hadn't happened. If only she had never set eyes upon Nigel Farnham, or let him hold her, or kiss her, or awaken her to desire. No, she could not turn back time, but she could go forward, wiser. First she must own up to what she'd done, however. As soon as Lady Greenway arrived, she would make a clean breast of it all and go home. Facing her father would be the worst of it.

"He said he loved me," Lady Clara sobbed.

"If only you had confided in me, told me what you were planning, I would never have gone to that masque," Alice said. "I would have done everything in my power to prevent you from making such a foolish mistake, even before I knew who and what Lord Chesterton was. I was curious, blinded by the glamour of a life I can never know. We are all who we are. I forgot that. I had no right to pretend I was someone else—even for a moment."

"What am I going to do?" Lady Clara wailed. "Who will have me now?"

Alice hesitated. She could offer advice that might save the foolish chit's reputation, but to do so she would have to ruin her own. While she didn't feel the selfish little flibbertigibbet deserved saving, she did need to make reparation for her own sins in the matter, a by-product of her upbringing. She was hardly blameless in this, and it was no more than she deserved to be cast out in disgrace. But would the gel learn her lesson from it if she had her salvation handed to her on a silver platter? Weighing the improbability of that, she breathed a ragged sigh.

"Does anyone know you were in that coach with Chesterton?" she said. "Were you seen?"

"No . . . I don't know. I don't think so. Why?"

"How did you get home?"

"By post chaise."

"It's all over town that Chesterton eloped with someone to Gretna Green . . . someone other than his betrothed, or his mistress. But nobody seems to know who it was. You can salvage something of this if you make yourself very visible about town for the rest of the season. That should put paid to any rumors that might crop up, and you could make a match, into the bargain. Of course, I will not be with you, but that won't matter. Your lady aunt will be here shortly, and she will take my place . . . or hire another companion for you."

"What of you?"

"Think, my lady!" said Alice. "The moment your aunt arrives, I will be sacked for my part in this. I shirked my duty to you. I failed you. I have been going about pretending to be you. You will have to expose me as an impostor in order to take your proper place amongst the ton. There is no other way. Countess Pembroke, Lord Romney, and a viscount friend of his all met me thinking they were meeting Lady Clara Langly. You began this ruse. That I am sacrificing myself to get you out of it is more than you deserve, I'm sure, but I am willing . . . provided that you will grant me two small favors in exchange."

"What sort of favors?" Lady Clara queried guardedly. Wiping her swollen eyes, she sat up on the bed. "You want money, I suppose?"

"No," said Alice, resisting the urge to throttle the

girl. It was becoming harder and harder to justify self-sacrifice for the likes of Clara Langly, but she was resigned. "I want no money," she went on. "It saddens me that you would think it. What I wish is that you do me the courtesy of waiting until I have left London to expose me. The missive I wrote to your aunt was sent by special messenger; she should be en route here as we speak. It shan't be too much of a hardship for you to wait a day or two longer to make your debut in public and mingle with the other hopefuls. You haven't missed much. Under the circumstances, you are fortunate to be having a season at all."

"And the second favor?"

"That you do not tell Nigel Farnham where I have gone."

"You needn't worry about that!" Lady Clara snapped. "I only hope you haven't ruined my chances with the man. And when I get my hands on Isobel Rutledge, I shall scratch her eyes out! He could have been mine!"

"There is one more thing," said Alice.

Lady Clara rolled her eyes. "You said only two conditions. Now there are three. If I allow three, there will be four—"

"Be still, you foolish little twit!" Alice shrilled, glad that she could speak her mind now that she was leaving. "It is not a condition. It is a bit of sound advice. I know I am only three years your senior, and I am certainly no sage, but I was raised differently, and sometimes such a difference can be beneficial in situations like this by giving a fresh

perspective. If you do align with someone, whether
it be . . . Lord Romney or another, you owe it to
that person to be honest about your relationship
with Chesterton. One's indiscretions have a way of
coming back to haunt one later on. Chesterton is a
rakehell, a blatant scoundrel. You do not want to
give him anything to hold over your head, my lady.
You do not need to name names, mind. It would be
best that you don't. But you do owe it to whomever
you accept as a life partner to be honest. Aside from
the fact that it is the moral thing to do, if your partner already knows, Chesterton can never harm you
with the telling of it."

"Yes, yes. Is that all, then?"

"Not quite," said Alice, hesitating. "I tell you
these things because I will no longer be here to help
you, and I doubt your lady aunt will be inclined to
broach such an intimate subject with you. I do not
hold her blameless in your . . . situation. If she had
taken her guardianship of you more seriously and
instructed you in the proper conduct for a young
lady, you mightn't be in this predicament."

"I find it amusing that you know of such things,
raised without a mother and in a Methodist rectory,
of all places. Perhaps you are not so lily-white as you
pretend. Perhaps your knowledge in these matters
stems from firsthand experience."

"Every sin and sorrow knocks upon a minister's
door, my lady," said Alice. "To that extent, if nothing else, I can boast of firsthand experience. And
this is my last advice: you should wait an appropriate time to be certain there have been no . . . conse-

quences from Chesterton, before you align with another. These prospective suitors gadding about town join the marriage mart to perpetuate their line. It is not too much to ask that it *is* their line that is being perpetuated, if you follow my meaning, my lady."

Lady Clara vaulted off the bed. "I hadn't thought of that!" she said, discovery in her voice. "Thank you for bringing it to my attention, Alice—but I shan't take that bit of advice to heart. What do I care for the bloodlines of these popinjays? What of *me*? Men are all alike. They use and abuse. They shall get no special consideration from me. To the contrary, I shall make it a point to 'align' myself with one of them straightaway, just in case of . . . consequences."

Nigel approved the larded-pheasant course the liveried footman presented to him. Then he leaned back, sipping his wine while the man served Alistair McGovern and himself. He hadn't returned to the fete, and the viscount had bowed out early. This intrigue at home was far more stimulating.

They had gotten through the soup and fish courses, with lemon-flavored ice between to cleanse the palate. The pheasant was the last before dessert. While the footmen arranged the takeaways, there was a lull in the conversation, which unfailingly returned to the same topic: a certain little flaxen-haired, green-eyed lady of mystery.

"So, what do you think of her, Al?" Nigel said, as they resumed their meal.

"You'd barely introduced us when she swooned. How could I possibly form an opinion?"

"I just wish you hadn't blurted it out about Chesterton as you did," Nigel said. "That was rather insensitive, don't you think?"

"I *didn't* think. Sorry, old boy, it just slipped out. She doesn't look the sort to go about unescorted, though, and she certainly seems intelligent enough not to get herself compromised. Yet she's done just that. Who can tell with women these days? I daresay I'm no judge. You know what sort of luck I've had with the birds of late."

"That could well be because tact is not your long suit, old boy," said Nigel over the rim of his goblet.

"Ouch!" McGovern responded. "But that's quite possible, though I'd rather like to think it's because I haven't met a gel who could turn my head the way Lady Clara has evidently turned yours. This is some kind of a record for you, isn't it? You're acquainted with the lady for less than a sennight. I've never known you to leap without looking before, and quite frankly, I'm worried about you."

"I've never met anyone like her before," Nigel said, his fork suspended. "I was taken with her the minute I collided with her in Lady Pembroke's ballroom at the masque. It isn't just her looks, though she is a beauty. Those eyes! She is exquisite. But that aside, there's something mysterious about her. She isn't like any of the other debutantes I've met. You've made the rounds. There's a certain . . . almost desperate air about them. Not so, Lady Clara. She thwarts me at every turn, and you know how I love a challenge."

"I wonder why we haven't seen her before?" McGovern mused. "This cannot be her first season. She's twenty-one, at least."

Nigel laughed. "Ready to put on her caps, hm?" he chided, wagging his head.

"No, no, there's nothing wrong with that," McGovern defended. "I'm simply making an observation. You know as well as I that most families trot their daughters out at eighteen . . . or nineteen, and even that is considered late these days. Why, I've known a few who made their come-out as young as seventeen. When a lady is still unspoken for past twenty, it's usually one of two things. It's either lack of blunt to bring her out sooner, or she's had a season or two with no takers. Whichever, there's something wrong here, and since I cannot imagine such a stunning creature as Lady Clara being passed up at first airing, that leaves only one alternative. The family's in dun territory, and she's swimming at low tide. Beware. You could be facing another Isobel Rutledge, old boy."

"Heaven forefend!" Nigel blurted. "Though, I doubt that. She wouldn't be running from me if she were scorched, she'd be running after me. And since you've brought Isobel into this, I've news in that regard that might amuse you."

"Oh?"

"She's spread tales all over town that I'm a hawk-nosed toady who relies upon leg pads and corsets to cut a good figure, and toys with young ladies with no good intentions of offering for them."

"Oh, Nigel! You've got to put a stop to that."

"Why? Anyone who's met me knows it's pure balderdash."

"But what of those who haven't? The gel could ruin you socially. If it goes unchecked, and you don't defend yourself, it's as good as an admission of guilt. You could be cut from the best affairs—struck from the guest lists—simply on principle. Nobody courts controversial guests. Artificial embellishments are one thing, but once word spreads that you know how to play the ladies, you'd be committing social suicide to ignore it."

"You're out of touch, old boy. Everyone courts controversial guests these days. Just look at Chesterton. By all accounts, I don't see him suffering ostracism because of his escapades."

"Oh, well, if you want to include yourself in *that* company. Dash it all, Nigel, you're a decorated war hero! You've had your share of escapades, I'll grant, and so have I, but we've always been discreet. You cannot allow a vindictive little chit to slander you all over town. You're thirty-four years old. I wish you'd just choose someone suitable and bow out of this marriage-mart madness. That's what I'm trying to do, and I'm a year and a half younger than you. It's downright uncivilized. Why, if your parents were living, they'd be on you like ticks on a dog for you to settle down and get an heir."

"What would you have me do, take out an advertisement in the *Times*? 'To whom it may concern:

Contrary to popular belief, Nigel Farnham, Earl of Romney, does not wear corsets or leg pads. His nose, though a bit Roman, is quite acceptable, and his sterling character is above reproach'? Really, Al, you're fast becoming a Sassenach."

"And you've become infatuated with trouble. This gel may be above reproach, and guilty of nothing more than bad judgment, but you cannot deny that she's put a blot on her copybook by associating with Chesterton. Her reputation is in question, and I hate to see you settle for damaged goods."

"I told her I'd come to call on Sunday," Nigel said, thinking out loud.

McGovern uttered a strangled sound as he nearly choked on a morsel of potato. Rolling his eyes, he tossed his serviette down.

"I think I shall go round on Saturday instead," Nigel went on. "There's something to be said for the element of surprise, especially since I have a feeling she might just bolt and run in earnest. She has that look about her, like a frightened doe staring down the barrel of a hunter's musket. You've no idea what that look does to me, old boy. If bones could melt . . ."

"You haven't heard one word I've said," McGovern groused.

"Oh, yes I have," Nigel replied. "I've just dismissed it out of hand."

Chapter Eleven

*C*ountess Greenway arrived from the cottage in Wiltshire before dawn on Saturday in the well-appointed Langly barouche. The coachman had driven through the night on the last lap of the journey in order to reach London by the weekend. The appearance of the sharp-eyed, fragile-looking woman in her sixties was deceptive. She walked with a cane, which she used more often as a weapon than a means of support. Alice had realized this early in her employ, and gave it a wide berth. She'd seen the deadly stick knock the wind out of more than one footman when the countess applied it broadside to the belly to enforce an order, and the rapid-fire tapping of its silver tip had gotten her attention on more than one occasion. It was most dangerous, however, when standing idle, while Her Ladyship's gnarled fingers worked the silver repoussé-embellished handle, just as they did now.

Alice had not come down to breakfast. She had opted for a tray in her room. When it arrived, the summons that she meet with Lady Greenway came with it. Alice was not taken by surprise. She hadn't slept. She was curled on the window seat in her chamber when the carriage entered the mews just before first light. Her food uneaten, she went downstairs.

They were seated in the drawing room. The countess had already interviewed Lady Clara and sent her to her room. Alice heard the muffled sobs leaking through the girl's chamber door on the way down, and she almost pitied her. Almost. Now Alice was sitting ramrod rigid in a gilt and brocade Roman Empire–style chair that matched the sofa across the way, where Lady Greenway had been studying her for some time.

Though she expected it, Alice gave a lurch when the woman's cane banged once on the floor, indicating that the inquisition was begun.

"Well, miss," the countess began, tight-lipped. "What have you to say for yourself?"

"I'm sure Lady Clara has given an accurate account," Alice replied. "I doubt I could add to it. I am ready to take full responsibility for my actions. My bags are packed. I shall leave at once, of course."

"Without notice?"

"There is nothing I can do here now but add to the problem, my lady. It would be best if I were just to go."

"Not before I hear your side of this. I want the truth, Alice. Sparing Clara isn't going to help her. Only the truth will do that. I cannot trust her to tell it, but I've never known you to lie to me. What happened here?"

Alice hesitated. The countess was right, of course.

Sugarcoating Lady Clara's involvement would do more harm than good. Her loyalties were divided, however, and struggling with that, she kept a close eye upon the silver-headed cane in the woman's grip.

"I am waiting," the countess intoned.

"Perhaps it would be best if you tell me Lady Clara's version. That way I could—"

"Ohhh, no, my dear," the countess interrupted. "It is your version that I am interested in."

"Very well, my lady," said Alice, squaring her posture. "Lady Clara heard rumors that Lord Romney was too repulsive for a suitable candidate. She did not wish to attend the masque and suffer the introduction to him that you had arranged with Lady Pembroke. She coerced me into going in her place and begged me to discourage him. She argued that no one knows her here, and even if perchance there were someone with whom she was acquainted, it wasn't likely that I would be found out, not so elaborately costumed and masked. It was only supposed to be that once. Unfortunately, things got out of hand."

The cane banged again. "Explain!" the countess demanded.

"I did not know until it was too late that the real reason Lady Clara wanted me to go was because she intended to elope with a man she'd been seeing in secret for some time."

"You were aware of this association?"

"I suspected something, yes," said Alice. "But I did not know the man's identity."

"Do you know it now?"

"Yes."

"What is the bounder's name?"

Alice hesitated. Evidently, Lady Clara had not confided his identity. If Alice were to do so, the consequences could be catastrophic.

"I do not know that it would be prudent for me to say, my lady," she said, "or that it would solve anything."

"We shall leave that for the moment. Did you broach the subject with Clara once you 'suspected something'?"

"I did not."

"And you certainly didn't broach it with me, did you? You should have done. If I had known . . . Well, it's too late now. Continue."

"When I returned from the masque, Lady Clara had gone off without a word to anyone. We waited a reasonable time, hoping she would return. When she did not, I sent for you. Meanwhile, with Lady Clara gone missing, and Countess Pembroke and Lord Romney thinking I was she, I had no choice but to continue the deception. In defense of my intentions, however, I did try to tell Lord Romney the truth. I told him who I was and that I was my lady's companion on two separate occasions. He simply refused to believe me. I am sorry, my lady. It was wrong of me to pretend to be something I am not . . . even for a moment. I should have resisted the temptation. If I had, I might have been able to prevent what has happened to Lady Clara."

"The jackanapes has ruined her, of course," the countess said, banging the cane in punctuation.

"She can be salvaged, my lady," Alice said. "I have given her the means, if only she will heed my advice."

"And what sage advice has the likes of you given my niece that might affect her salvation, pray?"

"That she take her place in society as if nothing untoward had occurred—become visible, attend the affairs, the balls, and fetes. That will dispel the rumors and curtail any on-dits that have begun in the meanwhile. And lastly, to lay the blame for the deception upon me, where it belongs."

"How noble, Alice. I applaud your performance. You actually believe this sacrifice is enough to excuse you?"

"That I forfeit my own reputation to salvage hers? Yes, I do," Alice replied, a close eye upon the countess's grip on the formidable cane. "Your niece, my lady, is a supercilious little ninnyhammer. She is a selfish, self-serving creature undeserving of such a redemption, because she will learn nothing from it, while someone else suffers the pain of her mistakes. I do her no favors. The 'sacrifice,' as you say, is for *me*, not her. We learn from our mistakes, my lady; it is how we grow. If our errors go unpunished, there is no benefit, and they will most assuredly be repeated."

"And . . . what have you learned from yours?"

"I have learned who and what I am, and where I belong. That is certainly not here. I have led a sheltered life, my lady, being motherless and raised by my minister father in austere circumstances. It is no excuse, I'm sure, but I have always wondered what my life might have been like if I were born a fine lady. I've air-dreamed it in my mind since I was a child. Such are the idle fantasies of the poor. My mistake was in taking advantage of an opportunity to make that dream come true, if only for a moment. I yielded to temptation, a grievous sin for the daughter of a man of the cloth. I have regretted it from the moment this unfortunate episode began."

"Did you beg my niece to exchange places with her at the masque?" said the countess, banging her cane, which had become an integral part of the conversation.

"I did not, my lady."

The cane banged again. "Did you deliberately set your cap at Lord Romney when you realized he wasn't the odious creature my niece supposed?"

"I did not, my lady—quite to the contrary. I have done naught but discourage Lord Romney's attentions. Is—is that what she told you?"

"Never you mind what she told me! I do not know which of you to believe."

"Believe whatever you like, my lady. I am well out of it. I shall be off on the noon coach to trouble your house no more."

"Mind your tongue!" the countess shrilled, surging to her feet.

Alice rose also. "It is enough, I think, that I take the brunt of this upon myself. What more than my ruin would you demand of me, my lady? What more than being sent down in disgrace will appease you? I offer myself up gladly, asking only that you have the compassion to allow me to make my

departure before you expose me . . . and that you
not disclose my whereabouts to Lord Romney. That
alone should show my honorable intentions in his
regard."

"I could never in good conscience recommend
you," the countess said, frosty voiced.

"I would not expect you to, my lady."

"I shall have to dispatch a full report of your
shameless conduct to your good father."

"That is your prerogative, my lady," said Alice, her
head held high. "I intend to make a full confession
to Father the minute I arrive home."

"Oh, I could throttle you!" the countess shrilled,
brandishing her cane. Alice didn't flinch, though
she fully expected the deadly thing to come crashing down upon her head. "You were good for Clara!"
she raved on. "How could you betray my trust in
you with such treachery?"

"If you strike me with that weapon, I will have
the guards in," Alice warned her. It was an idle
threat. She hadn't the funds to back it up, but the
countess couldn't know how much of her wages
she'd put by. "You have used it on your niece," she
went on. "Do not dare deny it, my lady, I heard her
cries. They were cries of pain in earnest. You shan't
do the same to me."

Countess Greenway sank back down on the sofa
and burst into tears.

"You may expect Lord Romney to call tomorrow," Alice said. "I told him I would not be here,
but he refused to take no for an answer. You might
want to prepare Lady Clara. I shan't see her again.

We have said our good-byes. If you will send someone up for my portmanteau and trunk, and be good
enough to have Groom drive me round to the
coaching station, I will leave straightaway."

"She . . . is . . . ruined!" the countess sobbed.

"I had no hand in that, my lady," Alice said.
"Though I shall take the blame, I'm sure. Do your
worst. I only hope and pray that what I do in her
behalf is not for naught. Good morning, Lady
Greenway."

"Oh, miss, ya can't be leavin'!" Mrs. Avery wailed,
helping Alice collect the last of her toiletries from
the vanity in her chamber. "How will we ever do
without ya?"

"The same as you did before I came," said Alice,
packing her precious Pears soap and rose water in
the last portmanteau. "You knew this would come.
I couldn't possibly stay now."

"But what about him?"

"Who?"

"*Him*, the Earl o' Romney. Ya can't tell me you
haven't a care for him, Miss Alice, and he's smitten
with you. Ya can't deny that, the way he keeps
comin' round here, even after ya told him not to!"

"I have no right to care for him. The man is rich
as Croesus. He has fortunes invested in Threadnee-
dle Street and properties all over England. He
thinks I am a lady of means. If he knew that in
truth he has been squandering his attentions upon a
poor little church mouse with pockets to let, you
would see soon enough how well he cares. He would

think me a fortune huntress, just like that dreadful
Isobel Rutledge, who has slandered him all about
town. Ton marries ton, or very close to it, Mrs. Avery.
They do not marry the poor. They take women
from my class as mistresses readily enough, but they
do not marry them. I shall never settle for such as
that."

"Is there nothin' ta be done, then?"

"We are from two different worlds, so far apart
on the social scale it would be impossible. I've
learned a hard lesson pretending to be what I'm
not—too hard a lesson to pretend something could
be, when there is no possibility of it. No, I'm
through pretending. It is much better to accept my
lot and move on. I have no choice now in any case.
Once Lord Romney comes round tomorrow, he'll
know the whole of it. He thinks I'm on the way to
becoming a fallen woman, and he means to save me
from myself. Imagine his embarrassment when he
finds out the truth! I mean to be away before that
occurs. I couldn't bear the humiliation of *his* humiliation, knowing that I have brought it on. That's
why I must leave now—today. I have the countess
and Lady Clara's word that they will not put me to
the pillory until I've departed . . . and that they will
not tell Lord Romney where I've gone. That was all
I asked in exchange."

"In exchange for what, miss?"

"In exchange for taking the blame for the whole
bumble-broth, so that Lady Clara can salvage something of her life, and her season."

The housekeeper gasped. "You're throwin' yourself ta the dogs?" she cried. "She ain't worth it! Why, you're worth ten o' the likes o' her. Good breedin' don't know no class, miss, same like blunt don't make a gentleman. It's what's inside of a body that makes their measure."

"God bless you, Mrs. Avery," Alice murmured, clouding. She would not let the tears fall. She would not! She'd gotten this far without becoming a watering pot, and she wasn't going to give in now. "I shall miss you most of all," she said.

The footmen, Higby and James, were carrying down the last of her luggage, her trunk. It was finally sinking in. She would never see Nigel Farnham again. He'd asked her to call him Nigel. She'd only done so once, though over and over she'd said it in her mind. It sounded soothing, like the music cool water makes rushing over pebbles in a stream. How she longed to lose herself in the serenity of that sound. How she ached to feel the urgent pressure of his lips upon hers, the strength of those sinewy arms drawing her to him. His scent came without bidding now, threading through her nostrils at odd moments when it was least expected. She drew a ragged breath. Would it always be so?

All at once a loud *bump! bump! bump!* echoing along the staircase outside brought her to her senses.

"The buffleheads have gone and dropped it!" the housekeeper said of the trunk. "I'll go see. I hope they haven't put a dent in it."

Alice glanced about—one last look around the room where it had all begun. A deep sigh brought her posture down. She did not regret leaving the town house, only leaving it in disgrace. What would her father say? He had always been a hard taskmaster, and she had suffered his wrath in the past for much less. She could just imagine the contents of Countess Greenway's missive, written with a quill dipped in venom. Hopefully, she would reach the rectory and make her confession before it did.

She took one last stroll about the room, running her gloved finger over the widow seat, over the foot of the polished mahogany sleigh bed. She stroked the vanity table, where her toiletries had been, and caressed the frame of the cheval glass, where she'd gazed at her image as Marie Antoinette in the tall powdered wig and feathered mask—where she'd yielded to the temptation that had changed her life forever. She could almost see herself, like a wraith in the polished mirror. Her hand fell away as the image dissolved before her eyes. *Good-bye . . .*

She would have finished the thought, but for Mrs. Avery, who came flying through the door at a speed Alice would have thought impossible in view of her girth, her arms carving circles in the air.

"What's happened?" Alice cried. "Is one of them injured?"

"No . . . miss," the housekeeper panted. "But you'll never guess who caught that trunk before it run clean over ol' Higby on them stairs down there." She didn't wait for Alice to answer. "'Twas him! The Earl o' Romney, come ta call!"

"B-but, he wasn't due until tomorrow!" Alice breathed. "What shall I do? I cannot see him. I cannot face him. I cannot!"

"Take ease, Miss Alice. He's not out in the hall no more. Her Ladyship is receivin' him in the salon."

"And . . . Lady Clara?"

"I haven't seen her."

"I have to leave. I have to go now!"

"Her Ladyship wouldn't have ya leavin' by the front, the sour ol' peahen. The carriage is round back o' the mews. Ya can go out through the servants' entrance, and—"

"But I shall have to pass by the salon to reach it," Alice interrupted. "Oh, Mrs. Avery!"

"Just go—quick and quiet, like a mouse."

Alice threw her arms around the woman. "I shall never forget you," she murmured.

"Nor I, you. Now, go if you're goin'," said the housekeeper, steering her toward the door.

Alice's legs were trembling. She inched up the skirt of her blue silk twill traveling costume just enough to keep from tripping. The last thing she wanted then was to go tumbling down those steep stairs just as the trunk had done. Reaching the landing, she steadied herself against the newel post and held her breath. Voices! *My stars! Is the salon door ajar?* Yes, just barely. She crept close, keeping to the shadows.

She had all good intentions of darting right by until she heard his voice, that deep, sensuous voice that reverberated in her soul and turned her knees to jelly. This was the last time she would hear it.

"I wasn't due to call until tomorrow, Your Ladyship," he said. "But I was in the neighborhood and thought to chance it. She isn't ill? She took a sick spell at the fete, but she was quite recovered by the time I escorted her home."

Alice held her breath, certain they could hear her heart, which was thundering in her ears. What was she doing? She could have reached the mews by now. She should be safe and away, but her feet wouldn't move. Her legs wouldn't carry her through the green baize-lined door that marked the servants' quarters only a few feet away. Not until she heard what he would say when he learned the truth, as painful as that would surely be to bear.

"Lord Romney," the countess intoned. The sound of that frosty voice crackling with arrogance filled Alice with disdain. "I am afraid that you have been the victim of a cruel and reprehensible hoax."

"My lady?"

"You have been duped, sir," the countess shot back. "Gulled by a brazen little nobody I employed as companion for my niece."

"I beg your pardon?"

Bang! went the countess's cane, despite the Aubusson carpet underneath it. Unprepared, Alice lurched, thankful that her back was against the wall, for then she had need of support.

"Have you a hearing impediment, my lord?" the countess snapped. "The gel you thought to be my niece, Lady Clara, was in fact her companion, Alice Jessup, a deceitful little commoner, the daughter of a poor country minister in whom I mistakenly placed my trust while I was indisposed. You have been bamboozled, sir. The gel you have been courting is a commoner, a liar, and a thief! She sought to steal my niece's season from her—her very identity, come down to it—and you, my lord, were her dupe."

There was a long silence, the kind that is tasted like death. It crawled over Alice's skin on a wave of gooseflesh that rooted her to the spot. Hot blood rushing to her temples starred her vision, which was already distorted by unshed tears. It was as if she'd been cast into a vacuum—until that evocative baritone rumble tore into it, erupting in a crescendo of heart-stopping guffaws. The last thing she would have expected. They cut her to the quick.

All at once, another sound bled into the rest. Another burst of laughter funneling down the staircase from above spun Alice around to face Lady Clara at the top of the landing, decked out in the same pink pongee-silk frock Alice had worn to the fete.

She could bear no more. With the mocking laughter ringing in her ears, and the rapid-fire thudding of the countess's cane keeping time with her runaway heart, she blinked back the mist in her eyes, inched up her skirt, and fled.

Chapter Twelve

*L*ord Romney, remember yourself!" the countess shrilled. The hollow thuds of her cane assaulting the carpet finally captured his attention. "Have you gone addled, sir? I find nothing amusing in this unfortunate affair."

"Forgive me, my lady," Nigel said, the words riding a chuckle. "Might I have a word with Miss Jessup?"

"No, sir, you may not!" said the countess, banging her cane again. The weapon had lost its effect and become downright annoying. Nigel resisted the temptation to snatch it out of the woman's hand and break it over his knee. "This is no public house," she went on. "I do not grant audiences between the aristocracy and hired help in my salon. You came here today to call upon Clara, my niece. Don't you think you should attend to that?"

"Did I hear someone mention my name?" said a voice from the doorway that turned Nigel around. For a moment, the frock blinded him to the woman wearing it. He almost thought it was Alice Jessup standing there. They were both fair and handsome-looking women, but this one was no frightened doe.

There was a cold gleam in her steely eyes that flagged danger. Those eyes were raking him from head to toe with the look of a street urchin salivating at the baker's window.

She floated nearer, extending her hand. It was a moment before Nigel rose to the occasion. Too much was impacting him to be absorbed all at once. This was by no means the woman he'd come to meet, but he was above all else a gentleman—to a fault, some would say, if such a thing could be a fault. Nigel couldn't imagine that.

Proprieties must be met. He took her hand and raised it dutifully to his lips, depositing a cursory kiss, and then released it without lingering.

"All right, Clara, sit," said the countess, "so that His Lordship may make himself comfortable."

"Thank you, but I'm afraid I cannot stay but a moment," said Nigel, taking a seat in a brocade chair the countess was nodding toward. "I only came by to inquire of Lady . . . of the other young woman's health—Miss Jessup, I believe you said—after her upset at the fete."

The conversation was strained at best, but Nigel wasn't about to leave until he'd gotten some sort of explanation and had a word with the lady in question. "I say, Countess, this is most awkward," he continued. "Might I have a clearer account of this . . . bizarre circumstance before I take my leave? I shan't settle well without one, as I am sure you can imagine."

"My niece's companion coerced her to exchange places at the masque," said the countess. "I've no

idea what she threatened her with to achieve her
dubious ends. Clara is too much a lady to reveal it
or to speak ill of the gel. But it didn't stop there. All
the while Clara was visiting her cousin across town,
the shameless creature perpetuated the hoax. You
should need no explanation of that, my lord, if you
give it thought, since you were the reason for it."

"I beg your pardon, my lady?" said Nigel, nonplussed.

"Aunt Regina," Lady Clara warned through rigid
lips. The sight sent shivers racing down Nigel's
spine.

"Clara was misled as to your . . . countenance
and character, my lord," the countess said. "In view
of that, Clara was reluctant to meet you. Once the
Jessup girl clapped eyes upon you and realized
Clara's error, she set her cap for you herself in hopes
of beguiling you before Clara realized she had been
led astray in the matter."

It was all Nigel could do to keep from blurting
out *Your foolish niece was led astray, all right, but I
had naught to do with it.* Instead, he forced a smile,
and swallowed a lump that had suddenly constricted
his throat. *Alice Jessup! Dash it all, she told me, and I
didn't believe her—dismissed the notion out of hand,*
he recalled. It served him right. He wanted to burst
into laughter again at his own colossal stupidity, but
he didn't. He wanted to streak out into the hall and
call Alice Jessup at the top of his voice, but he didn't
do that, either. She was a woman of mystery, all
right, and that mystery wasn't solved yet. These two
facing him now weren't going to solve it, either.

He scarcely heard what they were saying. They had taken on animal form in his mind's eye. Countess Greenway resembled a barking seal, chattering on and on, clacking her acid tongue in a scathing assault upon the girl, meanwhile banging that infernal cane so often in punctuation that he could anticipate the blows. Lady Clara seemed like a hawk, about to peck at the countess in a blink of those cold, steely eyes, then swoop down and latch onto him with her talons in a trice.

He'd begun to perspire. As addled as his brain was then, what was afoot was crystal clear. Whatever had happened between Lady Clara and Chesterton, they meant for *him* to redeem her. This was worse than Isobel Rutledge. Dash it all, Alistair was right! He needed to choose a wife and settle down. He was getting too old for this sort of mingle-mangle.

"I see," he said as the countess paused for breath, having no idea what had winded her. "I am sorry, my lady, to have had an unwitting part in this . . . charade. I thank you for enlightening me, but now I really must take my leave." Why did he feel as if someone had lit a fire beneath his chair? He surged to his feet as if his britches were aflame and took up his beaver, gloves, and walking stick from the pedestal table where he'd left them.

"Won't you stay for tea, my lord?" Lady Clara urged. "I've already asked Cook to prepare it."

"Forgive me, but I cannot, my lady," he said. "I thank you for your most gracious invitation, but I am already behindhand. And, as I said, I only meant to put my head in for a moment to inquire as to . . . Miss Jessup's health."

Both women stared, their blanched faces directing pleading looks of desperation toward him, and toward each other. Nobody spoke. When Nigel finally broke the awful silence, the words seemed to rumble up from the floor beneath his polished Hessians.

"I *would* appreciate a word with your Miss Jessup before I leave, however, Countess Greenway," he said. "It is rather necessary, you understand, in order to put paid to this unfortunate business."

"She is not *my* Miss Jessup any longer, my lord," said the countess. "I couldn't let you speak with her even if I wanted to. She no longer resides in this house."

The words hit him like cannon fire. "You've dismissed her? When? How long ago?"

"This morning," the countess intoned.

"Do you mean to say that the trunk I helped your footmen with when I arrived just now was *hers*?"

"It was."

"I believe I saw her leave just after you came in, my lord," Lady Clara remarked. "She was eavesdropping right outside that door, while you were talking with Aunt Regina when I came down. Shameless creature. She took one look at me and dashed out the back."

Nigel's jaw fell slack. Had he lost her? Worse yet, had he helped her slip right through his fingers? He'd been sitting here all this while listening to twaddle, while . . . Bloody hell!

"Where has she gone?" he gritted out, his eyes oscillating between the other two females.

"I'm sure I do not know. Nor do I care," said the countess, surging to her feet.

Uttering a string of blue expletives under his breath, Nigel streaked toward the door.

"My lord," the countess called after him. "May we expect you to call again soon, once you have recovered from this regrettable affair?"

"Thank you for your kind invitation, but I think not, my lady," he called over his shoulder. "I shall be leaving London shortly . . . on estate business. I cannot say when I shall be returning. Good afternoon, ladies."

Sketching a bow, he burst from the salon, nearly knocking over a plump housekeeper he'd flushed from the shadows, where she'd evidently been eavesdropping under the pretense of polishing the woodwork. Wailing like a banshee, Lady Clara was the next to vacate the room, her sobs echoing along the corridor in concert with the countess's cane thumping behind. Nigel scarcely heard as he bounded down the front steps to his waiting carriage.

"So, there you have it," Nigel said. He was seated on the lounge in his town-house study, sipping brandy and drawing on his clay pipe, with Alistair McGovern, whom he'd literally abducted from White's. Once they'd eaten, drunk too much, and made the rounds of the gambling hells, he'd dragged the viscount home to confide his news.

"What now, old boy?" said McGovern.

"I've got to find her," Nigel returned. "Haven't you heard me? The butler opened the door, and I no sooner set foot inside when a trunk came crashing down the stairs—her trunk, mind you—with dead aim upon one of the footmen. I rose to the occasion, shoved the churl aside, and eased it to the bottom, where I helped them get a grip on it and sent them on their way. If I'd known it was her trunk, it never would have gotten past the landing. I let her get away, Al—I *helped* her get away—and I didn't even know it."

"Perhaps that's for the best, as I've been saying all along."

"It doesn't ring true," Nigel said, ignoring the reply. "They made her out to be a woman on the prowl who'd set her cap for me. You met her, Al. Did she appear the aggressive type to you? No, I'll never believe it. She has done naught but try to run from me since we met at the masque." Tossing back the contents of his snifter, he poured another, and offered the decanter.

"No more, old boy," the viscount said. "I'm in danger of casting up my accounts as it is."

"Not on my carpet, Al. There's a chamber pot behind the folding screen."

"You shouldn't have any more, either," said McGovern. "You're passing castaway."

"I'm not foxed—I'm trying to make sense of all this."

"You can't prove that by me, the way you let the ivory hunters empty your pockets in the hells tonight. You must be in love. You're usually a bang-up-to-the-mark gambler, old boy. How much did they scorch you?"

"My mind wasn't on the game," said Nigel.

McGovern gave a guttural chuckle. "Keep that up, and you won't have long to worry over your legendary fortune."

"She tried to tell me the truth, and I didn't give her a chance," Nigel reflected. He raked his hair with rough hands. "I mishandled her while trying to teach her a lesson, when I found her on Chesterton's doorstep. She told me the truth about that, I expect, as well. Al, I never would have taken liberties, except to make the point that such was what she could expect, going about unescorted. I've got to find her."

"What then?" McGovern said. "You can't be serious about pursuing this gel. She's a nobody. You can't marry that far beneath you. Those sorts of unions never work, old boy. Take her for a mistress if you must, but marry someone of your own class, someone with bloodlines worthy of perpetuating your line."

"She's not a nobody, Al. She's a minister's daughter, quite well to pass."

"Hah!" McGovern erupted. "So you're jumping into the parson's mousetrap in the literal sense, are you? Nigel, that is priceless!"

"Stubble it! If you weren't in your cups, I'd plant you a leveler. And who said anything about marriage? There's something about her . . . just *something*. I can't put my finger on it, but I've never felt before the way I feel when I'm with her. I've had a taste, and I want more. I want to find out where she's gone. I need to see her, talk to her. I must, regardless, before I can lay it to rest. You're either with me in this, or you're against me, Al. I need to know right now."

"Whoa! I'm always with you, Nigel. You know that. Why do you suppose I'm trying to steer you clear of trouble? You should have been leg-shackled long ago. What is it that you want? What are you looking for? Why are you knocking about like a knight errant, championing everyone else's women, when you should be settling down with your own? Don't give me that look. You know I'm right. We had a purpose when we were fighting for king and country. We seem to have lost it now that that's behind us. I know I have, but at least I'm making an effort to find a new direction, and, by God, that's something for me. . . . But then, I've got a father lighting a fire under my breeches."

"I'm looking for someone to care about, who cares about me," said Nigel. "I'm not cut out for one to wed and one to bed. I've had mistresses, Al. You know that. It isn't the life for me, and this come-out madness every year is a travesty. If someone such as Lady Jersey or Countess Pembroke makes an introduction, you feel obligated to follow through. Just look what happened to me last season with Isobel Rutledge, and it's still going on. I've come to dread it all."

"You're a romantic, old boy. That's the trouble with you."

"I've been over at Tattersall's looking at stock,"

Nigel said, ignoring the observation. "They've got some good dams, and they put me onto a couple of horse farms out in the west country—one in Dorset, the other in Wiltshire—where I might find a few exceptional studs. I'm good with horses, Al. I'd like to raise them for racing and for hunting, just as Father used to do when I was a lad. I thought I might open my estate out on the coast. It's been shut up and forgotten since Father died. Cornwall is good country for raising horses. The climate is milder on the coast than anywhere else in England. I grew up out there. We had fine stables. I sold off the stock when I bought my commission."

"About as far from town as you can get, eh?"

"I'm serious, Al, but I have to make my marriage arrangements first. I haven't been out to the coast since I mustered out."

"That was a while ago, old boy. It's probably falling to ruin by now, what with the storms out that way."

"The house dates back to the Norman Conquest. It's built like a fortress. I doubt it's crumbled to dust. I do pay a caretaker to look after the place. I'm sure he'd have sent word if that was the case."

"You really are serious."

Nigel nodded. "But I cannot begin to deal with that until I've settled this here. I have to find her, and I have no idea where to begin."

"You say they were taking her trunk out. Did you speak with the coachman?"

"I did. He drove her round to the coaching station, the Swan with Two Necks in Lads' Lane, but she didn't go post. She wasn't on the passenger list. She must have hired a coach or shared with someone. Probably the latter, as hired coaches come too dear for a companion's wages. No one seems to remember her, and I couldn't even say what she was wearing to narrow it down."

"I don't suppose you could wring it out of Countess Greenway?"

"The woman is a menace. She wields that cane of hers like a lancer. She won't give up any information, Al. She has designs upon me as a match for Lady Clara. That was obvious. She'd hardly point me in Alice's direction."

"I take it there isn't any hope of a match there—with Lady Clara, that is?"

"No, none at all," said Nigel. "Chesterton's ruined her, more than likely, and she's desperate. She wouldn't care if I were all that Isobel Rutledge accused at this point. She'll find no takers now. I've half a mind to call the bounder out for it on general principles. Somebody has to put a stop to men like Chesterton going about gulling young ladies into giving up their virtue just for the sake of conquest. There ought to be consequences."

"You cannot take on all the knaves in England, old boy," said McGovern.

Nigel was about to reply, when the butler appeared in the doorway. "Begging your pardon," the man intoned. "A person to see you, m'lord."

"At this hour?"

"I put her in the study, m'lord."

Her? Nigel put his pipe aside and surged to his feet, dizzy from drinking, and cast the viscount a hopeful glance. Could it be?

"A Mrs. Avery, m'lord," the butler went on. "Housekeeper at Langly House, so she says."

Nigel's heart sank and rose all in one beat. "Thank you, Archer. I shall come directly," he said, snatching his frock coat from the lounge where he'd discarded it earlier. He shrugged it on, raked his hair into place with hands as clumsy as bear paws, and straightened his neckcloth. "How do I look?" he asked McGovern.

"Like a lord in his cups," said the viscount, flashing a wry smile. "Dash it all, it's only a housekeeper at the gates, Nigel, not the Queen of Sheba."

"Yes, yes . . . Of course it is. Foolish of me. For a moment I thought . . . Well, never mind. Just don't move from that spot!"

"Wild horses couldn't move me from this spot, old boy, if the house were afire."

"Forgive me for comin' on so late, my lord," Mrs. Avery said as she jumped to her feet when Nigel entered. "But I had ta wait till the house was asleep before I dared ta leave. If the countess knew I was here, she'd sack me for fair."

"Please," he said, gesturing. "Sit, Mrs. Avery. What can I do for you?"

"I've come about Miss Alice, my lord," she said, sinking back down in the chair she'd sprung from. "I don't even know if I'm doin' the right thing.

'Twas part o' the bargain that neither the countess nor Lady Clara tell ya where she'd gone, but she never asked *me* ta make such a promise. That's why I've come."

"What bargain?"

"Miss Alice promised ta take all o' the blame for Lady Clara's . . . situation, go down in disgrace, in exchange for two things: that the countess not hold her up ta public ridicule, but wait till she'd left ta come out with it, and that you not be told where she'd gone."

"But why? Why wouldn't she want me to know?"

"She was too ashamed, my lord."

Nigel's posture collapsed, but he'd balled his hands into white-knuckled fists at his sides. His head was pounding from the liquor he'd consumed, though the housekeeper's words had sobered him.

"I'm not sayin' what she done wasn't wrong, my lord. She never should have let Lady Clara talk her inta goin' to that masque in her place. It was only supposed ta be for that one night, but then Lady Clara run off—went missin', that is—and things got outta hand."

"Why are you telling me all this, Mrs. Avery?" Nigel said, almost afraid to hope.

"Because she was heartsore over foolin' ya like she done. It's none o' my business, I know, but I come here ta speak my mind, and I'm goin' ta do it! Unless I miss my guess, that lass is also heartsore over never seein' ya again. Beggin' your pardon, my lord, but I think, judgin' by what I seen and heard when ya come ta call taday, that you might feel the same, in spite o' who she is and what she done."

"Do you know where she's gone, Mrs. Avery?" asked Nigel, hanging on her every word.

"I do," the woman returned, giving a brisk nod. "She's gone home, my lord. Her father is the Methodist minister of a little valley church outside o' Warminster—Rood Chapel, 'tis called. 'Tis a poor wayside chapel, is what it is, mostly farm folk and them what lives way out in the wilds o' Wiltshire tendin' sheep, so she told me."

"Hah!" said Nigel. "Warminster . . . in Wiltshire?"

"Yes, my lord, why?"

"I'm supposed to be looking at horses in Wiltshire."

"You're goin' ta go out there?"

"Oh, yes, Mrs. Avery, and not just because of the horses."

"Oh, sir, I beg of ya, don't tell her I told ya! She'll never speak ta me again. And, please don't let Countess Greenway get hold o' it, neither, or I'll be sacked on the spot! Why, if she even suspected I'd come here, I'd be out in the street, I would—bag and baggage."

Nigel reached her in two strides—ignoring her strangled gasp—raised her up, and spun her around, despite her circumference. It was something he never would have done sober, nor would he have kissed the plump, rosy apple of her cheek. But he did that, too.

"Mrs. Avery, I adore you!" he said, returning her

to earth. "Please do not fret over your position, dear lady. If my plans come to fruition, you won't have to overset yourself over your situation at Langly House for long. And even if they don't, you have my solemn promise that you shall never want for employment as long as I draw breath."

"Oh, my lord! I don't know what ta say!"

"You don't have to say anything, Mrs. Avery," he said, leading her toward the door. "Have you a carriage outside, or shall I send for mine?"

"Oh, no, my lord. I mean, yes, my lord, the countess's groom drove me round on the sly. We all love Miss Alice. She was a bright ray o' sunshine in that sour old house."

"Very well, then, put your mind at ease. I cannot thank you enough for coming to me tonight. You have my eternal gratitude. Meanwhile, if you have any word, you'll let me know?"

"Oh, beggin' your pardon, my lord, but I wouldn't wait for word. Go after her if you're of a mind. The Lord alone knows what her father's goin' ta do when he gets the countess's letter. She sent it off by special messenger right after ya left this mornin'. One thing's sure and certain: she's goin' ta need a friend, is Miss Alice."

"I hope to become infinitely more than that, Mrs. Avery. Infinitely more, indeed."

Chapter Thirteen

Alice sat alone in her father's study. Waiting. She'd been there for some time. The worst had befallen her. If only she'd had the fare and hadn't been afraid to travel by post chaise for fear Nigel would follow, she might have reached the vicarage before the messenger delivered the countess's missive. She might have even intercepted it with no one the wiser! One more deception wouldn't have mattered after all the others she'd committed in less than a fortnight.

The mail coach might have been an option, but it didn't stop anywhere near her destination so far out in the country. And she would have had to travel the rest of the distance by night coach, which wasn't safe for a young lady alone, what with the threat of highwaymen still lingering. That left the stagecoach, which was neither the fastest nor the most comfortable means of travel. She had barely had enough for the fare.

Mrs. Sills, the thin, gray-haired housekeeper, scarcely spoke a word of welcome to her when she arrived that morning. Nor was food offered to her.

She was simply told to wait in her father's study. It was just as she remembered it, smelling stale of damp and decay and the penetrating must peculiar to old bookbindings. Not even the lemon polish Mrs. Sills slathered on the furniture could mask that sour smell. It reminded Alice of her childhood, for this is where she'd come whenever she'd displeased her father and he'd deemed discipline was in order. It all seemed so grave to Alice as a child: being remanded to her room for a span of time appropriate to her offense, going to bed without her supper, doing penance on her knees in the chapel. Those were the most popular choices. Being shut up in the rectory, denied access to her beloved mare, Treacle, and consigned to muck out the stables were reserved for the most serious offenses. Though the switch was seldom employed, there was that one time. . . . No, it was still too painful to remember.

All in all, James Jessup wasn't a cruel man, though he was cold and aloof by nature, but rather a strict authoritarian in every sense, and a cheeseparing miser when it came to showing affection. Faced with raising a daughter alone, he truly believed his hardness in meting out discipline was for the good, and he had always made his views plain in that regard. That punishment, tempered by the inherent love that ought to exist between father and daughter, might have taught a more lasting lesson, but that thought never occurred to him. The child Alice had never been able to extract such an emotion from him.

Just knowing she had disappointed him was

enough to throw her into the dismals. Pleasing him had always been so difficult, hence her air dreams of a different sort of life. What would her penance be now, for her most grievous offense to date? All the ghosts were gathering. She hadn't been in residence an hour, and she was already sorry she'd come home.

The door creaked open, and there he stood in his threadbare cassock, his shock of thick white hair, and his pallid skin, which rarely saw the light of day, in stark contrast to the dingy black cloth. For as long as she could remember he'd worn a cassock, while many of his contemporaries chose to go about in less conservative attire. As a child, it had always frightened her. Even now, her heart took a tumble. He seemed older somehow for the six months that had passed since she'd seen him last. That disapproving look had not altered, however, as he raked her with the gelid eyes she so vividly remembered.

"So you are come home, Daughter," he said, taking a seat at his desk. "And in disgrace. I cannot say I am surprised."

"If you will let me explain, Father—," began Alice.

He unfurled the countess's letter with flourish. "This quite explains it, I think," he interrupted.

"I have heard the countess's explanation of what occurred, Father, and it is inaccurate, pure gammon," Alice braved, determined to prove she was no longer the child he remembered from other study interviews. What could he do to her, after all? She was too old for the usual punishments to be effective. She could not imagine him switching her now.

"I'm guilty of yielding to the temptation to see for myself how the aristocracy lives, as if I were one of them," she said. "I allowed Lady Clara to coerce me to attend a masked ball, pretending I was she in order to discourage an unwanted suitor. It was only supposed to occur once, but she used me to effect an elopement with a scoundrel who has ruined her. I chose to take the blame in order to salvage what could be redeemed of her life, and her season. She has ruined her chances, Father. I had no hand in that. Once I realized what she had done, I did everything in my power to help her as a self-imposed penance for my fault in it, even to allowing the distortion of truth that you hold in your hand there—and for my pains I am cruelly slandered."

Her father brandished the missive. "Countess Greenway takes a different view," he said.

"Let me see that," Alice returned, reaching out.

"I think not, Daughter," he replied. "It is not addressed to you."

"But it concerns me, Father, and it is *false witness*. How many times have you drummed the importance of not bearing false witness into your congregation from that pulpit"—she gestured toward the chapel—"and forewarned of the strictest repercussions in the hereafter for the breaking of that commandment?"

"I only have your word that it is false witness, Daughter. In these circumstances, what else might you say, after all?"

"Have I ever lied to you, Father?"

"You have exaggerated upon occasion—"

"All children exaggerate. I shall restate my question. Have I ever in my adult life failed to own up to my shortcomings, or blamed them upon another?"

There was a long silence.

"Father?"

"Not that I can recall," he said.

"Good! Now I shall tell you something that you will not find in that letter. When I suspected what Lady Clara had done and learned the identity of the blackguard she'd run off with, I went so far as to go to the man's home in hopes of persuading her to come to her senses. But it was already too late. He pretended he was taking her to Gretna Green to wed her. Instead, he took her virtue and left her to find her own way home. She is fortunate to be alive, Father, and while I was so despairing of her predicament that I wanted to throttle her, I allowed her and that wicked aunt of hers to slander me to save face for the foolish twit. That woman beat her with her cane, you know, Father, and raised it toward me as well!"

"She didn't . . . *strike* you?"

Alice hesitated. She knew he hadn't asked that question out of compassion. She knew his mind. It was a barometer of guilt or innocence. If the countess was moved to deliver a blow with her cane, his daughter must surely be guilty indeed.

She pulled a face. "No, she did not, because I threatened her with the guards. Father, I am not the little girl you dragged to this study for punishment years ago. I allowed Countess Greenway to place the blame upon me as a means of vindicating Lady Clara in the eyes of the ton in London, not here in Wiltshire County. Here, I am myself—innocent of wrongdoing, with the exception that for a blink in time's eye I pretended to be something I am not. And that sin, if it is a sin, is not a public one. It lives in the privacy of my heart. I am not perfect. I have never pretended to be."

"Do you imagine that your indiscretions have remained behind in London, Alice?" her father said. "Are you forgetting whose cottage lies on the other side of this hill? Can you be so bird-witted that you believe the servants in that cottage aren't privy to the scandalous affairs of their betters, or that they would keep such juicy tidbits to themselves?"

Alice drew a ragged breath. She had forgotten that the countess's cottage, on the far side of the patchwork hills that she called home, was the very place where she'd been hired. She'd spent her first five months in service there. The servants all knew her well. They must surely know she'd been sent home in disgrace. The on-dits would be spreading through the parish, just as ripples spread in still water when a pebble breaks the surface.

"Did Mrs. Sills welcome you with open arms when you arrived just now?" he said.

"No, she did not, but I imagined that was your doing, Father—and that woman and I have never been close."

"No," he replied, wagging his head. That he did it slowly, in concert with a cold half smile, as he always did when making a point, chilled her to the marrow. She'd almost forgotten how this one particular mannerism held sway over her, how its simplicity spoke louder than his voice might have done and possessed the power to intimidate. "Mrs. Sills is on friendly terms with the countess's staff at the cottage, Daughter," he continued, dissolving the unpleasant memories that look had conjured. "I had no part in your cold reception."

"What could they possibly have said of me, other than that I am guilty of a foolish misjudgment?"

Again he brandished the missive. "That you have seduced a gentleman intended for Lady Clara. A man with a . . . re-pu-ta-tion," he pronounced, curling pursed lips. "An odious fellow who pursues young ladies with no good intentions of marriage. It is all over London. It says here that you beguiled him so thoroughly, he fled Lady Clara's company, once the truth was out, in search of you. A man far above your station. Now, what purpose could an *earl* have to pursue a dirt-poor little church mouse like yourself, but to take her for his mistress, Daughter? Or has that already begun? *That* is the tale circulating here, and what might you expect, considering the man's checkered past. Your association with him alone has damned you. You have been tarred by the same brush, my girl! Had you not one thought of me? Of what your shameful behavior might bring to bear upon Rood Chapel? You are come home in disgrace, a ruined woman! Well, he had better not come sniffing round here seeking you, Daughter, or he will rue the day he ever set eyes upon you. After I've read him from the pulpit, I shall fire up the tar vat and mete out a bit of sound medieval justice on the bounder—earl or no—with the whole congregation behind me! He shan't turn my daughter into Haymarket ware!"

Gooseflesh chased the blood from Alice's face, and she swayed where she sat as if her father had dealt her a blow. White pinpoints of light starred her vision. She hadn't expected the countess's vengeance to go this far. For a moment, it was as if she were struck dumb.

"Well? What have you to say for yourself now, Daughter?" her sire demanded.

"I . . . we . . . It isn't true, Father," she said, low voiced. "H-how could you believe such a thing of me? Can you not see what they've done? They've taken Lady Clara's indiscretion and transferred it to me to save her reputation! Lord Romney has never presented himself as anything but a gentleman, Father." The words had barely passed her lips when the memory of Nigel's intimate embrace in the carriage sent hot blood rushing to her cheeks. Her ears were on fire. Why had she removed her bonnet? She could only imagine their color, hardly the shade of innocence.

"Why, h-he thought all the while that I was Lady Clara," she went on, hoping her father wouldn't notice that her hands had begun to tremble, "and set himself up as my protector . . . to save me—

her—from the bounder that ultimately ruined her, because, you see, it was already too late. I—I wasn't she, and he had no idea who I really was, even though I tried on several occasions to tell him! Oh, dear, I'm not putting this well. It's complicated, and you have quite muddled my brain with these— these horrid accusations."

"Even if all that you say were true, it doesn't change the fact that you are ruined, Alice. Guilty or innocent, your reputation is besmirched. I am ashamed of you!"

"I do not have a care what you think of me, Father," said Alice. "You have always thought the worst, but you are wrong about Lord Romney. He is not the jackanapes you accuse him of being. False witness has damned him also. I know, because it was the reason Lady Clara begged me to go to the masque and give the man a cut direct. She had heard the on-dits, and believed them. They couldn't have been further from the truth, and when she realized that, she set out to have him at any cost— especially now, since no one else will have her after what she's done. All this is at his expense as well as mine. She hardly knows the man!"

"Neither do you, yet you defend him well enough, Daughter. And you expect me to believe there's nothing to all this?" He rattled the countess's letter.

"I shall always defend right, Father."

"You have been willful since a child," her father said, his words riding a sigh. "When you were still in leading strings, I saw the seeds of this . . . this shocking independence in you. The defiance, the deuced curiosity that always led you astray. It is why you were so often summoned to this room for . . . correction. You take it from your mother, God rest her soul. She was an air dreamer, too—never satisfied with her lot. Never accepting her place in the fabric of God's plan, always reaching for the unattainable. You have never known your proper place, nor have you proper respect for you elders or your betters."

"Father, rail at me all you like, but it is so unfair to accuse Mother when she is no longer here to defend herself."

"Do you intend to remain under this roof, Daughter?" her father said, tucking the parchment into his pocket. It was plain that bringing up the topic of her mother had overset him.

Alice nodded. "This is my home," she murmured. "I have nowhere else to go."

"The countess will not recommend you. Who do you imagine will offer you employment after this? You are a pariah, Daughter. How will you make your way? I shall not live forever. What will become of you when I am gone? You went into service to better yourself, to have a future. You have thrown away the only opportunity you shall ever have."

"So, what shall my punishment be this time, Father?" Alice asked haughtily. "I am too old for being sent from the table to be effective, or being put to bed with no supper. Neither will keeping me from my horse, or forcing me down on my knees in that chapel until my bones splinter. And mucking out the stable is too lenient a punishment for the nature of my latest offense, I should imagine. So, tell me. What will you do to me this time, Father?"

It was a bold outburst, and she'd purposely omitted the switch lashing in her account. It would not do to bring that to his attention. She shuddered, reliving the crack it made when he'd broken it over her young back. No. She couldn't let herself remember, though the incident had crept into her memory twice now since she'd entered the rectory, coming in rampant flashes to her mind's eye.

In all her life, she had never spoken to her father thus. Maybe it was time. What hurt her most was that he believed every word the countess had said against her, and no matter which punishment he settled upon, the worst of it was that she had no choice but to remain under his roof. She hadn't a halfpenny to her name, and she was regretting now that she'd spent on her fare home the last of the wages she'd put by.

"Do you recall the choice I gave you six months ago, when we discussed your future, Daughter?" her father intoned. It was a voice she'd heard booming from the pulpit next door on more than one occasion, his fire-and-brimstone voice, which always filled her heart with terror. "Let me refresh your memory," he went on, folding gnarled hands atop the desk. "The only two avenues open to you were going into service or marrying one of the locals and settling down. You tried the former and failed. Now you have no choice. There is only one avenue left. You will marry."

Alice jumped to her feet. "You cannot make me

marry a man I do not love!" she cried. "That and
that alone is why I consented to go into service in
the first place."

"It is already arranged, Daughter," her father said.
"John Mapes is willing to have you. He's a widower
now, needing help with the chores. He will call upon
you tomorrow. He is a respectable sheep farmer,
and—"

"He is one of the countess's crofters! You cannot!
I won't—"

"That cannot be helped," he said, his voice raised
over her bluster. "He is a respectable man of the
old school. He will succeed where I have failed, and
settle you down in a trice, my girl, in true Wesleyan
tradition: 'Salvation by grace through faith.' You
are far from a state of grace, Daughter, and at this
point even your faith is suspect. There is much to be
done within you to achieve salvation, and mark my
words, you will be humbled!"

"He is twice my age, Father! You cannot shackle
me to an illiterate old man. You cannot be that
heartless! I shall die of humiliation—of shame!"

"*You* have brought all this to bear, Daughter," he
sallied. "You have proved to me that you cannot
manage your life on your own. What other choice
is there? None. You should be grateful John Mapes
is willing to take you on, because no other here will
have you. No, Daughter, you've sealed your own
fate. I had precious little hand in it. I am giving you
a respectable way out of your dilemma, which is far
more than you deserve, bringing shame upon this
house—upon this church!"

"I will not marry John Mapes!"

"Oh, but you will, Daughter. It is already arranged. I will read the first banns from that chapel out there on Sunday next."

Chapter Fourteen

Nigel decided not to go the whole distance to Wiltshire on horseback. He couldn't. Alistair McGovern was traveling with him. Refusing to be left behind, the viscount persuaded him to allow the tagalong fancy, arguing that he could use a jaunt in the country as well. He also pointed out that he might tour the horse farms and look the horses over while Nigel courted his lady fair.

The carriage arrived in Warminster just before midnight, too late to pay a call at the rectory. They would spend the night at the Old Bell coaching inn and in the morning rent horses and go their separate ways.

They were seated at a scarred corner table at the inn and served plates of hot venison stew, which meant one of two things. Either the Old Bell was on the mail route, and therefore served late, or the food was so bad, there was plenty left over from the supper hour. Unfortunately, the latter proved to be the case. Wolfing his meal down with a tankard of dark, nutty ale, Nigel didn't care. He was famished. The sweet country air that hinted at hills and vales laden with lush herbaceous foliage burgeoning all around them had charged his appetite. It was always thus when he traveled in the country.

"You'll want to get an early start, I expect," McGovern said around a mouthful of the stew.

"I will," said Nigel, tearing off a piece of crusty bread to sop up the gravy. His table manners had suffered somewhat since they'd left London, but then they hadn't stopped that often. It didn't matter. Nothing did, except that he find Alice. He wouldn't be himself again until that was behind him.

"It shouldn't be too hard to locate," he went on. "Mrs. Avery said the chapel is atop a hill, and there's part of a ruined castle in the vale below at the edge of a pine grove. A stream threads through it, an offshoot of the Willy River. She started her service at the countess's cottage on the far side of the hill."

"It sounds a place enchanted, old boy, but typical of the land round these parts. There are groves, stones, ruins, hills, and vales aplenty in Wiltshire. You'll need an early start, indeed."

"Ahhh, but only one Rood Chapel, Al, and I shall inquire of the innkeeper before I set out, you can count upon it. I have a sinking feeling in the pit of my gut that's flagging danger. I never ignore my gut instincts; they've served me all my life. How do you suppose I got through my tour of duty relatively unscathed? I can only hope that's where she's gone. To hear Mrs. Avery tell it, her father is something of a tyrant."

"Look here, old boy, is all this wise? It isn't too late to turn back, you know. We could go and have a look at your horses, take a day or two, and return to town. There are other fish in the ocean."

"I haven't come all this way to turn back now," Nigel returned. "But you can leave any time it suits you."

"Ohhhh no, old boy. You shan't get rid of me that easily. I intend to see this through to the bitter end. Somebody has to ride point for you out here. No battle ever fought was won with a captain at the helm whose sanity has slipped all its moorings. At least I'm levelheaded. That's more than you can say at the moment. Odds fish, old boy! I think this gel has bewitched you!"

"It started out as a challenge," said Nigel. "But it's become something . . . more. I have to know what lies in her heart of hearts concerning me. I will know when I see her again, hold her in my arms again, now that it all has come out in the open. To that extent, I am bewitched indeed."

The first gray streamers of a cheerless dawn had begun to creep over Alice's windowsill when she woke. For a moment she was disoriented, searching the soft semidarkness for more familiar surroundings: the velvet cushioned window seat, rosewood vanity, and matching oval cheval glass in her Langly House bedchamber. Then it struck her. Like a deadly blow to the pit of her stomach, it raised her upright in the small, handwrought bed of her youth. Her heart sank. She had come home.

The only thing that would save her from a severe case of blue devils awaited her in the stable: her beloved Treacle. She threw off the counterpane, leaped from bed, and padded to the wardrobe, where she'd hung her frocks when she unpacked them. There weren't many. Two muslin frocks—one white, one a lovely robin's egg blue—several twilled silks, a serviceable bombazine, and a brown twill traveling costume that would be perfect for riding in the fall but much too hot for the warmer months.

She snatched out the blue muslin and dressed without the aid of a maid or a mirror. The only servant in residence was Mrs. Sills, who had no time to take on lady's-maid duties, and there were no mirrors in the rectory. "Vanity is an affront to God, and a mirror is the devil's tool," her father had drummed into her as a child. Until she'd taken up her post as Lady Clara Langly's companion, Alice had never looked into one. Although, there was that day when she'd strayed to the stream at the edge of the wood and seen her reflection in the cool, clear water. No. She wouldn't think of that awful day. Why did it keep creeping into her thoughts since she'd come home? She was heartsore enough as it was. She would cling to the only bright ray in her homecoming, a ride on the sorrel mare.

James Jessup didn't employ a groom. He did, however, retain a young boy, Davey Epps, a member of the congregation, to come around on a daily basis to tend the two horses in his stable and to milk the cow if Mrs. Sills's duties prevented her. He had just arrived when Alice reached the stable. His surprise at the sight of her didn't go unnoticed. Was he privy to the on-dits too? Alice shuddered at the thought, waiting somewhat impatiently for him to saddle Treacle.

After practically no discourse with the lad, the awkward episode was quickly over, and she was mounted and leading the horse toward the patchwork hills of rolling green she loved so. This was just the tonic she needed, food for the soul. Inhaling the heady sweetness of wildflowers, so much more potent while laden with dew, she gave Treacle her head, soothing the horse with a gentle voice, whispering the secrets of her heart as if she had never been away. Except that now, those secrets were deeper and heavier. How she had missed riding! How she had missed the keen understanding that existed between herself and this horse.

The animal knew her haunts. Alice let the ribbons go slack as the sorrel led her to the thicket at the edge of the wood, where she could see her reflection and order her hair in the mirror-bright stream. No one would punish her now. Her punishment would come in the afternoon, when John Mapes came to call. She wouldn't think about that, however. It was hours away. Now she was free . . . or was she? Alice didn't travel alone. Nigel Farnham traveled with her—in her thoughts, in her heart, in her senses, where his scent came without bidding and overpowered the best nature could offer on that dull, dreary morning.

Nigel rode out after breakfast in search of Rood Chapel. Armed with a crude map the innkeeper had drawn, he traveled south-southwest in the direction of a hillock crowned with oak trees. Squatting in their midst was a small stone church with a square bell tower. He nudged the rented gelding with his knees and, tugging on the ribbons, made straight for the building, as giddy as a schoolboy.

There was a hitching post on the side of the rectory. Ordinarily, he would leave one of his own mounts untethered, standing, bridle down to graze, with complete confidence once he dismounted. This being a hired horse unfamiliar to him, and skittish besides, he opted to tether it to the post. It would be a long walk back to the Old Bell if the beast took a notion to wander.

He removed his beaver hat and right-hand glove and raked his hair into place, then donned the hat again. After tugging the glove back on, he ordered his gunmetal gray coat of superfine and pearl gray breeches, then strode down the crushed-stone walk and up the front steps with well-mustered confidence. He banged the knocker twice, and waited.

Presently, the door came open in the hand of a pinch-faced woman of middle age, whose pursed lips were deeply scarred with wrinkles. A wiry little thing, she scrutinized him with the steeliest pair of eyes he had ever encountered. They looked like two dull black raisins beneath her withered eyelids.

"Who knocks?" she said, jutting her chin in punctuation.

Nigel doffed his beaver. "Lord Romney, madam," he said. "I wish a word with Miss Alice Jessup, if you please."

"I don't please, and she ain't at home, m'lord," the woman replied.

"Can you tell me when she will be returning?"

"I couldn't say, m'lord."

"She does reside here?"

"She does."

"And you don't know when she is expected?"

"I will handle this, Mrs. Sills," said a deep voice from the shadows inside. The man who owned it emerged, almost seeming like a disembodied head, since his dusky cassock matched the dark interior. He shoved the housekeeper aside and filled the span, visible now in the glaring gray light of the cheerless morning.

Nigel sketched a bow that wasn't required, but judging from the stern-faced minister's deportment, it couldn't hurt to show respect for the man's office, considering his mission. "I wish a word with your daughter, sir," he said, his confidence flagging. James Jessup seemed a man to be reckoned with, standing ramrod rigid, his square chin thrust over his clerical collar. "I shan't take but a moment of her time," he hastened to add.

"My daughter is not at home to you, my lord," said Jessup. "You shall do us both a favor to get back upon that horse there and leave."

"I assure you, sir, that I have nothing but the most honorable intentions toward your daughter. There has been a . . . misunderstanding that I wish to clarify. You are most welcome to bear witness. I have nothing to hide."

The man's eyes were positively sinister, raking him from head to toe—an odd countenance for a man of the cloth, thought Nigel. He had never seen the like.

"That being the case," said Jessup, "if you have a piece to speak, speak it now—to me—and have done."

"Very well," Nigel said. "Will you have it here, on this doorstep?"

Jessup nodded. "You are not welcome here, Lord Romney. I shan't ask you into my home. My daughter is not in residence, at any event, and even if she were, I could not permit you an audience with her. All that is ended. There shall be no assignations here, no trysts to bring more scandal to my very doorstep! Kindly state your business and leave, sir. My patience ebbs low, and you have already worn out a welcome you were never granted."

Nigel cleared his voice. Speaking his piece in these circumstances was useless. She would never hear his words from this hard man glaring at him through hooded eyes. Deciding that his only hope, if she were in residence, might be for her to overhear this conversation, he began his discourse with raised voice.

"An unfortunate situation has arisen, sir, because I mistook your daughter for someone else—"

"You may as well lower your voice, my lord," Jessup interrupted. "Unless, of course, you address the livestock. My daughter is not at home."

"I beg your pardon, sir," said Nigel. It was evident that the man wasn't interested in anything he had to say. Why he was allowing their meeting to continue, Nigel couldn't fathom. There was a sting at the end of it, he couldn't help but feel. Nonetheless, he went on speaking, in a lower tone of voice this time. "Your daughter has done nothing wrong, sir," he said. "And neither have I. After the truth of the . . . mistaken-identity situation became known, she left London before I could tell her that it didn't matter. That is something I need to convey to her in person. I am asking only for an opportunity to do so."

"Your reputation precedes you, my lord. How could you possibly imagine I would let you within a mile of my daughter? You have gone beyond the pale coming here, Romney. You may have duped Alice, but you shan't dupe me. What motive could a man of your distinction—classwise, of course—possibly have for pursuing the daughter of a country minister, except to the purpose of grooming her for his mistress? I clarify 'classwise,' sir, because I find nothing distinctive in the character of a rake who goes about seducing young innocents."

"So that tale has reached Wiltshire now, has it?" said Nigel, more to himself than to James Jessup. Well, of course it had. The servants would have spread it, unless Alice . . . ? No. He wouldn't believe. "It is untrue, sir," he said. "A young woman I was introduced to last season imagined that the introduction was an ironclad promise of betrothal. It was never that. We were not suited to each other, and when I pointed that out to her, she retaliated by spreading untruths." Why did it sound so shallow, so improbable—so utterly false? "And as to my having designs upon your daughter as a candidate for a mistress, that is preposterous, sir! I do not need to defend myself in that regard. Anyone who knows me—"

"I do not wish to know you any further!" Jessup thundered. "I told my daughter what would be if you were fool enough to follow her here. Only, something a shade more definitive comes to mind after having met you, something more of a permanent nature. There you stand in all your aristocratic glory with your fine clothes and regal bearing. The devil was handsome, too—the most beautiful of all God's angels. Do you presume to imagine that I cannot see through that elegant facade to the deceiver underneath? You will not see my daughter again!"

"Your daughter, sir, is of an age to decide such matters for herself," said Nigel.

"And so she has," Jessup triumphed. "Alice is betrothed, sir. She marries a man of her own class as soon as the banns are read. Get off this holy ground!"

The blood drained away from Nigel's scalp, and cold sweat ran beneath his neckcloth, which had begun to chafe. She couldn't be betrothed! How could she be, so quickly? Before he could marshal his thoughts and reply, Jessup's right hand rose from behind the folds of his cassock, gripping a deadly flintlock service pistol, cocked and at the ready.

He took dead aim and pronounced unequivocally, *"Now!"*

Chapter Fifteen

The morning passed too quickly to suit Alice. It was glorious to ride again, to commune with nature, to listen to the voice of the wind as it stirred the tall grass, sharing ancestral secrets of the land in hushed whispers. It was the only saving grace in coming home.

She slowed Treacle's pace when they reached the bottom of the hill Rood Chapel sat upon. Overhead the sun was trying to break through the cloud cover, a faint glow of gold beneath the gray. It was nearly at its zenith, bringing her closer and closer to the dreaded interview with John Mapes that would finalize their betrothal. How she wished she could give Treacle her head and ride—just *ride* over the undulating green landscape before her, ruffled by the wind, with no sense or purpose except to put as much distance between herself and Warminster as was humanly possible. Instead, she walked the horse on. There was nowhere for her to go except home. Her heart was breaking.

Nigel knew what she had done, and he had laughed at her, mocked her for it. Those hearty guffaws would haunt her memory until she died. She had shared the innermost secrets of her heart that morning with her beloved horse, and with the wind. It would whisper her tales for all time now, for it was said by the elders that secrets shared with the wind were one with God and nature. They had become part of the wind song, the litany of joys and sorrows of the ancients.

How could she bear never to see Nigel again? Her heart would wither and die. That was the secret she shared that morning. There was no place for one such as she in his life—no respectable place, that is, and she would not consider the obvious alternative, if there even was an alternative after those mocking belly laughs. Was this love? If it was, the phenomenon was grossly overrated. It wasn't the glorious mystery of the universe Lord Byron would have one believe in his romantic writings. It was cruel and painful . . . but there it was. She had given up the secrets of her heart to the wind. Such was supposed to unburden the soul. Why did it still hurt so?

Lost in thought, she had nearly reached the summit of the hill when a shot rang out, startling Treacle and jarring Alice back to the moment. The horse, breaking stride with a shrill whistle, reared back, her forefeet pawing the air. Skilled horsewoman though she was, Alice nearly lost her seat. It was a moment before she could manipulate the ribbons and bring the animal's churning forelegs back to earth, albeit facing back toward the valley. She turned the mare in a trice and rode at a gallop over the path in the direction of the sound, past the sweet-smelling bramble bushes, laden with fruit at the top of the rise, and the hedgerows bearding the crest.

She reached the hilltop, only to rein Treacle in again at what met her eyes. The animal's shrill complaints, siphoned off on the wind, drew the attention of another rider likewise trying to gain control of his mount as it pranced in erratic circles in front of the chapel. Horrified, she stared. It was Nigel, and her father was standing on the rectory steps brandishing a pistol.

All at once, Mrs. Sills came running through the open rectory door with another pistol. James Jessup thrust his spent iron at her and took fresh aim with the other. Both men were shouting, but Alice was not near enough to make out their speech. Her father hadn't seen her, but Nigel had, and she turned the horse around again and fled down the hill toward the valley below as another shot ripped through the quiet morning. Then an outcry! Her heart nearly stopped. Had her father killed him?

The thunder of hooves hammering the ground in pursuit answered that question. Alice glanced over her shoulder as Treacle carried her back down the hill. She could still hear her father's shouts, as well as a familiar baritone voice barking a string of expletives at the horse underneath him. Thank the stars there wasn't murder done!

Had her father seen her at the last? She neither knew nor cared. She glanced over her shoulder. Nigel was coming on at a full gallop. Something red striped the thigh of his light gray breeches, which mirrored very color of the day. Blood!

Alice sucked in her breath and leaned low over Treacle's neck, letting the ribbons go slack. "Go, girl!" she cried. "Like we used to do! Go like the wind!"

The horse gave a whistle as if she understood, and Alice was transported back to the days of her girlhood, when she and Treacle would play this game. She had ridden shamelessly astride then and been called to her father's study for it on more than one occasion. It was much more difficult a task keeping one's seat during such a maneuver riding sidesaddle, she was finding out, especially when she turned her head to monitor another's pursuit, as she was doing now. Nigel was gaining on her, and she slapped Treacle's neck with the ribbons and urged her onward.

The wind had claimed her bonnet. It was just as well. She could see her pursuer much clearer now without the encumbrance. He was close—too close—and Treacle's stamina was flagging. Six months without this sort of exercise in Alice's absence had softened the animal's muscles; she wasn't in shape for such a ride. She was lathered, breathing hard. Her nostrils were distended. White foam hung from her lips and streaked her neck and withers. Alice's hands were slippery with it, clinging to the horse's mane.

The grove loomed up before her. She would have to slow the horse's pace. She glanced over her shoulder again. It was no use. He was nearly upon her. She could hear him calling her name, albeit tangled into other words that she was certain were part of his naval vocabulary. If the blood hadn't already rushed to her cheeks from the sheer circumstance, she would have blushed at such profanity.

It was quite hopeless, but she plunged headlong into the copse anyway, heading for the stream and the far bank, where there were places to hide deeper in. The advantage here was that she knew the terrain and he did not—that is, until a low-hanging bough caught her off guard and evened the odds. Striking her a glancing blow to the shoulder, it unseated her, and she landed hard on her bottom with a thud and a splash in the center of the stream.

Dazed, she felt herself lifted in strong arms. She was drenched to the skin from head to toe, since recent rains had raised the water level in the tributaries that flowed from the Willy. Nigel set her down on a patch of moss at the edge of the stream, brushed the wet tendrils from her face, and began feeling her limbs.

Alice swatted his hands away. "Stop that!" she snapped.

"I'm only feeling for broken bones," he replied. "That was a nasty spill you took."

"My bones are quite intact, my lord," she said, struggling to rise. "My dignity is all that is injured." She slapped at the skirt of her best blue muslin frock, and a strangled sound escaped her. Clinging wet to her body, it defined every curve. The thin fabric had become transparent. He could see . . .

everything. She may as well have been standing there naked. She didn't have to meet his eyes to see that he was devouring the sight, and she crossed her arms in front of her breasts. The shock of cold water had hardened their tawny tips, and they were very visible through the wet muslin.

Nigel stripped off his superfine coat and wrapped it around her. It was warm, and his scent wafted toward her nostrils: leather and lime, and that familiar musky maleness that was distinctly his. In spite of herself, she moaned. It was barely a sound, though it raised his eyebrow.

"Where did you learn to ride like that?" he murmured.

The seductive tone of his deep voice did not match the spoken words. They seemed a caress, riding that deep, bone-melting baritone timbre. His breathing seemed shallow, and rapid, but not from the ride. A moment ago, it had seemed normal enough, despite the exertion. She was lost in his coat, and his hands were shaking as he tried to adjust the fit. Alice snatched the lapels out of his hands and ordered it herself. At least it covered her charms, and it was oh, so warm.

"I could ride before I could stand," she said, "which goes to show how little you know about me, my lord." Glancing down, she spied the tear in his breeches along his right thigh and the blood seeping through. She gasped. She'd almost forgotten. "You are wounded!" she cried.

"'Tisn't serious. Just a graze," he said.

"He *shot* you!" she said. Gasping again, she covered her gaping mouth with her hand.

"I suppose I shouldn't have called him an anti-quated old tyrant," he said, flashing a lopsided smile that crippled her defenses. "I expect I have his call-ing to thank that he wasn't more skilled with a flintlock. If he couldn't do better than this at close range, I believe I am safe enough trespassing in your domain, Miss Jessup."

"I wouldn't count upon it, sir," Alice said. "You should never have come here! You do not belong here. Why did you come? To mock at me, to gloat?"

"We need to talk," he said, the smile fading from his lips.

"There is nothing to talk about, my lord."

"I have come all this way. The least you can do is hear me out."

"I have heard all that I need to hear," she snapped. "I tried to tell you the truth, my lord, but you wouldn't believe me. I was outside in the hall at Langly House when you learned it from those whom you would believe, because they are your equals. I heard your laughter, sir! It spoke louder than any words you might have spoken, or might speak to me here now."

Nigel took hold of her upper arms through the jacket and drew her to him. His closeness was heaven. His body, all male, hard-muscled angles and planes, pressed up against her, and the heat he generated warmed her like a furnace.

"I was laughing at *myself*," he said, shaking her gently. "You told me the truth, and I dismissed it out of hand, because you had duped me so thoroughly.

You were telling the truth the night I found you at Chesterton's town house, too, weren't you? You don't have to answer. I've been such a fool! Alice—"

"Please refrain from the intimacy of addressing me by my first name, Lord Romney," she snapped. "I have not given you leave to do so."

"Forgive me. It is just that—"

"It is just that I am a commoner, and I do not have to give you leave, is that it? You do not have to answer. I see it in your eyes."

"No, Al—Miss Jessup, that is not it," he returned. "What you see is a man you have humbled, come to make amends."

Alice couldn't meet his haunting, glacier blue stare. He towered over her, and she fixed her eyes upon a swirl in the pattern of his wine-colored brocade waistcoat, monitoring the rise and fall of his chest underneath. His hot breath puffed against her moist skin in a most alarming manner.

All at once, he ran the back of his hand along her jawline and captured her chin, tilting it upward, forcing her to meet his hooded eyes. Passion and longing lived there . . . and something more, something she dared not probe too closely for fear of being captured by it. He didn't mean it, after all. Yes, there was an attraction. There had always been that. Now, however, he evidently thought to take advantage of it—of *her*—because of who she was. Or rather, because of who she wasn't. There was no more need for propriety, not with a poor country church mouse. Did he think he could do as he pleased?

Lost in those dark thoughts, her eyes brimming
with tears, she didn't anticipate the kiss until his
warm lips gently came to rest upon her own. For a
moment she melted against him, opening to the
silken tongue that glided past her teeth and teased
hers after it. He moaned, and she pulled back, both
hands braced against his chest. The thunder of his
heartbeat hammering against her open palms sent
rivers of liquid fire racing through her anatomy to
places hitherto virgin territory.

"No!" she cried, struggling against his grip. "I
beg you . . . *no*. Do you imagine that I am not aware
of your intentions, sir? Do not delude yourself.
There could only be one reason for your coming
here, and I am not for sale! Gentlemen of your class
do not take up with women of mine except to take
advantage, sir. Let go of me!"

"You little goose, I've come—risked life and limb
into the bargain, *literally*—to tell you that it doesn't
matter."

"But it does matter, my lord. You are a fool to
imagine otherwise. I do not belong in your world,
and you certainly do not belong in mine. I think we
have proven that just now. Go back to your ton, to
your fine ladies and parties, all the glitter and pomp
that the season offers. That is where you belong, not
here in provincial Warminster. You have just been
shown that, sir. Here is where *I* belong. Our worlds
cannot commingle. Society will not allow it, and I
am not bachelor fare for the taking."

She shrugged off his jacket and returned it. "I
must get back," she said. "That wound needs tend-

ing. I should see to it without delay if I were you, else you court infection. That flintlock of Father's hasn't been fired in years. To my knowledge, the last recipient of his pistol ball was a fox that invaded the chicken coop when I was thirteen."

"You cannot remain here with that . . . that brutish barbarian," Nigel said, raking his hair back from his brow. He'd evidently lost his hat to the wind as well. She almost laughed aloud: at least their headgear was united on common ground!

The clouds were thickening. They had swallowed the sun, casting an eerie green darkness over the grove. Alice was cold now, with the warm superfine coat removed. She shuddered, craning her neck in search of Treacle, who had found a grazing spot beside the stream. Alice started toward her. The animal needed cooling down first.

"Oh, I shan't be here for long," she said over her shoulder. She had to put distance between them. It was the only way. The association had to be severed for good and all right there in that grove with the wind as witness, wailing like a woman through the rowan trees. Then her sacrifice would be complete. "I am to be wed, my lord, once the banns are posted, to trouble society no more." These were the hardest words she had ever spoken or ever would speak. But they were the right words to send him home where he belonged.

She mounted with ease, sitting her horse like a queen, her head held high despite her soggy frock and bedraggled hair. And what had become of her slippers?

Oh, how she wanted to climb back down and rush into his arms. How she wanted to bind his wound, to ease his pain—for he was surely in pain, though he tried not to show it. His wound was still weeping, his sensuous mouth had formed a hard, lipless line, and his face had gone gray of a sudden.

Glancing down to order her frock, her hand stopped midstroke. He'd crushed her so close in his arms that her skirt was stained with his blood.

"It would not be wise for you to pass by Rood Chapel on your way returning," she said, walking Treacle past Nigel. Why was he just standing there like that, as though he'd been struck dumb? "If you follow the stream eastward, thus"—she pointed—"you will come out near a lane that skirts the hill near Lady Greenway's cottage. You cannot miss it. It is the only three-story Tudor hereabouts. The servants there will gladly bind your wound, considering your alignment with Lady Clara. Do not think to ride back up that hill to Rood Chapel, my lord. Nothing will be served, and I am the one who will suffer for it, although that suffering would be deserved. I mean it, sir. You have tasted my father's wrath. No matter what you think of me, I am trusting your honor as a gentleman not to be the cause of such as that which would be visited upon me."

As though he'd just awoken from a trance, Nigel grabbed Treacle's bridle. "Why did you do it?" he gritted. "What were you playing at? What made you come to that damnable masque?"

"I wanted to see how it felt to be a lady," she said emptily. "Something I have air-dreamed about since

I was a child. I had an opportunity, and I took it. That was wrong of me, and I am paying for my mistake. But it ends here. Unhand my horse, sir, and stand aside! My betrothed awaits me at the rectory, and this poor animal is in need of tending, lest she suffer from bloat." She dug her heel into Treacle's side, setting the mare in motion. "Good-bye, Lord Romney," she said, riding into the thicket.

"Alice! Wait!" he called after her.

Her name riding the wind echoed in her ears as she drove the horse back to the lane. *Please, God, don't let him follow!* she prayed. She would not look back, though she ached for one last glimpse of him. It would never have worked. They were just too different.

Yes, he'd been attracted from the very first, there was no denying that, but he'd thought he was courting a lady. She had looked the part, and acted the part. What else was he to think? If he had met her as herself, he would have walked right on by without giving her second glance. It would never have worked. They were just too different—worlds apart. He had met the real Lady Clara now, and he could go about the business of championing her honor, just as he'd thought he was doing with Alice all along. Alice knew him well enough to know that was exactly what he would do. He was the professional gentleman, in every sense of the word. Lady Clara Langly did not deserve him.

Alice uttered a dry sob at that thought. Something tugged her heartstrings like hot pincers. It was a certainty that the match was already made.

Countess Greenway and Nigel's sponsor, Lady Pembroke, would have seen to that. Both wanted their charges settled. There was only one reason for his visit to Warminster: to prepare her for a call from some lady patron of his acquaintance—Lady Pembroke, more than likely—for the purpose of brokering their arrangement. She would arrive with a contract and a list of the assets he was willing to settle upon her for becoming his mistress. That is how such things were finalized. Alice envisioned Countess Pembroke dodging pistol balls on the front walk, and would have laughed if her heart weren't breaking.

Treacle was laboring when she reached the bramble bushes. Hadn't they exercised her during Alice's absence? Evidently not, for the poor horse was pitifully out of shape. She needed cooling down badly. Once they passed through the hedgerows to the little courtyard surrounding Rood Chapel, Alice delivered the mare into young Davey's hands in the stable behind and entered the rectory.

She was relieved that Nigel must have taken her advice, for he hadn't followed her. Now all that remained was to steal up to her room under the eaves and try and repair some of the damage before her father came to collect her for her interview with John Mapes.

She'd nearly made it to the staircase when the study door opened and James Jessup stepped out into the hall. Her heart sank. Gooseflesh prickled her scalp. She had been caught out, and she looked a fright. The ride home had not dried her stained frock completely. The hem was dragging. How had it gotten torn? The satin ribbon sash that marked the high waist had gone limp, and she'd lost her slippers in the stream. She could just imagine the condition of her hair. When wet, her natural curls always seemed to have a mind of their own that was hardly ever flattering.

Anticipating a session in the rectory study, she started to back down the stairs, but her father reached her in two strides, grabbed her arm, and propelled her up the stairs instead to her chamber. Shoving her inside, he closed the door, raking her from head to toe with his eyes.

"Look at yourself!" he seethed. "You've been with him! Is that his blood there . . . or is it yours, Daughter?"

Alice swayed as if he'd struck her. "How dare you, Father." she breathed.

"Oh, I dare," he returned. "I have to dare. I will not have my daughter running wild throughout the parish to bring shame upon this house. Was it an assignation? It was, wasn't it? So that is how you imagine it will be, do you? You two had arranged to meet, hadn't you? And he came here first. He will not make that mistake again, my girl. That trench I sliced in his thigh will serve as a reminder of just what he might expect if he returns. Only next time, I will take better aim."

"There was no . . . assignation!" cried Alice. "I took Treacle for an outing. The poor horse is badly in need of exercise, and I was so lonely for her in London, I couldn't wait to see her again. I was returning from my ride when I heard the shot. You ought to be ashamed of yourself—a man of the cloth bearing arms? What will the elders say?"

"A man has the right to protect his domain and daughter, minister or no. I have exercised that right." He pointed to his neck. "This collar does not prohibit the wearer from his inalienable rights."

"And what of my inalienable rights, Father?"

"You have none. What rights you had, you forfeited. While you live under this roof, you will abide by my rules, Daughter. That is how it has always been, and it will be so now. Your six-month absence hasn't changed that. You have brought enough shame upon us. There will be no more rides."

"You cannot stop me from riding, Father. Treacle is mine! You gave her to me years ago!"

"Oh, but I can, Daughter," he thundered, triumphant. "And I shall. 'The Lord giveth, and the Lord taketh away!'"

With that, he stomped through the door and locked it behind him.

Pounding upon the scarred oak panels, Alice called after him at the top of her voice. She heard the study door slam shut downstairs, and then the front door. She ran to the window. It faced the north, toward the stable and paddock behind the rectory. Staring below, her heart froze in her breast as if an icy hand had clenched around it. James Jessup was striding toward the stable, his cassock spread on the wind. He had a flintlock pistol in his hand.

The clouds burst overhead, and a flurry of raindrops battered the window, obscuring her view.

Screaming at the top of her voice, she pounded on the glass until she'd broken it. She scarcely felt the shards prick her hands, or the sting of the rain. Her wide-flung eyes were focused upon her father as he disappeared inside the stable, and upon young Davey bursting through the open doors seconds later as if hellhounds were upon his heels.

Shrieking through the broken glass, her own voice echoed back on the wind. "No, Father, *nooooo*!"

Chapter Sixteen

Nigel heard the gunshot from the valley below, just as the threatening clouds overhead gave way to a steady downpour. He reined in momentarily, his heart turning over in his breast, and he waited, straining his ears. The sound didn't come again.

Could it have been thunder? No, too shallow for thunder. A pistol shot, sure as check. He shook his head, exciting vertigo.

No, the bufflehead wouldn't shoot his own daughter. That was preposterous. Nigel shuddered nonetheless and took a firmer grip on the ribbons. The aftershock of being shot that had kept the pain at bay was now fading. Agony was breaking over him in waves, especially when he flexed his thigh muscle. Urging the horse forward with a grimace, he continued on his way.

He hadn't done exactly as Alice bade him; he'd followed behind at a discreet distance, until he saw her break through the hedgerows. Then he'd turned his mount down into the valley by way of a path that wound between Rood Chapel and a wider lane to the south.

He only passed one other rider along the way: an older, gray-haired man with deep lines carved in his weather-beaten face, which resembled tanned leather. The man was clutching a bunch of wild-flowers. Could this be Alice's betrothed? He was tempted to stop the man and ask, but he did not. He passed him by with a cordial "Good day, sir" and a nod, since he no longer possessed his beaver hat. Then he continued on his way, as if it were the most natural thing in the world to be riding along hatless in the pouring rain in torn breeches, his thigh bound with his blood-soaked neckcloth.

Why had he let her go? Why hadn't he told her what was in his heart? Why did he just stand there like a colossal dunce while she presented him with her list of wrong assumptions? Was it because he'd been transfixed by her beauty? Or was it because she'd seemed unreal in that primeval setting, like a wood nymph, in all her nearly naked glory in that transparent frock? There was no doubt that she had enchanted him. If truth were to be told, it was more likely that he held his peace because he realized that anything he might have said to her then would have done more harm than good. She actually believed he wanted her as his mistress! The thought had never entered his mind, but now, as he rode through the patchwork hills of her home, he could see why she'd imagined such a thing. She would never be-lieve him without proof. Perhaps that was what had tied his tongue.

Well, that could be remedied. An interview with Countess Pembroke should put it to rights . . . after he'd explained the situation to her, of course. He would ask her to pay a call at Rood Chapel, or arrange a meeting elsewhere—somewhere safer—to plead his cause. Yes, that would be best. Somewhere out of range of pistol balls.

With that decided, he rode on with confidence, passing Countess Greenway's cottage. He gave it a wide berth, though his wound was still oozing and he was dizzy with pain and blood loss. That alone might have fogged his mind back in the grove. He'd fought so hard to hide it from Alice. Were the pain beyond bearing, Countess Greenway's cottage was the last place he would go for tending. He wanted no more truck with the Langlys. How could Alice even suggest it? Could she actually believe he would take up with the likes of Lady Clara once he'd tasted *her* sweetness, held her in his arms, known the pure delight of Alice's innocent awakening to desire?

If this was love, he didn't think much of it. Such alliances were far simpler when heart and loins were disjoined. When aligned, they had the power to addle a man's mind, tie his tongue, break down his defenses, and reduce him to a blithering bedlamite. Ruefully, he saw himself afflicted with all four symptoms. Whatever it was, he had no experience with it. It had never happened to him before. It was a very uncomfortable thing, and there was only one cure. He had to have her. Somehow, no matter what he had to do to accomplish it, *he had to have her.*

"Good God, old boy! Have the French invaded?" McGovern cried, lending Nigel his arm in support as he left the coaching-inn stable. "What have you done to yourself?"

"Her father wasn't receiving callers," said Nigel. "He was rather heavily into target practice." The wound was deeper than he'd thought. He could barely stand. Waves of nausea impeded his vision, and there was fever, though he was quaking with chills. The soaking he'd taken in the cloudburst hadn't helped. It was raining still, a stubborn, steady downpour that had soaked him to the skin.

"He *shot* you?" the viscount breathed. "What did you do to provoke that?"

"His attitude reduced me to name-calling, though, by God, it was deserved. The man's a pompous ass, Al. Alice wasn't in, though I thought otherwise. She'd gone riding, and was just return-ing when it . . . happened."

"Well, go on, go on. Don't keep me hanging," the viscount urged.

"Out . . . of . . . breath," Nigel panted.

"Well, of course you are, old boy. What's wanted is a surgeon. Let's get you inside and deal with first things first, eh?"

There was no surgeon in the immediate vicinity. They had to settle for one Jonathan Pypes, a bleary-eyed veterinarian they found at the inn who treated most of the locals as well, or so the innkeeper told them. Though the man's primary patients were cows, horses, and sheep, and he was half-castaway on the inn's superior ale, he cleaned, cauterized, and dressed Nigel's wound as if he did such things daily as a matter of course. After dosing Nigel with laudanum, the disheveled little man repaired to the lower regions of the inn to spend his fee in the ale room. Meanwhile, Nigel recounted the events of the morning for his friend's benefit.

"So you see," he said in conclusion, "I'm not about to give up. She's come to all the wrong conclusions, and I shan't rest until I've convinced her of that." He slurred the last. His tongue seemed too thick of a sudden, and there was a wavy aura about McGovern's tall, angular form. Why wouldn't the man hold still? It was so difficult trying to talk to a moving target.

He groaned. The laudanum, of course.

"Look here, old boy, why don't you rest while I fetch you some new togs. You cannot go about in these." McGovern picked up Nigel's soggy, torn breeches, drawers, and coat and tossed them down again. "They're tatters. You're fortunate your shirt is still wearable! At least you got yourself shot within range of a market town. It won't be Bond Street, but I shall try to find something that's not too shocking."

The viscount hesitated, staring down at Nigel, who sat reclining in a wing chair in his shirtsleeves bundled in a counterpane, the injured leg propped on a stool. "You ought to call the guards in. A tad one way and the blighter would have severed the artery. A jot the other, and you could have bid goodbye to your cods."

"No guards, Al," said Nigel, with a shake of his head. "Jessup is a clergyman—"

"Hah!" the viscount blurted. "Sink me, old boy!

If it's all the same to you, I shall refrain from allowing him to welcome *me* into the fold!"

Nigel almost laughed. "If I call in the guards, Alice would be the one to suffer for it," he said. "Jessup has heard all the gammon. He's convinced that I'm a jackanapes—Isobel Rutledge's handiwork—and he thinks there's something . . . more between Alice and myself. He's of the same mind as she . . . convinced that I'm grooming her to be . . . my . . . mistress."

"Not a half-bad idea. I've said it all along. You're fading, old boy. Let me help you into bed. You heard Pypes, that's a nasty wound. Unless your clergyman strays out of character on a regular basis, God alone knows when that gun last saw a cleaning tamp. You're courting infection. What's wanted now is sleep. Let the laudanum do its job. I'll be back in a trice. Then later, when you've rested, we'll sort it all out."

Alice was numb. She lay across her bed in her ruined blue muslin frock, exhausted. She had sobbed her heart dry. It wasn't happening. It couldn't be happening! It was a dream, a horrible nightmare. She would wake and go to the stable with a treat for Treacle—an apple from the larder, cold and juicy. How Treacle loved apples. She would throw her arms around the sorrel's neck and stroke her and groom her and whisper the secrets of her heart in the silken ear that always listened as if she understood every word. Then she would ride. She would ride like the wind, just as she'd done so many times before.

But it wasn't a dream. One glance at the shattered windowpane where the rain was leaking in, puddling on the bare wood floor, at the cuts on her hands that she was too numb to feel, at the glass shards littering the floor, told the tale. Treacle was dead. Her father had shot the horse just as he'd shot Nigel.

Nigel! Her heart sank. She should have helped him tend the wound. He was bleeding so, and he was in pain. She'd seen it in those ice blue eyes, though he'd steeled himself against it, against betraying himself in her company. Instead, she'd left him there like that in order to put an end to an impossible situation before it went any further. Besides, she didn't trust herself to chance the intimacy of such close personal contact with the man. Not after the shocking emotions he'd awakened in her.

She struggled to a sitting position, still giddy from shock. Her hands were trembling as she smoothed out the wrinkles in her bloodstained frock. She would never see him again. Fresh tears welled in her swollen eyes. How had one foolish mistake come to this?

The sound of a key turning in the lock brought her to her feet. Her heart leaped as the door handle turned, and the door came open in her father's hand.

"Your betrothed is downstairs in the parlor," he said. "Why haven't you prepared yourself?"

"I have no betrothed," she snapped. "You cannot make me marry John Mapes, Father."

"It's just as well that he sees you thus," he said,

seizing her by the wrist. "We shall prepare him for just what he's getting, hmm? He will tame you, Daughter. He will teach you your place. He will show you what comes of queening it up in town— of imitating your betters."

Alice's mind was racing as he propelled her toward the narrow staircase. She never should have come home. She should have known that the on-dits would reach Warminster before she did. Knowing her father, she also should have known how he would react. One thing was certain. She was not about to marry a man twice her age whom she didn't love. She dug in her heels.

"Father, please!" she cried. "You can see through this wet frock . . . M-my hands are bleeding . . . see? And I'm barefoot! My slippers were lost when I fell in the stream."

"Whose fault is that, Daughter? Let go of that banister! It is all arranged. He has agreed upon the settlement."

"Y-you've given me a dowry?" Inspiration struck.

"I've proposed a marriage settlement, yes," her father said, still struggling with her on the landing. Alice's hands were sore from the cuts, but her grip held true. "To be paid upon your wedding day. You didn't think he'd take you for naught, did you? It's more than you deserve, and more than I can afford, but well worth it to be rid—To have you settled at last!"

"How much?"

"That is none of your business. Let go, I say!"

"All I ask is that you give me a moment to change

my frock and order my hair. Please, Father. Surely you can occupy John Mapes a moment longer while I minister to myself?"

There was a long silence before he let her go.

"Oh, thank you, Father!" she cried, darting away before he changed his mind. "I'll be down in a trice!"

Alice didn't go directly to her room. The storm had brought the twilight early, and she hid in the shadows along the balustrade until her father entered the parlor. He wouldn't leave John Mapes alone, for fear the man would have a change of heart and leave. He would sit with him until she went down, and probably remain during their interview, come down to it. Confident in that, she padded to her chamber on feet that made no sound—but not to change her frock and order her hair. She snatched a hooded pelerine and a fresh pair of slippers from the wardrobe, stole down to the study, and tiptoed to her father's desk.

The study and parlor were in close enough proximity that the need for silence was paramount. Noises carried in the drafty old house, and boards creaked with little or no provocation. The echo of John Mapes's and her father's voices seeped in through the door she'd left ajar behind, and cold chills gripped her. If he ever caught her now . . .

James Jessup kept an accounts ledger in the top left-hand drawer of the desk. He also kept a coffer there with funds for household expenditures inside. He always kept it locked, but Alice knew where he hid the key: underneath the fronds in the fern on the plant stand beside the window. She had it in a flash, unlocked the drawer, and opened the coffer.

She hesitated. Borrowing Lady Clara's frock was one thing. What she was contemplating now was really stealing. How had she sunk to this? To what other sordid depths would her one foolish mistake take her? The coffer contained pound and two-pound notes, several guineas, silver crowns, a few farthings, and a handful of copper pence. She fingered the notes absently. Did her father not just say he had settled a dowry upon her? The whole contents of the coffer would not equal whatever that sum might be. Still she hesitated, until the sound of creaking floorboards made up her mind for her. Snatching only the cost of her fare on the night coach and enough to eat, if she did so sparingly, while she looked for a new situation, she tucked that inside the little pocket she wore suspended from her frock and put everything back as she'd found it. She'd taken so little, perhaps he wouldn't notice. No, that was ludicrous. James Jessup knew every dust mote on every coin and note in that coffer.

Regardless, it was done. If it took her the rest of her life, she would repay every penny, but now it meant freedom. "As long as you live under my roof," he had said. Well, she would live under his roof no longer.

The sound of her name funneling up the staircase outside set her in motion. He was going up to fetch her! There wasn't a moment to spare, and she sped along the little hall and out the door without a backward glance, praying Mrs. Sills hadn't seen her.

They had never been on friendly terms. The woman was mean-spirited.

Alice couldn't help but compare her relationships with Agatha Avery and the stern-faced Betty Sills. Tears stung behind her eyes, for she recalled Mrs. Avery's kindness to her while she was employed at Langly House. There was one friend who would never turn her away, but she dared not go near the Langlys again.

It was still too light to make her escape, so she scurried down the hill into the valley, where she could pick her way eastward inside the copse until dark. Then she would make straight for Warminster village by way of the lane. Granted, it was a long distance afoot, but if she cut across Lady Greenway's property surrounding the cottage, she might just make the coaching inn before the night coach departed. With this as her goal, Alice began her journey.

Chapter Seventeen

There was still an hour before the night coach arrived, and Alice took a table in the far corner of the inn to wait. She had toyed with the idea of passing the time well hidden in the grove that hemmed the road, but rain was still falling, and she was exhausted from climbing over hedges and stiles and fording brooks along the way.

A bowl of hot, salty broth of uncertain composition and a chunk of crusty bread were brought. The fare was cheap and satisfying. Alice devoured it. She hadn't realized until the greasy brown liquid trickled down her throat how hungry she was. She hadn't eaten all day.

She did not remove the hood on her indigo pelerine. It wouldn't do to take chances. There was only one person at the inn whom she knew— Jonathan Pypes, who had doctored Treacle many times in the past and her as well upon occasion, when she was a child. There was no danger that he might recognize her now, however. He was passed out—drunk as a wheelbarrow—at a table nearby.

She had nearly finished her meal, when a gentleman approached Pypes. He was tall and slender,
with golden brown hair and angular features, a rug-
gedly good-looking man who might be deemed
handsome, but for the scowl that spoiled his appearance. There was something vaguely familiar
about him. He hadn't come from out of doors. He
wore no coat or hat. Alice decided that he must be a
traveler stopping at the inn in need of Pypes's
services. She almost smiled. He'd have no help
there. Pypes was sleeping off his stupor, his deep,
shuddering snores loud enough to rouse the dead.

"Wake up, you jug-bit nodcock!" the newcomer
barked, shaking Pypes's shoulder. The veterinarian
moved under the assault as if his bones had gone to
jelly, the rhythm of his snores interrupted momentarily, but he made no reply. "Get up, I say! I'd plant
you a facer, if what's in that tankard there hadn't
already planted you a leveler, by the looks of it." He
shook Pypes again. "Wake up, blast you, man.
You're a disgrace to your profession!"

The gentleman's voice was vaguely familiar, too.
Where had Alice heard that delivery before?

Issuing forth a spate of blue language, the man
called to the innkeeper for a bucket of water, which
he promptly dumped over Pypes's head. That pro-
duced a string of unintelligible mumblings from the
veterinarian's drooling mouth, but failed to bring
him around.

"It ain't no use, cove," the innkeeper hollered
from the ale barrels across the room, where he was

filling a tankard for one of the few patrons remaining. "When he's cup-shot, he'd sleep through a cyclone."

The gentleman raked his fingers through his hair and slapped the bucket down on the table. An exasperated sigh flared his nostrils. He glanced about the room, and Alice lowered her eyes and concentrated upon the empty soup bowl before her. Even at that, she sensed a hitch in the man's breath as he settled his hard gaze upon her. Then her heart took a tumble: he was striding toward her, and she was trapped with no hope of escape. Her table was situated beside an archway that led to the upper rooms, too far from the entrance for her to flee.

Recognition broke over her like a wave. It was Nigel's friend, Alistair something or other! She'd scarcely met him at the fete when his news spiraled her into a dead faint. He looked different without his coat and beaver, and the sand-colored stubble forming on his angular face was similarly deceiving.

"Miss Jessup?" he said, strolling nearer. "Odds fish! *It is!* Fancy finding you in such a place as this, and at this hour! Are you traveling so soon after returning home? Well, of course you are. Silly of me, why else would you be here?"

"Please," Alice whispered. "I must ask you to lower your voice, my lord. None here knows me, save Mr. Pypes, and he is no threat at the moment. I beg that you as a gentleman will preserve my anonymity."

"You can't be considering the *night coach*," he said, his voice dutifully lowered. "You are! Well, this is a most fortuitous meeting, then. Sink me, dear lady, if I'll allow you to set foot inside that dubious equipage, when I have access to a most excellent coach. It is at your disposal, my dear, and I will be delighted to take you anywhere you wish to go. First, however, I have need of your help, if you will give it. It shan't delay you long. I had intended Pypes there to assist me, but as you can see, he's quite castaway. May I presume upon our short acquaintance to enlist your able assistance? I assure you, my request is quite honorable, if it's a matter of trust . . . ?"

"Trust you?" she murmured. "Forgive me, my lord, but we are of such short acquaintance that I'm afraid I don't even remember your name."

He flashed a broad smile. "Is that all?" He bowed from the waist. "Viscount Alistair McGovern at your service, Miss Jessup. I hate to speak for myself, but since there is no one in the immediate vicinity to speak for me, you have my word that you shan't hear of my name being bruited about with disfavor in polite company or otherwise. My character is quite sterling, and the help I seek is of a strictly benevolent nature."

Alice hesitated. Should she trust this man? He seemed sincere, but why wouldn't he tell her what sort of benevolence he required? Something was not as it should be. He was evidently holding whatever it was back because he knew that if he disclosed it, she would refuse.

She was just about to decline, when a figure in the doorway set her heart pounding like a triphammer. It was John Mapes.

"Please, my lord," she whispered on the tail of a strangled gasp. "That person who has just come in . . . He must not see me!"

McGovern gave a passing glance toward Mapes and raised her to her feet. Alice's first instinct was to resist, but something in McGovern's eyes fostered trust. Before she knew what had happened, he'd whisked her through the arch wrapped in his strong arm, voicing something about it being time that they retired, and propelled her up the staircase to the upper chambers.

"Look here, where are you taking me?" she snapped, struggling against his grip as he hurried her along the upper hallway.

"Judging from the look on that pretty face of yours when you clapped eyes upon that latecomer downstairs, whoever he is, somewhere decidedly less dangerous." He turned the knob on a door on the south side of the hall. "We have arrived," he said, ushering her inside. "Now you can see for yourself why I need your help, Miss Jessup."

Alice's hand flew to her lips as if it had a mind of its own. She gasped. Her throat had closed over any words that might have tried to escape. Before her wide-flung eyes, Nigel lay unconscious in the bed beneath a counterpane, his right leg protruding from it, his upper thigh carelessly swathed in a bloodstained linen bandage.

"I am in hopes that you are a better hand at doctoring than I, dear lady. Women tend to have a natural talent for it that we men lack. I'm counting upon that, you see. We've got to bring his fever down."

Alice threw off her pelerine and approached the bed. She placed her hand on Nigel's brow. It was on fire. He stirred but did not wake. She'd had no idea the wound was as serious as all this.

"I shall need strong spirits," she said, turning to McGovern. "Preferably gin."

"Oh, I doubt you'll be able to coax him to drink it as he is," the viscount replied.

"Not to drink, my lord. His fever is raging. We shall need to rub him down with it . . . to bathe his face and wrists and feet, to cool his skin. It will bring the fever down."

"It seems a dreadful waste of blue ruin, but I shall see what I can do," the viscount said, turning to leave.

"Y-you shan't betray me?" she asked, her eyes pleading.

"I'm sorry you even felt it necessary to ask," he said, taking obvious note of her ruined frock and mussed coiffure. The rain, and being crammed beneath the hood of her pelerine, had reduced her cap of natural curls to an impossible tangle of wayward tendrils falling into her eyes. "But I shall hold you to filling me in on that mysterious fellow below and your shocking state and condition, once I return," he added.

Alice managed a feeble smile and returned to her charge. She reached toward the bandage on his thigh and drew her hand back several times before her fingers touched the linen. The wound was precariously close to his private areas, and he was naked below the waist beneath the counterpane. He

groaned as she unbound the wound, and her eyes
smarted with unshed tears as she looked down at
the ravages of her father's stupidity. The wound had
been cleaned and cauterized skillfully enough, but
an aura of angry redness surrounding the burned
flesh worried her. There was infection. She'd feared
that from the first, considering the condition of the
weapon that had delivered the wound. It should
have been treated at once, not left to fester for hours
and subjected to every kind of exertion over hill and
vale on horseback, collecting dirt along the way.
Oh, why hadn't she seen to it back in the valley?

Guilt washed over her in damning waves. This
was beyond her skills. She'd seen infection take the
limb of a stable hand once. Left too long to fester,
there had been nothing to do to save it, and that
wound had been much less severe than the one facing her now. Jonathan Pypes had put more than
one animal out of its misery for such a wound. But
she wouldn't—couldn't—think about that now.

She shouldn't be here, either—not *alone* with
him. The man was nearly naked. That he was unconscious didn't seem to matter. What sight of that
exposed physique was doing to her equilibrium was
scandalous. He was all masculine muscle and sinew,
lightly furred with dark hair about his chest. It
came peeking out through his open shirtfront each
time he drew a deep, tremulous breath. There was
no need of leg pads and corsets here. He was perfectly formed.

The bandage needed changing. She had to concentrate upon the task at hand and not the object of

her affection himself if she was to maintain any semblance of emotional control. There was a pile of bandage linen on the chiffonier, and she carried a length of it to the bed and stared down toward the wound. It needed some sort of salve to address the infection, but she had none. If only Jonathan Pypes were conscious! He must have something suitable. She'd seen him slather unctions on Treacle's abrasions.

Treacle. She hadn't thought of her horse since this new press had come upon her. Treacle was dead, and so horribly, after such a fine reunion and ride. Tears welled in her eyes. She could scarcely see Nigel through them. Blinking the sadness back, she was debating whether to bind Nigel's wound or wait, when McGovern entered with the gin, the sound of the closing door spinning her around with a start.

"I've got it," the viscount said, exhibiting the bottle. "The best blue ruin in Wiltshire County, to hear the innkeeper tell it. It came dear enough, and I still say it's a waste, but—" He stopped in his tracks. "Good God, old thing, bear up!" he said. "Belay that Friday face. He's not exactly knocking at death's door. I've seen him in far worse shape, during battle on a man-o'-war, with none save a bleary-eyed ship's cook to tend him. We fought together at Copenhagen, you know. That's a decorated war hero you're tending there!"

"That's just it," Alice sobbed. "I'm not tending him. I've nothing to tend him with, but this." She brandished the bandage linen. "It needs something to fight the infection . . . a salve or ointment to keep that gauze from sticking to the wound. It's bleeding again from just removing the dressing."

"Mrs. Davies and her herbal cures are what he needs," the viscount said. "She keeps a capital herb garden, and she's patched us both up more times than I can remember."

"That awful housekeeper at his town house? She hung rue about my neck!"

McGovern threw back his head in laughter. "She's hung worse around mine," he warbled, "and I've survived. Her remedies are legendary. Even the local physicians consult her. You've led a sheltered life, m'dear, growing up in a rectory with a man who could do such as this." He gestured toward Nigel's wound, and his friend began to stir and moan. "Not all mysteries are evil, and not all superstitions unfounded. Mrs. Davies's remedies are aeons old. Folks have been healing with herbs since time out of mind. She'd have this under control in a trice, but it's a long journey for someone in his condition, and we have to make do until he's fit for travel."

"*You* have to make do, my lord," Alice corrected him. "I must away. It is not safe for me to remain here. The night coach has come and gone, and now I shall have to wait until morning to take my leave. I needed to be on my way before then. In daylight, someone will surely recognize me. My father—"

"Where will you go, and why are you going?" the viscount interrupted. "Who was that fellow downstairs earlier? He's gone, by the way. You promised you'd explain."

"I—I will. Once this is bandaged and we've wiped him down," Alice hedged.

How could she put it into words? Her eyes ached for holding back the tears, and her fingers trembled as she finished removing the bandage from Nigel's wound. He moaned when her hand grazed his thigh precariously close to his manhood, still covered by the counterpane, which all at once rose up and gained volume in that area.

Alice jerked her hand back and reached for the gin. Soaking a towel with the alcohol, she began stroking Nigel's brow and throat, as far from dangerous areas of the man's anatomy as she could range herself.

So many uncomfortable emotions were running riot in her then that she could barely stand. She was grieving for Treacle, terrified of being caught out, embarrassed about being in such a situation and at the prospect of confiding in a virtual stranger. Meanwhile, she was wrestling with the shocking sensations Nigel's closeness had set loose in the regions of her most secret self, heretofore virgin territory.

Her heart was thumping against her ribs. She was certain McGovern could hear it as he leaned close, helping her spread Nigel's shirt wide enough to sponge his shoulders and chest with the cooling gin. Pulsating spirals of warmth attacked her belly and thighs at the touch of Nigel's hot, dry skin and silky chest hair beneath her fingers. He was burning up, yet he responded to her touch, leaning into her strokes, meanwhile writhing—but not in pain, from the look of the hooded eyes that had come open a crack. They were dilated with desire. How could they be, when he was in such a state?

"Look here," said McGovern. "You aren't about to swoon again on me here, are you? I'm ill equipped to handle more than one crisis at a time."

"No, I am not!" Alice snapped. "I am no milk-and-water miss, my lord."

"Yes, well, I can certainly see that," McGovern replied, with a skeptical arch of his brow.

"I'm sure His Lordship has told you everything," she replied. "You must know that it was what you said at the fete . . . about Lord Chesterton that rendered me inert. What I was trying to prevent had come to pass. Lady Clara was on her way to Gretna Green with the blackguard, and I was left to face her aunt. That, coupled with the ridiculous deception, was enough to bear, without the appearance of Isobel Rutledge, whom I had been introduced to early on in my employment. Had she confronted me, the whole coil would have unwound then and there, and I would have been mortified. I am not good at deception, my lord. I made a dreadful mistake, but believe me, I'm paying for it."

Tears streamed down at last. She could no longer hold them back, and before she knew what had happened, the whole tale spilled from her—everything he couldn't have known, from the moment she left Langly house to their meeting that night at the inn. McGovern hung on every word without interrupting. Only his facial expressions responded to each element of her story.

She was still standing beside Nigel's bed when

she finished, the gin-soaked towel clutched in her fingers. When McGovern spoke, an audible breath preceded his words.

"You have feelings for him, don't you, my dear?" he asked softly. "You needn't answer. I see it in your eyes and hear it in your voice. That throaty little tremor betrays you. It's none of my affair, of course, but that's never stopped me from sticking my oar in where it's not wanted, and I shan't break tradition now. Would it ease your mind any to know that those feelings are returned, my dear?"

"I have no right to . . . any feelings, my lord," Alice flashed. "And as for what he feels, that is quite obvious—and I am no man's Cyprian, sir!"

"No, I can see that," McGovern agreed. "Though I must confess I pressed for such a situation. But that was before I was fully acquainted with you," he hastened to add. "I daresay he all but called me out over the suggestion."

"I should have been gone—would have been gone, but for this," she murmured, gesturing toward Nigel. "I had bid him farewell, as was good and just. I did it more for him than myself. It was the only way. We are from two very different worlds. Now I must go before he wakes, before he ever knows I've been here, or all I have suffered since will be for naught. Had I known, I never would have let you bring me into this room. You could have managed without me. How is it that you came to be here at the inn? Were you traveling together?"

McGovern nodded. "And fortunate it is that I insisted upon accompanying him. I didn't think he ought come on his own. I feared something like this might occur. He's all about in the head over you, m'dear. He'd planned a trip to Wiltshire to look at horses for some time. I thought I'd look them over for him while he paid a call upon you at the rectory and be close at hand if he had need of me. We've always watched each other's backs. It's paid off splendidly in the past, for the both of us."

"His Lordship is fortunate to have such a friend," said Alice. "And he needs your assistance more than I do. You needn't keep your end of the bargain. I shall find my own way. You cannot leave him, and I must not stay."

"Where will you go? Have you a place?"

Alice shook her head. "I shall find a situation. I shall go into service, if needs must. Scullery maids and laundresses are always in demand. I shall find something, my lord—I am quite enterprising. But it cannot be here in Wiltshire. If I remain and Father finds me, he will force a marriage to that person you saw downstairs earlier. He thinks all the on-dits are true—that His Lordship is a philanderer and a rakehell, and that he has . . . taken advantage of me."

"But, my dear, surely you know—"

"Have you not heard me, my lord?" Alice interrupted. "Father *shot my horse* because he believed I had ridden her to an assignation with Lord Romney and meant to keep me from the means to have another. All lies! My Treacle is dead in her stall in the stable, shot with the same pistol that did this mischief here, for naught but lies! He may as well have

shot me as well. I shall hear that gunshot until I die.
I must go, my lord, while I can. Where matters not."

All at once, a scorching hand captured hers in an
iron grip, and Alice gave a lurch. Nigel pulled her
closer, his hooded eyes glazed over with . . . Could
those be tears?

"She's right, Al," he murmured, meanwhile not
taking his gaze from hers. "She cannot stay here.
I . . . cannot help her as I am." He searched Alice's
face. The look in his eyes turned hers away. "If I had
known he was going to . . . If I had known, I never
would have let you go. . . ."

"How long have you been conscious, my lord?"
Alice breathed.

"Since you unbound my wound," he murmured.
"I dared not let on. You would have run again. . . .
But I'd best tend it myself from now on."

"*Oh!*" she cried. "How could you, sir!"

"Look here, old boy," McGovern put in. "You've
a fever. There'll be time enough for all this argle-
bargle once you're on the mend."

"I'm well enough for what must be done," said
Nigel through a grimace as he moved the injured
leg. "Go and wake Carter. Have him bring the
carriage round. We leave for town at once."

"You cannot!" Alice and McGovern chimed in
together.

"And I am not going anywhere with you, Lord
Romney!" Alice cried.

"Do not argue with an injured man," he replied.
"It . . . taxes the strength I shall need to pull this
off. I'm well aware of the fever. That deuced rusty

pistol ball has had its way with me, but I've been shot before, with lead left behind, and survived. Now then, you are my houseguest, Miss Jessup, until I can sort all this out. Every propriety shall be observed . . . and, by God, I know just the person to enforce that!" The last was expressed in the nature of an epiphany.

Nonplussed, Alice stared.

"Well?" Nigel barked at McGovern. "What are you waiting for?"

Chapter Eighteen

The first thing Nigel did before he committed himself to Henrietta Davies's care was send Carter to Langly House for Mrs. Avery. It was done with the utmost secrecy by way of the servants' entrance at the Mayfair residence. Nigel received her in his study, despite Mrs. Davies's vehement protests that he should be abed where he belonged, while he could still boast of two legs underneath him.

Exertion had caused the wound to weep again. Sitting stiff-legged in his favorite wing chair, wearing a dressing gown over his shirt and bloodstained breeches, he tried to stagger to his feet when Mrs. Avery entered, but she promptly rushed to his side and sat him down again.

"Oh, la, my lord! What have ya done ta yourself?" she cried, stepping back from him, her plump fingers splayed out on her cheeks.

"I've had the misfortune to make the acquaintance of Miss Jessup's father," Nigel quipped.

Her gasp replied.

"Please be seated, Mrs. Avery," Nigel said, flashing a lopsided smile meant to put her at ease. "I've enough mother hens fussing over me here. Our business must be settled before I succumb to them."

"Our business, my lord?"

"Yes, dear lady. I have brought you here to make you an offer—an offer of employment. I had Carter come round secretly, because I would not presume to anticipate your answer and did not want to disrupt your situation should you not wish to accept the position I have in mind."

Mrs. Avery's jaw fell slack, and the round apples of her shiny, veined cheeks blushed crimson.

"Miss Jessup is my houseguest," he went on. "I rescued her from . . . God only knows what would have become of her, but she suspects me of ulterior motives, and all proprieties must be met if she is to remain under this roof until I can convince her otherwise."

He paused. She was too dumbfounded to speak, though her jaw worked as if she meant to.

"She shall need a chaperone, a companion. I have maids to assist her with the menial tasks. You have befriended her, and she will trust you before she would trust any in my employ to see that . . . proper decorum is upheld." He was fading again. He'd only had one dose of Mrs. Davies's yarrow tisane, and it was past time for another.

"Y-you mean . . . you want me to do like she done with Lady Clara?"

"That is precisely what I wish, yes."

"But . . . I'm not suited! It's above my station, my lord!"

"You are exactly suited, Mrs. Avery, and you shall

be paid accordingly. She needs you. *I* need you. Making wrong assumptions, her father shot me when I tried to pay a call upon her, and then shot her *horse* because he thought she'd ridden the animal to an assignation with me, which couldn't be further from the truth. I brought her here because she was fleeing from him, and from a marriage with one of the locals that he had arranged for her— fleeing with nowhere to go. I shudder to think what might have become of her if our paths hadn't crossed so fortuitously. I brought her here, but she will not stay unless you help me persuade her that my intentions are strictly honorable. If you agree to my proposal, it will mean leaving Langly House without giving notice. I need you now, tonight. And regardless of how this turns out, you shall have employment with me as long as you desire."

"H-he *shot* you, my lord . . . and her horse?" the housekeeper cried.

"That he did. She'll tell you all about it. Can we strike a bargain?"

"Oh, my stars! Well . . . If you're sure, my lord."

"I'm sure."

"I can hardly take it all in," the woman murmured, clearly trying to do just that. She gave a start. "I'll go back round to Langly House and fetch my things at once. Countess Greenway is a termagant of the first water, the old peahen. She'll fly up in the boughs at me for fair, leavin' on the spot and all, but that don't matter a whit to me, after the way she done ta Miss Alice. I'll be glad ta see the last o' her—of the whole lot o' them."

"Thank you, Mrs. Avery," Nigel said, his words riding a sigh of relief. "I've put Miss Jessup in the blue suite on the second floor to the right of the landing. Your apartment adjoins it. Go on up and tell her the good news. When you've done, I'll have Carter drive you back round to Langly House for your things."

"I don't know how ta thank you, my lord," Mrs. Avery said after a breathless moment. "You won't be sorry, I swear it!"

"I'm sure I won't. Now then, you can do me one more kindness before you go. . . ."

"Anything, my lord."

"Just pull that bell rope there beside the door. I'm afraid I shall need the footmen to help me to my chamber."

It was a sennight before Nigel's fever subsided, and a fortnight before the doctor would allow him to be up out of bed for long periods. The wound was healing nicely, though he walked with a limp and would, so the doctor told him, for some time. Henrietta Davies was credited with his recovery. Puffed with pride and singing the praises of her yarrow remedies, she strutted about the town house like a queen. This was her greatest victory to date, and she made sure all in residence were aware of it.

Nigel deliberately avoided Alice, though he met on a regular basis with Mrs. Avery to keep abreast of her settling in. Alice had come to his suite on a number of occasions, begging news of his condition from the staff in attendance, but she was refused admittance to the sanctuary at Nigel's orders, though she was kept apprised of his progress. There were several reasons for this. He wanted her to relax in her new environment with Mrs. Avery, for one thing. He was counting upon absence making her miss him enough to work in his favor, for another. Last but not least, he couldn't trust his body not to betray him as it had done at the Old Bell coaching inn at Warminster, when her gentle touch so near his manhood had brought him to a full arousal, despite the pain and fever. Just thinking about her made his loins tighten and his blood race.

So far the strategy seemed to be working. He kept his distance, sent cordial messages by way of Mrs. Avery, and took his meals in his apartment alone, except when Alistair McGovern came to call. But the viscount had been absent for many days, until one afternoon at the end of the month of July, when he arrived late in the day and stayed to join Nigel in his rooms for dinner.

It was a balmy night. Their dinner was served on the little terrace off Nigel's sitting room, which overlooked the town-house garden, with two footmen in attendance. The air, though a trifle damp, was infused with all manner of fading and burgeoning botanicals. Nigel employed a skilled gardener, who planted in such a way that something was always blooming right into fall. The result was breathtaking. The last perfume of one dying species mingled with the first awakening of another. The exotic result was hypnotizing. Nigel couldn't even name all the varieties, but the sweet fragrance drew him to that terrace like a magnet since he'd come home. It reminded him of Alice.

"Well, old boy," McGovern said, stirring his julienne soup. "You're looking a damn sight better than you did at our last meeting. So, how long are you planning to shut yourself up in this self-imposed tower of yours, hiding from the world? This isn't like you, Nigel."

"I'm not hiding, Al, I'm trying to foster trust."

"Look here, old boy, you cannot keep her on here indefinitely. Tongues have already begun to wag. What? Do you think you're invisible here? When I came in just now I took notice of a suspicious-looking cloaked fellow loitering about. Like it or not, you're being watched. One slip and the murmurs become full-blown outcries. I do not have to remind you how the ton loves a scandal, and what becomes of those whom it scandalizes."

"You know all proprieties are being met here."

"Yes, *I* know it, but as long as Miss Alice Jessup resides under this roof, those tongues are going to wag regardless. My point is that you're fast becoming fodder for the tongues of the ton, old boy. You will never make a legitimate match after this. You need to stand back and take stock. It isn't just one issue. You're contemplating marriage with a commoner—Don't give me that look! I know it's been done. It's hardly a crime, and I mean no disparagement against the gel. She is utterly charming and very much in love with you, I'm sure, but she is far beneath you socially, Nigel, and one of you needs to see reason. This sort of thing isn't for you.

She knew it, and she was doing something about it, until you interfered. I give her credit for that. Now you've got her here at your residence with a displaced housekeeper acting as her companion, of all the unlikely foibles. That is bizarre. The Avery woman is East End born and bred, gotten up in silks. It's like trying to teach a mule to perform dressage. One word from her mouth condemns her. Why, you'll be the laughingstock of the season if they walk out in town. If it weren't so . . . so . . . pathetic, it would be comical. You could stage it in Drury Lane! What can you be thinking? What would your sainted father say?"

"Father was no saint, Al, and when have you known appearances to rule me, or convention—or the bloody ton, either, for that matter? Don't be such a snob. I once accused you of becoming a Sassenach. I rescind that. You *are* a Sassenach."

"What of it? Look here, old boy, I'm just looking out for your best interests. Do you know what's being bruited about, old boy?"

"I don't know, and frankly I don't care, Al."

"Well, I shall enlighten you anyway, because *I* care. You have Lady Clara to thank for this, I have no doubt, but rumor has it that Alice Jessup deliberately misled you in order to snag you for herself, and that it evidently worked, because she's here in this love nest with you and you've taken her for your mistress. By the time Lady Clara and that harpy aunt of hers are through, the pair of you will be blackballed for good and all! That you don't have a care for yourself is one thing. At least have a care for the poor gel. Let her go, Nigel. Either set her up as your mistress in earnest, or let her go."

Nigel let the footman take his soup plate with the soup untouched. Alistair was his friend, but he had gone too far. All that he had said was factual enough, but the viscount had put it in the most unflattering light possible. Couldn't McGovern see what he was trying to do? Couldn't the man see that if he wasn't very careful how he handled the situation, he could lose Alice? Didn't he know that if Nigel did lose her, part of him would never be the same again? The only part that mattered, the part he'd just gotten to know—his heart.

There was something about her. He'd seen it from the start: an ethereal something that bound them with tethers of the soul, as if they were already joined in another lifetime and were destined to meet again in this one. He had fallen in love. Cupid's dart made no allowances for class distinction, and if the deuced fogs set loose by that unexpected happenstance hadn't crept in and addled his brain, he'd have figured out how to settle the matter by now.

"I am well aware that she cannot remain here, Al," he said at last. "Have you done what I asked you to do? You've been gone long enough. Did you make the purchase?"

The viscount heaved a sigh. "Yes, yes, I bought the lot. They didn't come cheap, but I haven't rolled you up. I think you will be pleased. Your friend at Tattersall's didn't play you false. He put you onto some top-shelf horseflesh—excellent dams, and a few studs I wouldn't mind owning myself."

"And you've been out to the coast?"

"I have. I've brought you some French contra-band brandy from one of the wrecks, compliments of your man out there—and the local smugglers, of course. You can bet your blunt that your cellars are stocked. The manor house is livable, and your man has his instructions. I hired a drover and riders. The horses will be delivered in a fortnight. I'll go back out to Wiltshire and accompany them, if you like, just to be sure there's no havey-cavey goings-on afoot. You never can tell nowadays with such trans-actions. Hah! Those horses tempted me, I'll be bound! Do you think you can unwind this coil here by then?"

"Not without help," Nigel admitted. "I've sent a message to Countess Pembroke. Her footman came round with a reply just before you arrived. She's coming to call tomorrow. Once I've explained the situation to her, I shan't have any difficulty convinc-ing her to broker the match. Under the circum-stances, that's what's wanted."

"Are you sure you know what you're doing, old boy?"

"I've never been more sure of anything in all my life, Al."

Alice stepped back inside her sitting room from the little balcony attached to her chamber. She hadn't meant to eavesdrop. The night was so starry and fine, and the garden scents so inviting. She had just come up from dinner, and it was much too early for bed. She only meant to indulge herself for a little while, to collect her thoughts and search her heart for answers that had thus far eluded her. How could she know that just next door, Nigel and Alistair McGovern would be dining late together on the balcony attached to Nigel's rooms?

Voices carried on the gentle breeze, and though she hadn't heard all of that conversation, she'd heard more than she'd bargained for—certainly more than they would have wanted her to hear. She was a captive audience, not daring to move and betray her presence. Her worst fears were realized. She had been right all along. This is how such arrangements were brokered. Not between a gentleman and his ladylove, but through a third party, a patroness of some distinction, who would finalize the arrangements, propose a reasonable settlement, and present the contract. Such procedures were all very civilized and proper, and acceptable amongst the ton, when a gentleman selected a mistress. But they were not acceptable to Alice.

She closed the French doors soundlessly and backed away from them. Nigel and the viscount went on speaking, but she had heard enough, all she needed to hear to come to the only conclusion possible in this hopeless situation. She wouldn't be there when Lady Pembroke arrived to broker the match. She still had most of the money she'd taken when she fled the rectory. Now she was preparing to flee again, and the only casualty of that decision was Mrs. Avery. Trusting that Nigel would do right by the woman, she went to the wardrobe and threw it open.

The ruined blue muslin she'd arrived in wasn't amongst the frocks hanging there. It had been consigned to the dustbin when she arrived. Nigel had provided several replacements, but she hadn't even tried them on. They were much too fine. They were for a lady. That was how the whole mingle-mangle had begun, when she'd put on clothes she had no right to wear! She would not make that mistake again. If she knew nothing else when all was said and done, she knew her place, and it was not at Nigel Farnham's town house in Grosvenor Square. She didn't belong in the wilds of Wiltshire, either. Where she did belong—if she did belong anywhere—didn't matter at the moment; the only thing that did was stealing away just as she was, in the borrowed costume of a housemaid. That this time the frock she'd put on was beneath her station somehow seemed fitting and just.

Now would be the ideal time to leave: while Nigel was occupied with the viscount, and Mrs. Avery had gone early to bed. Alice snatched her pelerine from the armoire, shrugged it on, and rushed to the door. The narrow hallway outside was deserted, and she'd nearly reached the landing when she spied Nigel ascending from the first floor gingerly on the mending leg, a candle branch in his hand. Could it be that the viscount had left, and Nigel had seen him out?

There was no time to puzzle over it. She was caught out—too far from her chamber to reach it in time, and too close to the landing to avoid being seen. A soft sound escaped her when their eyes met, and she stopped in her tracks as he turned stiff-legged at the landing and limped closer.

"Where might you be going at this hour, Miss Jessup?" he asked with a playful smile. There were those irresistible dimples, so much more provocative in the dimly lit darkness of that hallway.

Bathed in the candle glow, there was an ethereal look about him. Something seized her heart and loins at the sight of him so casually attired. He'd shed his coat, vest, and neckcloth. His Egyptian-cotton shirt was open at the throat, revealing a glimpse of silky dark hair in the shadows beneath. It reminded her of the sight of him half-naked in the bed at the Old Bell coaching inn. Hot blood rushed to her temples as the fingers of a blush crawled up her cheeks. She could just imagine their color, and that of her earlobes. It was as if they'd caught fire.

"I—I—It is such a fine evening," she murmured, mentally begging her voice not to crack. "I—I fancied a walk in the garden before I retire. That is . . . if I am allowed?"

His posture collapsed, and the hypnotic smile faded from his lips. "You are not a prisoner here, Ali—Miss Jessup," he corrected. "Would you like me to join you?"

That was the last thing Alice wanted and the thing she wanted most, rolled into one. But it was something she couldn't have—dared not risk. If she were to venture into the garden alone with him now, she would never be able to leave him. No, Alistair McGovern was right. She knew any sort of alliance between herself and Nigel was impossible, and she had done something about it. Now, owing to his persistence, and her weakness, she had to do something about it again . . . for both their sakes.

"I saw you struggling up that staircase just now," she said. "I wouldn't presume to have you descend again. You are too soon out of bed, my lord."

His wince at the *my lord* drove her eyes away. *Please don't let him press for it!* she prayed. *And do not let him come any closer.* The latter prayer, however, was spoken in vain.

"Alice, please," he murmured. Setting the candle branch on the hall settle, he took her hands in his. "Don't reprimand me for the familiarity of calling you by name. I know it's a breach of convention, but I have never been a conventional fellow. And don't shrink from me like that. You have naught to fear from me. I should think you would know that by now."

Alice wanted to scream *It isn't you I fear, but myself!* She bit the words back and swallowed hard.

"Have I imposed upon you once since you arrived here?" he asked. "You know I've not. I have deliberately kept my distance. If my motives were not above reproach, would I have done that? No. I think not." He stroked her cheek with the back of his hand. "You're feverish, yet your hands are cold," he observed. "Perhaps you oughtn't chance the night air after all. . . ."

Feverish? She was on fire, caught in the radiant lava flow his body heat generated between them, aching to be enveloped in those strong, sinewy arms she strained to keep at a distance. His scent rose in her nostrils, that leather and lime laced with clean male essence and the heady ghost of recently drunk wine. It was all she could do to keep from turning her head and pressing her lips against the hand lightly caressing her face. The instinct came as naturally as drawing breath. How could something that felt so right be so wrong?

"Perhaps you're correct," she murmured, unable to meet his hooded gaze. "There will be . . . other nights." But there wouldn't be—couldn't be—and her heart was breaking. She had left him once. Was she brave enough to do it again? She had to be.

He tilted her chin up until she could not avoid his dilated eyes. "You're trembling," he noticed. "Come, I shall light your way back to your rooms." He picked up the candle branch. "Can't have you taking to your bed just when I am vacating mine. Tomorrow, my intentions will be made plain in such a way that there will be no question as to what I have in mind for our future."

They had reached her chamber door, and he pulled her close in his free arm, gazing down into her misty eyes. She tried to blink the tears back, but in a way she was glad of them. They blurred his image.

"Until then . . . ?" he whispered, grazing her temple with his warm, moist lips. It was no fraternal kiss, that, for all that he'd obviously meant it to be. It was charged with a tender passion filled with restraint that made her heart race and her knees wobble. When those scorching lips began sliding along her cheek with her mouth clearly in mind,

Alice lowered her head and pulled back, spoiling his aim. Had those lips touched hers, her resolve would have crumbled. She would have yielded to that single kiss, unlocked the gates that held back heaven only knew what pleasures. But no, she dared not yield. She dared not lose herself in his glacier blue gaze. She had already lost her heart. Looking into those riveting eyes would mean losing her very soul.

"Good night, my lord," she murmured. And with the grace of a dancer, she reeled out of his embrace and through her chamber door.

Chapter Nineteen

The door snapped shut, and Alice sagged against it. Outside, a deep sigh fractured the silence. She held her breath, waiting for the sound of Nigel's ragged gait receding along the hallway. It was some time in coming, and she didn't draw an easy breath until the click of his own door closing down the hall drew her shoulders down even farther.

Her instinct was to run just as fast as her trembling legs could carry her while she still possessed the courage. Common sense, however, bade her wait. She had excused herself brilliantly just now. If he were to catch her leaving again, it would all have been for naught. He would know.

It was the hardest half hour she had ever endured, but at the end of it, confident that Nigel had indeed retired, she eased her door open and stepped back into the shadowy hallway. It was still early, though well past a respectable hour for a young lady to be abroad alone in the streets of London, but Alice didn't think about that now. Nor did she pay close attention to her surroundings as she pattered down the town-house steps. She knew the general direction she must travel in order to reach the nearest coaching inn.

Pulling her hood close about her face, shielding herself against a fine sheeting mist that had suddenly settled in over the square, she passed the parked carriage without noticing. It wasn't until the door flew open and a cloaked figure leaped down to the cobblestone street and began stalking after her that fear raised the fine hairs at the back of her neck and her quick step became a scurry.

She'd been caught off guard, however. The split-second hesitation it took her to set her trembling legs in motion was costly, and her pursuer closed the gap between them with ease. All at once, a gloved hand seized her by the arm and jerked her around, while the other clamped tight over her mouth. The man propelled her back toward the carriage waiting at the curb.

Struggling against her captor's bruising grip, Alice tried to scream. Sadly, only breathless whimpers escaped, and he shoved her into the coach and slammed the door.

"Drive on!" the villain bellowed to the coachman, and the carriage lurched forward at the crack of the man's whip.

With the jingle of rattling tack and the rasp and creak of rusty springs, the conveyance turned down a lane cloaked in the fog, and her captor shook her none too gently. "So, little trollop, you are found!" he triumphed. "Steal from me, will you? I shall soon show you the error of your ways. It seems that you have two options once again, but fortune hasn't smiled upon you, if that is what you suppose. You shall marry John Mapes and be glad he is still willing after this, or—"

"Never!" Alice cried, twisting her mouth free of her father's pinching grip.

"Or," he went on, with raised voice, "I will have you to St. Mary's of Bethlehem Hospital—*Bedlam*—straightaway, there to be committed amongst the rest of the insane. I shan't have any difficulty persuading the physicians there that you are quite mad enough to certify, after your bizarre behavior and the scandal you've brought upon my house because of it. Or perhaps you would prefer to go before the magistrate and be shut up in Newgate for theft, Daughter? That makes three options, doesn't it? Well, I would think carefully if I were you before you decide, because either alternate choice to a proper wedding in Rood Chapel for all to view will bring reprisals upon your lover in that house back there. I promise you, Daughter, if you do not act just exactly as I say, I will ruin the bounder! And as for *you*? Do not think to put me to the test."

Nigel was standing at the terrace doors, gazing into the empty garden hidden in the mist that hadn't abated with the dawn, when Archer, his butler, admitted Countess Pembroke. He'd nearly forgotten she was coming to call. It didn't matter anymore. Alice was gone. She hadn't been headed down for a

stroll in the garden at all last night; she'd been running away. That possibility had never occurred to him
when he stopped her in the hallway. If only it had.

He'd searched the house and grounds. He'd ridden like a madman from one coaching inn to another, interrogating the innkeepers at the Angel, in
St. Clements, Strand; the Swan With Two Necks,
in Lads' Lane; at the Bell and Crown, in Holborn;
the Golden Cross, in Charing Cross; the Bull in
Mouth; the Spread Eagle. None had seen her. All
he'd accomplished was grieving his newly mended
thigh with the reckless exertion. She had vanished
without a trace.

"Good heavens! What has happened to you?"
the countess cried, turning him from the French
doors with a start. "You were so much improved
when I called a sennight ago, dear. Why, you look
like death itself! You're unshaven, your hair all
mussed . . . And your togs! They look as if you've
crawled through a coal bin. What catastrophe has
befallen us?"

"Please be seated, my lady," Nigel said, sweeping
his arm toward the lounge. It was his only append-
age that didn't ache.

The countess sat ramrod rigid, her flawless bearing above reproach in her ecru muslin frock and
wine-colored spencer, her silvered hair contained
within the confines of a fashionable ecru bonnet
with plumes to match the spencer. The delicate
feathers drew Nigel's eye. They seemed to be moving in slow motion, just as his world was. Nothing
seemed real. It was as if a great fissure had split his

world apart, and he had fallen through the crack but not yet struck bottom. He was floating in limbo. He had lost her.

"Forgive me, my lady," he said, easing himself into an ornately carved Jacobean chair, whose stiffness suited his condition. "It totally slipped my mind that you were coming to call this afternoon."

"Slipped your mind, Nigel? When I was summoned so urgently? Your missive was so vague and mysterious, I could scarcely contain myself until this afternoon. How could you have forgotten?"

He heaved a sigh and raked both hands through his hair as if the motion would keep his brain from bursting. She had already made her opinions plain regarding Alice Jessup. If Alice were still in residence, he might have been able to convince her to help him persuade the countess. Now that she was gone, all hope of that was lost. Still, he did owe an explanation, and though he was in no humor for the lecture that was imminent, he steeled himself against a foregone conclusion and drew an audible breath.

"My missive was vague, because I feared you wouldn't come if you knew the real reason for my invitation, my lady," he began. "I know you are opposed to a match between myself and Miss Alice Jessup, but that is exactly what I wanted you to broker."

"You wish to take her for your mistress, of course."

"No, my lady, I did not," said Nigel levelly. "I wished to take her for my wife."

There was a long silence.

"You speak in the past tense, Nigel?" the countess said at last.

"She is . . . gone, my lady," he replied. "Without a trace."

"Gone? How, gone? What do you mean?"

The words came pouring out of him as though a floodgate had been opened. Before he knew what had happened, he'd told her everything that had occurred during his last meeting with Alice, and since.

"I've been to every coaching inn in town, and then some," he concluded. "Nothing. No one has seen her. Mrs. Avery is beside herself. She's convinced she herself is to blame because she retired early last evening, and will not be consoled."

The countess opened her mouth to speak, closed it, then after a moment opened it again. But still she hesitated.

"I know what you're about to say," he murmured. "Forgive me, but this is not the moment, my lady, believe me."

"Nigel, I dandled you on my knee before you could walk without your knees buckling," she said. "I couldn't love you more were you my own son, which is why I shall speak my piece, whether you wish to hear it or not. I told you when you brought her here that it was madness, dear. You knew the ton would pounce upon such a scandalous situation. You were duly warned."

"I had no choice but to bring her here, my lady." He took a swipe at his thigh, which he instantly regretted. "Her father did this to me," he gritted out around the pinpricks of pain shooting through the wound. "He is a tyrant, and she was trying to escape him with nowhere to go. You would have done the same."

"Ahhh, but if I had taken her in, there would be no wagging tongues, no on-dits circulating. . . . No *scandal*, dear."

"That is why I took on Mrs. Avery. You know that."

"A common scullion to act as the gel's companion? What could you have been thinking?"

"Mrs. Avery is hardly that, my lady. She was housekeeper at Langly House. She had been kind to Alice . . . Miss Jessup. There was a bonding there that I thought would put the girl at ease under this roof until her coil could be unwound. Unfortunately, I was indisposed until just recently. I was in hopes that you might have persuaded her of my true feelings. She was convinced I had designs upon her for my mistress."

"Which is the only capacity I would have sanctioned, Nigel. I would have brokered such an alliance gladly, but I would never have intervened for the purpose of convincing her to become your wife. I am well aware that you have feelings for the gel. I knew that before you did, but I would not see you waste yourself on common baggage. Think of your responsibility, dear. You owe it to your poor deceased father to perpetuate the bloodline with a suitable mate—one of class and breeding. A candidate of your own station, Nigel, not some common bit of fluff pretending to be something she isn't just to snag herself a lord. Take whomever you wish to your bed, dear boy, but you must marry a lady."

"That wasn't how it was," said Nigel, on the defensive.

"Oh? And how was it, dear? Explain it to me."

"Alice Jessup is far more a lady than Lady Clara Langly ever was, and I seem to recall your beating a path to Langly House to take Lady Clara under your wing. I didn't presume to ask you to do the same for Alice, because I knew you would refuse me, so I brought her here. Nothing is served in going over it again. Miss Jessup is gone."

"Back to her father?"

"I should imagine that to be the last place she would go, my lady. The man shot her beloved horse because he suspected her of using the animal to carry her to an assignation with me. That, and because her father had arranged to marry her off to one of the local bumpkins, is why she fled the place. She would not be trapped in a loveless marriage, and her heart was broken over that horse. It was her only comfort there. I had hoped to replace the animal. Alistair McGovern has just made a capital purchase of fine horses from Wiltshire for me. I haven't even seen them yet. They're on their way to the coast the first of next week. I plan to reopen the Cornwall estate and breed fine steeds for racing and hunting, and for the army, just as Father did when I was a child. We had the finest stables on the coast. I wanted to wed Miss Jessup and offer her a home there. She would have wanted for nothing. My man out at the estate has already appointed a staff—subject to my approval, of course. I meant to remove to the coast just as soon as my courtship with Miss Jessup was complete and a marriage could be arranged."

"Madness," said the countess. "You are well out of it, Nigel. The gel has more sense than you do, dear. Let it go. You could have been killed, or . . . or maimed. You actually wanted to marry into that? And there's another thing! She isn't even Anglican. She's Methodist, and not even true Methodist, at that. Some renegade offshoot of that cult."

"Methodism is hardly a cult, my lady, and there are different levels in that persuasion, some more fundamental than others. But I should expect that religion would not have been an issue, what with the poor example of it she has been made to endure at the hands of that madman who calls himself her father. It doesn't matter. We shall never know. She is gone, my lady. She has made it plain that she does not share my feelings, though I could have sworn . . . Well, never mind. That's neither here nor there at this point."

He stiffly got to his feet. "Now then," he said, turning the conversation in a new direction. "If you wish, I shall ring and have refreshment brought. We are usually of like mind in all matters, Lady Pembroke, but not in this, and you cannot change my feelings or my mind. I was taken with Alice Jessup the moment I clapped eyes upon her at the masque. I told you that then, and my feelings have not changed. So, rather than risk a dustup or put our friendship to the hazard, I think it best that we speak of other things."

Countess Pembroke had scarcely departed when Alistair McGovern arrived. A black day, indeed: two reprisals, two separate I-told-you-so's. Nigel wasn't up for it, but on second thought, he decided, *Might as well get it all over with in one afternoon and have done. Then all I'll have to deal with is Mrs. Avery's acute case of blue devils before I shut myself up in the study with a full bottle of that French contraband brandy Alistair brought back from the coast, and try to drown my own.*

"Sink me, old boy! What's happened to you?" the viscount cried, flopping down on the lounge.

"She's gone," said Nigel, easing himself back down upon the carved Jacobean chair.

McGovern sprang off the lounge. "Gone?" he exclaimed. "Gone where?"

"I wish I knew, Al. I've searched everywhere."

Again, Nigel told the tale. When he'd finished, McGovern sank back down on the lounge, a hard frown pleating his brow and casting his steel gray eyes deep in shadow.

"I believe she was attempting to leave when I stopped her in the hall on my way back up from seeing you out last night," Nigel remarked. "If only I'd known what she was about to do . . ."

"Look here, old boy—"

"Al, if you open that mouth and presume to tell me it's for the best, I'll draw your cork, plant you a leveler, and you will wake out there in the bloody street!" Nigel made a wild hand gesture and thumped his sound leg with his fist.

"Take an ease, old boy, I've given that over," replied the viscount, his hands raised in defeat. "You're smelling of April and May. Any fool can see it. My tuppence worth doesn't matter. I was going to ask you if you're sure she's gone and not just . . . absent? Have you searched for a letter? Did she take her things with her?"

"Mrs. Avery and I—the entire staff—turned this house inside out. Nothing. And she didn't have any belongings. She wouldn't wear the frocks I had sent to replace her ruined one, only one of the maid's castoff service dresses."

"Did she have any blunt?"

"I don't know. I expect she had some. I just don't know."

"What say we clean you up and go for a drive? We could check at the coaching inns again. Who knows but that she might have waited and taken a coach this morning? The night coaches had already come and gone by the time I left here last night, old boy. It's something to try."

"I have to find her, Al," Nigel murmured.

"Well, you won't find her sitting here all Friday-faced," said McGovern. "Now ring for your valet and let's be about it, eh?"

Nigel did as the viscount bade him. He didn't deserve a friend like Alistair McGovern, his melancholy psyche told him. The man had been opposed to his association with Alice Jessup from the start, and yes, he had tried to dissuade him along the way . . . but not any longer. He accepted defeat—if not easily, graciously. It had always been that way with them, ever since Copenhagen. They each knew the other's limitations and never crossed the invisible line between them that, if breached, would sever their friendship. Right now, the viscount was doing the only thing that could be done. He was helping Nigel exhaust all possibilities. Nigel would never be able to say that Alistair McGovern had let him down.

Their unsuccessful search ended in the wee hours at the Spread Eagle coaching inn, in Gracechurch Street. They'd eaten earlier. Nonetheless, they took a table at the back of the inn and nursed tankards of the inn's strong, dark ale.

"I'm sorry, old boy," said McGovern. "I had hoped we'd see her walking in one of the lanes or find an innkeeper who had helped her board one of the posts or whatnot. She's got to be somewhere. She can't just have gone up in smoke."

"I was hoping you might think of something I haven't," Nigel returned. He'd removed his new beaver, and he ran his hand through his hair gingerly. His head was aching. His brain hurt from the wracking, the endless parade of possibilities—all dead ends—that kept banging around inside. They were possibilities he considered again and again, long after they had proven fruitless.

"You're sure she hasn't gone back to her father?"

"Al, if I thought for an instant that she could have gone back to that, after what I had to offer her, I would run mad."

"You're close to that as it is," McGovern observed. "Drink up. Let's get you home. It's late. Perhaps once you've rested, something will pop into your mind."

"I'm not going to rest till I find her," Nigel said. "I've held her, tasted her, inhaled her fragrance. She's inside me, Al, burning me up—consuming me alive. I know she felt something too. She responded. She did! I've been attracted to women before, but it's never been like this. This . . . it's madness."

"I should be so addled," McGovern quipped, drawing Nigel's glower. "Look here, old boy, not to change the subject, though it wants changing, but you didn't answer me last evening. Shall I go back to Wiltshire next week and keep an eye on those drovers I've hired? I've naught to do here in town— nothing pressing, birdwise. Wait! Why don't you come with me? We could both do with a change."

Nigel shook his head. "No, but I'd appreciate that you go, Al. I want to stay in town for a bit . . . just in case. I mean to keep searching. If I haven't found her in a reasonable time—a fortnight or so— I'll join you on the coast, if you've nothing pressing, and can stay on for a bit. Then, after I've gotten everything set with the horses and instructed the new stabler, I mean to continue my search for her, even if I must knock on every door in England."

"Very well, then, if you're sure you shan't need me here," said McGovern, rising. "I've a few things to tend to first. I owe Father a visit, for one. He's begun to refer to me as his long-lost son, and one does have to secure one's inheritance, old boy. As long as I leave by Monday, I shall be in Wiltshire in plenty of time for the drive."

Nigel tossed back the rest of his ale and got stiffly to his feet.

"The wound still bothers you, eh?" McGovern observed.

"It will mend." But it would always be a reminder of the love he'd lost, and that was far more painful than the dull nagging ache in his thigh.

"Don't stay here too long, old boy," McGovern said. "You've a whole new enterprise awaiting you on the coast." He frowned. "What of Mrs. Avery? You can't mean to leave her here with old Davies? I sense a bit of rivalry there. I don't think Davies approved of your elevating another housekeeper to companion status. There'll be more than pheasant feathers flying in the game room if you leave those two together. I think you might have made a mistake there."

"No. Alice and Mrs. Davies got off on the wrong foot when I brought Alice here from the fete. The chit had bonded with Mrs. Avery at Langly House, and I'd hoped having the woman here would put her more at ease. She certainly couldn't stay without a chaperone, and a stranger wouldn't do."

"Why didn't you ask Lady Pembroke to house the gel? It would have spared you the scandal. I must admit that's had me nonplussed."

"Lady Pembroke is not sympathetic to my feelings for Alice. I just had another go-round with her over it this afternoon. I was afraid she would drive her away—for my own good, of course."

"Will you keep Mrs. Avery on, then?"

"I promised her employment no matter how the situation played out, and I shall keep my word. I shall bring her out to the manor with me. That way, if I ever do find Alice . . ."

McGovern wagged his head. "Come on, old boy," he said. "Time to go home."

Chapter Twenty

O_n second thought, the visit to his father would have to be put off, Alistair decided. He wouldn't wait for Monday to travel to Wiltshire, either. Without a word to anyone, least of all Nigel, he hired a coach and set out straightaway. It wouldn't hurt to take a turn about Warminster in search of Alice Jessup, just in case, since he was going to be in the vicinity.

Of course it wasn't probable, but still, there was this gnawing feeling in the pit of his gut that wouldn't be denied. Since Copenhagen, he'd made it a point never to ignore such gut instincts—a strategy he'd cultivated from watching Nigel in the thick of battle. Their mutual perceptions had saved not only both their lives during the war, but a number of their shipmates' as well, and on more than one occasion. Now, he was counting upon those instincts to help his friend. He had to do something to make amends for his unsympathetic attitude toward Nigel's feelings for the Jessup gel. The bufflehead really loved her! Alistair was ashamed of himself for not realizing how much.

If he'd mentioned his gut feelings to Nigel, Nigel would have insisted upon coming with him. He'd had to extend an invitation, of course, but had been relieved when Nigel declined. James Jessup had shot him on their last encounter; he would recognize Nigel on sight. Knowing his friend, Nigel would probably get himself shot again, or worse, considering his obsession with the gel. But Alistair and the minister had never met. He would be able to walk about freely, beyond suspicion.

There was something else he hadn't confided. He couldn't help thinking about the cloaked figure he'd seen loitering about the town house when he'd arrived the night Alice Jessup disappeared. He hadn't thought anything of it then, except that the ton's spies were afoot with designs upon unearthing more juicy tidbits in the latest scandal. But now that Alice had gone missing, that mysterious figure haunted him. He wished he'd taken more notice of the man. He racked his brain trying to recall if that person was still lurking about when he'd taken his leave that evening, but he could not. His thoughts were elsewhere when he'd left the town house. He and Nigel had been on the verge of another dustup, and he'd been anxious to be away before it became a full-blown row. If Alice Jessup had met with foul play . . . No, he wasn't prepared to credit that, but he would be more observant on this gambit, and from now on in general.

He reached Warminster early on Saturday afternoon and stopped at the Old Bell coaching inn, just as he and Nigel had done before. After arranging for a room and indulging in a satisfying meal of mutton stew, crusty cheese bread, and black ale, he hired a horse and rode out to the stud farm to check on the purchase he'd made for Nigel. All was in readiness for the drive scheduled to begin midweek. Satisfied, he took a turn around the town proper.

Being a market town, Warminster was teeming with local folk making their Saturday purchases. Leaving his mount at the livery, Alistair strolled through the streets, past the stalls and carts and tables laden with every commodity imaginable, from silks to stickpins, from radishes to rashers of bacon. All manner of provocative smells—savory and sweet— perfumed the air. He chose an apple at the fruit vendor's cart and bit into the sweet, tart flesh as he browsed through the stall keepers' wares. But his mind wasn't upon the merchandise, rather upon the patrons. He was looking for Alice Jessup amongst them, fantasizing upon how fine it would be if he were to find her and cart her back to Nigel however needs must.

Alistair indulged himself in those thoughts for some time as he walked through the square, until all at once a female figure caught his eye. She was selecting ribbons across the way from the tobacconist's booth where he was examining snuffboxes. His heart leaped inside. Her bonnet hung down her back, the blue grosgrain streamers fluttering in the breeze, her short-cropped cap of golden curls gleaming in the midafternoon sun.

Discarding the snuffbox he'd been deliberating over, he reached her in two long-legged strides and laid a hand on her arm. "So, we meet again, my dear," he said. "Lovely to see you."

She spun around, and to his embarrassment he stared not into green eyes but brown, flung open wide in an unfamiliar face.

"O-oh! I beg your pardon, ma'am," he gushed. "I took you for someone else!"

"Somethin' I can do for you, cove?" a young man at his elbow said. Brushing past, this man took the girl's arm.

"Dreadfully sorry, old boy," Alistair replied. "I took the lady for my cousin! From the back, you see, eh . . . she . . . Yes, well, I do beg your pardon," he stammered. Tipping his beaver, he offered a bow.

"Aye, sure ya do," said the man. Then, to the girl as he steered her away, "What have I told ya 'bout talkin' ta strangers, May? Cousin, indeed! I seen him put his hand on ya—a cutpurse more than likely, or worse. Just because he looks like a gentleman don't make him one."

Chattering in her own defense, the girl responded, but Alistair had moved on. This was no way to do. He had to get a grip on himself. Everyone was staring. He sauntered back to the livery as nonchalantly as was possible under the circumstances, where he collected his horse, fed the animal the rest of his apple—it had lost its flavor—and rode out of the village toward the patchwork hills, which were like a piecework quilt of variegated green spread out wide in all directions.

The hill Rood Chapel stood upon lay to the west. Alistair rode by the building at a leisurely pace a good distance away, though close enough to make out anyone moving about the grounds. The chapel and rectory were shut up tight as a drum. Even the stable behind looked deserted in the light of the low-sliding sun.

All at once inspiration struck. "Nodcock!" he said, slapping his forehead with the heel of his hand. Tomorrow was Sunday. What better way to have a closer look than to attend Sunday service in the morning? But at what time? He shrugged. The innkeeper would know. And with that decided, Alistair turned his horse around and rode straight for the Old Bell.

"You've no one to blame but yourself, miss," Mrs. Sills said, standing arms akimbo in front of the door in Alice's chamber. The keys dangling from her chatelaine gleamed in the last rays of fractured sunlight streaming in through the broken window-pane. Chased by the clouds, it was gone in a blink, taking the warmth of the day with it. "Now you eat that," she admonished, her finger wagging toward the tray she'd set down on the table. "You're fortunate to get it after shamin' your father like you done. I've got more important tasks before me than standin' over you. Now, eat!"

Alice couldn't take her eyes off the keys clinking on the cord dangling from the woman's waist. If only she could snatch them and escape! She'd done that once; she wouldn't manage it so easily again. James Jessup meant to keep her locked in her chamber until the wedding.

"Why don't you be about them, then?" said Alice. "And take that with you." She gestured toward the tray. "I'm not hungry."

"Do you want me to fetch your father?" snapped the housekeeper. "He's writin' out his sermon for tomorrow. He won't take it kindly, bein' interrupted."

Alice snatched the tray and thrust it toward the woman. "Then we shan't, shall we?" she hissed. "Don't you dare presume to threaten me with Father. I'm not a child in leading strings any longer, Mrs. Sills. Get out! You have no right to keep me prisoner here—you, of all people, who would be cast upon the parish, but for your situation here. It was I who spoke for you when you came begging at the door. I should have known better, but then, I was a child at the time, wasn't I? A foolish, wide-eyed child, desperate for someone to fill the gap Mother's passing rent in my life. Father put her in an early grave and soured you—hardened you—and made you his spy.

"I recall the day you followed me to the folly in the valley, the old ruined tower that I loved to play near. It was my special place, my only refuge. You caught me making daisy chains beside the stream. What was it you said? I was 'adorning myself like a harlot in the temple'? Father broke a birch branch on my back for my vanity that day. And now you presume to hold me prisoner in my own house?" She hurled the tray to the floor. "I have quite outgrown the birch branch, you wicked old harpy! Get out!"

"Your father's put me in charge o' your redemption," the housekeeper said. "That's good food there gone to waste, when poor folk are starvin'. 'Tis for your own good, this—you'll see that in the end."

"*Get out*, I say!" Alice took a bold step toward her.

Delivering a garbled string of exclamations, the housekeeper fled through the door, her skirts spread wide. The rasp of the key turning in the lock brought Alice's posture down, and she threw herself across the bed and shut her eyes.

Outside, the birds were singing their last before sleeping—all but the nightingale. His song would still be sweet long after the others settled in after sunset. She'd forgotten how sweet. She hadn't heard a single one in town.

She longed for Nigel's strong arms around her, ached for his lips, the gentle touch of his hand stroking her cheek. John Mapes's hands were hard and gnarled like the twisted knots on the trees that grew on the moors. Tears flooded her eyes. The thought of those hands pawing her, touching her where Nigel's hands had been, was more than she could bear. But it was no use. Like it or not, this was where she belonged. This was her place. She'd learned that bitter lesson the hard way.

Her first instinct when her father had grabbed her outside Nigel's town house was to watch for her chance, throw open the carriage door, and run, but his threats were hardly idle. He'd proved that before they ever left London. He had the coachman drive straight to St. Mary's of Bethlehem, dragged her out of the carriage and up the front steps. His hand was on the knocker of the dreaded Bedlam before she gave in. A drive by Newgate after that was all it took to bring her to her knees. He meant what he said, and his irreproachable position as a minister would hold sway at either institution. Shut up in prison or in the asylum, there would be no hope of escape. She would be left there and forgotten, not to mention what Nigel would suffer. At least as things were . . .

The sound of a key turning in the lock stalled her brain and brought her bolt upright on the bed. Her father stepped inside, stopping short before the food scattered over the floorboards beneath the overturned tray.

He sidestepped the debris. "That mess will remain until you clean it up, Daughter," he said, pointing a rigid finger. "Mrs. Sills has enough to do in this house without cleaning up after your childish tantrums."

"Keep that woman away from me!"

" 'That woman' warned me years ago that you would come to this. Always reaching beyond yourself, always the air dreamer—rebellious, vainglorious. Well, you shan't have to suffer her much longer. Tomorrow I shall read the third banns. Saturday next, in that very chapel out there, you become Mrs. John Mapes and I wash my hands of you . . . unless, of course, you've had a change of heart in regard to the magistrate?"

Alice's glower was her only reply.

"No answer?" her father asked. "Good. Now, make yourself presentable. Wash your face and order your hair. Your betrothed is downstairs in the parlor. I shan't trust you to come on your own this time. You've proven that you cannot be trusted. I shall escort you down. He wishes to walk out with you this evening, a brief stroll about the grounds. Not to worry. I shall be but a few paces behind. There will be no more breath of scandal, Daughter, and there is nowhere for you to run. The sooner you accept that, the better."

There was no use in arguing. Alice rose, splashed water on her face, and followed him down the narrow stairs to the parlor below, almost glad of the reprieve. It was the first time she'd been let out of her room since he brought her home.

John Mapes was waiting, hat in hand. A silver-haired man more than twice her age, he was possessed of a leathered face, hunched stature, and lips that tried to smile, though his faded gray eyes did not. Once, he might have been handsome. The shell that remained was evidence of a hard, rugged life. Handing her over, her father—true to his word—followed several paces behind as they stepped out into the twilight mist.

"It's only fair to warn you that I am opposed to this marriage," Alice said to her would-be spouse. "I needn't tell you that I do not love you, sir. How could I? I do not even know you. What's more, I do not care to." He seemed unmoved. "M-my father has arranged this without my approval," she went on through his silence. "You would do well to re-think the betrothal, sir. If you do not, you will regret it to your dying day!"

"You're but a child yet," he said. "You'll mellow. You need a firm hand to settle you down. Aye, you'll mellow after your first shearin'. Raisin' sheep'll do that for ya, just like it done fer my first wife."

"And it put her in that graveyard early," Alice snapped back as they passed the churchyard. "If a farmhand is all you desire, why not hire one?"

"A farmhand comes dear—and it won't warm my bed."

Repulsed, Alice shuddered. He smelled of sheep-dip, rancid grease, and the shaving paste he'd slathered on to cover it up. The thought of sharing a marriage bed with John Mapes made her skin crawl. She glanced over her shoulder. Her father was still walking behind, the hem of his cassock hidden in the mist. If only it were thicker, like the London fogs rolling in off the Thames, it might cloak her escape. There was no hope of that, though. Mapes's grip on her arm, looped through his, was like a vise.

"Aye, you'll mellow," he said, with a nod. "You'll mellow right fine."

Ten o'clock in the morning came quickly. Alistair was up and dressed and on his way to Rood Chapel in plenty of time, riding through a fine sheeting mist that had turned the air cooler. He would pass himself off as a wayfarer, stopping over on his way south to the coast, if anyone inquired.

The little chapel was half filled when he reached it. Removing his beaver, he took a seat in one of the tall wooden pews at the back, where he could watch the congregation file in. He made a quick sweeping glance over those already seated. Alice Jessup wasn't amongst them. As others began trickling in, he resisted the urge to turn his head as they passed. Minutes later the doors slammed shut with a bang against the rain behind him, and James Jessup strode down the aisle, a sweeping black cloak over his cassock.

Cold chills gripped Alistair's scalp as recognition struck. The cloaked figure outside Nigel's town house: it was he! But where was Alice? The service was about to begin, and he squirmed in his seat, not wanting to look suspicious. But he surely would, being an Anglican in the midst of Methodists. He swallowed dry, certain he was about to make a complete fool of himself. She had to be here somewhere, but where?

Divine service was begun. To Alistair's surprise, it was quite similar to the Anglican ritual—similar enough that he was able to follow along without drawing the others' eyes. He was quite proud of himself until just before the offertory, when James Jessup took to the pulpit and quieted the congregation with a stern-faced look that turned Alistair's blood cold. This was a hard, embittered man, evidently the sort who intimidated his flock with fire and brimstone. When he spoke, there was no color in his lips. They had formed a thin, shapeless line.

"I publish the banns of marriage between John Peter Mapes and Alice Jessup of this parish," he said. "If any of you know cause or just impediment why these two persons should not be joined together in holy matrimony, ye are to declare it. This is the third time of asking."

Chapter Twenty-one

Alistair didn't hire a coach; he would reach London quicker on horseback. He rode through the rain and did not stop to rest or eat. One storm dovetailed another, and the horse was half killed when he reached Grosvenor Square.

He was soaked to the skin. Water dripping from the brim of his beaver drizzled down his soggy shirt-front. His neckcloth and saturated shirt points were so wet, cold rivulets ran down his back and chest beneath. Bounding up the front steps, his heart was thumping a ragged rhythm. The wedding was to take place Saturday next! His brain had been so numbed by the announcement James Jessup had made from that pulpit, he'd scarcely heard anything else. He'd sneaked out right afterward, hardly able to put one foot in front of the other. All else was a blur.

He hated to bring this news to his friend, but there was nothing for it. Nigel had to know. James Jessup had evidently abducted his daughter from his very doorstep. That he didn't see her with his own eyes at Rood Chapel didn't matter; Jessup had her closeted there somewhere. That was obvious.

What Nigel would do with the information, he shuddered to wonder.

The polished brass knocker in his hand addressed the door with a riveting rat-a-tat-tat-a-tat-tat that sent another wave of chills along his spine. After a moment, the door came open in the startled butler's hand.

"My lord!" the servant said. "Step inside, you're soaked through!"

"Never mind me, Archer," said Alistair. Brushing past him, he removed his beaver and thrust it under his arm. "Is His Lordship in? I need to see him at once. It's dreadfully urgent."

"Why, no, my lord, he's gone!"

"Gone? Gone where, Archer?"

"Why, to the coast, my lord."

"So soon? He wasn't to leave for at least a fortnight."

"He had a change of heart, my lord. When you didn't call, he went round to your lodgings. He didn't find you in, and left a message. He said if you called I was to tell you there was no point in his staying on in town at present, and that he would expect you at the manor."

"Damn and blast!" Alistair thundered, backing the butler up a pace. "How long ago did he leave, man?"

"Why, 'twas yesterday, just after the noon hour that they left."

"*They?*" Alistair repeated, hopeful.

"His Lordship, his valet Brewster, and Mrs. Avery, my lord. She is to keep house at the manor now that Miss Jessup has . . . left us."

Alistair brushed the wet hair out of his eyes. "He's got a whole day's head start!" he said, thinking out loud.

"My lord?"

"I have to catch up to him before they reach the coast. Did they go by hired coach, or did Carter drive them?"

"Why, Carter drove them in the carriage, my lord. Is anything wrong?"

"Everything's wrong, Archer. I'm going to leave my hired horse and take another from the stables. Have one of the footmen take him round to the livery once he's rested. I drove him hard. He'll need tending."

"You're leaving *now*, my lord? Like *that*? You cannot, you're soaked to the skin. You'll catch your death!"

"I've no time. Too much has passed already. Just do as I've told you, and if perchance they should return, tell His Lordship that I have set out after him. Tell him it is urgent that we meet. I shall be traveling the mail-coach route, assuming that is the route Carter has taken. The inns are two hours apart along the old post road, and they will surely stop, with Mrs. Avery aboard. I mean to seek him at the inns all along the way."

"At least let me fetch you a slicker, my lord. You are courting pneumonia."

"Quickly, then I must away. If he reaches the coast, there won't be time to get back to Wiltshire by Saturday next."

"Sir?"

"Never mind! Just fetch the bloody slicker—*and hurry!*"

"How long is this going to take?" Nigel said to the wheelwright. They were bogged down on the outskirts of Southampton. They'd been making good time until the coach struck a rut in the flooded post road. They had just left the coaching inn after nuncheon, and now this.

"I ain't no miracle worker, gov'nor," the man said. They were standing in the pouring rain. "She's gotta come off, and I can't do that while she's loaded."

"Very well. How do you propose we get back to the inn?"

"I could fetch the wagon, but it'll cost ya. I ain't no hackney service."

"An open wagon in this?" Nigel said, thrusting his palm upward in the rain. His gloves were soggy with it, and he was already soaked to the drawers. But he wasn't thinking of himself, he was thinking of Mrs. Avery. She was beside herself over leaving town without word of Alice. She'd been blubbering into her handkerchief since they left Grosvenor Square. The prospect of subjecting her to a drenching now was unthinkable.

"It ain't that far," the man said.

"Not for myself and my man, but too far for a woman. Have you nothing more accommodating?"

"I have, but—"

"I know, I know, it will cost me," Nigel interrupted.

"Who was it that said highway robbery was a thing of the past? Well, don't just stand there, man. Go and fetch it!"

Nigel was numb to the rain splinters. Alice was gone. He would never see her again. Nothing else mattered—not the rain that had ruined his togs, or the nagging ache in his thigh. Not the fine horses, soon on their way to the coast, that would begin his new enterprise. Nothing. Without Alice, life had no meaning, no purpose. . . . *He* had no purpose. He had no heart. She had torn it out and taken it with her.

The wheelwright soon returned with a closed carriage and drove them back to the inn. Nigel's promise of a vulgar bonus got the wheel repaired in record speed. They were soon on their way again, this time by a route less traveled—a narrower road on higher ground that did not offer the convenience that the mail-coach route did when it came to inns. They were few and far between off the main roads in that quarter, so the man told them. Word from an eastbound coachman that the main highway ahead was flooded and riddled with pockmarks as well, however, decided that. Supplied by the innkeeper with an assortment of meat pasties, bread, cheese, and fruit that could be eaten en route, along with several bottles of wine, they set out again, this time off the beaten path.

Would the blasted rain never cease? The slicker helped somewhat, trapping his body heat inside. But Alistair was still soaked to the skin underneath, dreaming of a hot bath and a warmed brandy as he drove the horse beneath him from one coaching inn to the next along the mail-coach route. At least he was on the right track. A lord traveling in his own carriage with his valet and a middle-aged female servant in the throes of the dismals was still fresh in the innkeepers' minds. Bless the old girl for that!

Why did Nigel have to go off to the coast so soon? If only he'd waited one more day. Alistair would bet his blunt that Alice Jessup had not gone willingly to Warminster. Should he have interfered? Should he have stood up in that chapel and stated a just impediment? If she and this Mapes person had been standing at the altar, turnips to toenails he would have, by God! But not in this instance. This was Nigel's coil to unwind, and there was still time. But it was dwindling fast.

When he reached the inn at Southampton, it was to find that the mail-coach route was closed for a stretch beyond. Several miles of washed-out road lay ahead, according to the innkeeper. He was delighted, since the inn was overflowing with wayfarers traveling west who were stranded until the rain stopped and the roadways became passable again. Alistair couldn't wait for that. He was too pressed for time. The whole valley was flooded. It could take days before the soggy ground absorbed the water.

"I'm looking for a friend," he said to the innkeeper, who was juggling tankards. "I'm certain his coach passed through here some time ago." He could hardly make himself heard over the din in the place. "A black and royal blue carriage, with three passengers. One was a female servant, about so tall." He gestured. "Heavyset, of middle age. There was a valet and my friend, the Earl of Romney. Did they stop here?"

"Oh, aye, they did, cove. They took their noon meal here—"

"*Yesterday* noon?" Alistair interrupted. "That long ago?" He loosed a string of expletives that broke the innkeeper's rhythm filling tankards. "Do you mean to say they set out over that road in *this*?"

"Not directly," the innkeeper said. "They busted a wheel on the coach tryin' to drive over them ruts, and come back here while the wheelwright fixed it."

"What time did they leave? Come, come, man! It's vital that I catch up to that coach!"

"I don't remember exactly. 'Twas late in the afternoon."

"Thank you!" Alistair said. Spinning on his heels, he pushed his way through the crowd and stormed out into the rain again.

The innkeeper was hollering something after him, but he couldn't make it out over the racket. There was no time to waste. He was closing the gap, but every second was bringing Nigel closer and closer to the coast. He mounted and rode off at a gallop until the road was no longer visible.

His horse was laboring, and he reined in to a canter, then slowed again when the moving water proved too perilous to navigate mounted. The horse beneath him shied and complained, stirring the rising water with prancing feet. He was almost unseated when an invisible crater caused the animal to rear. The stream ahead had risen over its banks, and he had to turn back when the little wooden bridge that had forded it floated by him in pieces.

"Damn and blast!" he hollered into the wind.

Carter was a top-notch driver, but could he have navigated the carriage through this? Alistair thought not. He'd scarcely traveled two miles on horseback, only to be forced to turn around again. For the first time since he set out from the town house, his confidence was flagging.

He glanced behind, shielding his eyes from the rain. The landscape looked more like a sea than green fields now, undulating all around him, complete with swirling eddies and froth. There was nothing for it but to retreat to the inn he'd just come from and wait it out with the rest. The skittish horse had evidently come to the same conclusion. They were already heading in that direction.

When he reached the inn, he stabled the horse and dragged himself, dripping and spent, to the taproom for a tankard of ale. Defeat left a bitter taste after it that the rich, nutty ale couldn't quell.

"So ya come back after all, eh, cove?" said the innkeeper. "I tried ta tell ya, but ya just kept on goin'. City folk. Always in a hurry."

"The road is impassable. The bridge is washed out," Alistair said, speaking from the tankard around breathless gulps.

"I tried ta tell ya—"

"Yes, yes, I know you did, but I had to try. I told you it's vital that I reach my friend."

"No, not that," the man said. "I called after ya when ya was leavin'. Your friend didn't go that way."

"What do you mean, he didn't go that way?"

"Jim Bishop, the wheelwright, put him onto the south road."

"What south road? Tell me, man!" Alistair slapped the tankard down on the bar and took hold of the innkeeper's ale-stained shirtfront.

"Here, now! Hold on, cove! Lemme go! It'll still be there when you've drunk that dry."

"Sorry," said Alistair, relaxing his grip on the man. "But I need to know now!"

"At the fork, there's a road goin' south on higher ground. It's narrow, and steep now and then. Not many inns, neither. We sent a few coaches that way, them what was goin' south ta the coast, that is." He gestured. "This lot in here now are headin' north, and there ain't no road north till the next junction west o' what's flooded, so they're stuck here till the rain stops."

Alistair seized the tankard and tossed back the ale. "I'll need a fresh horse. Mine's spent," he explained.

"Round back, cove, but there's no need ta hurry. Your friend's long gone. He's got clean ta Cornwall by now, I'll wager."

"Well, you'd best pray that he hasn't, innkeeper," growled Alistair. "You should have sent someone after me. I told you it was urgent."

The innkeeper gestured. "Who was I goin' ta send?" he said. "I'm busy as a cat coverin'."

Alistair didn't trust himself to speak. He slapped

a few coins down on the bar, spun on his heel, and stalked back out into the rain.

"Take an ease, Mrs. Avery," Nigel said. "We're nearly there." He almost laughed. Cornwall was notorious for storms such as they'd just come through, and now that they neared the coast, the rain had subsided. It was as if the whole world as he knew it had turned upside down.

"I'm goin' ta retch, my lord!" the woman choked, covering her mouth with her handkerchief. "Ridin' in carriages for long spells does it to me. 'Tis my own fault. . . . I never should have had that last pasty."

"But you've been doing so splendidly thus far, Mrs. Avery," Nigel said.

"Not no more!" she cried, giving a lurch. Her face had turned pastelike gray, and her plump cheeks were puffed out.

They were alone in the coach. Once the rain stopped, Brewster had climbed up top with Carter to give the woman more room. Nigel thumped the roof of the carriage with his walking stick, and the coach rolled to a shuddering halt. The valet jumped down, and they scarcely got her out of it in time.

Gulping air in spasms, meanwhile sputtering a string of apologies, Mrs. Avery finally righted herself. They were just about to help her back into the coach when a rider coming on at a gallop through a ghostly dawn haze stopped Nigel in his tracks. The man, leaning forward over his mount's neck, his slicker spread wide, was shouting at the top of his voice.

It was . . . Alistair?

Nigel ran back to meet him, slip-sliding in the ooze of the road in his mud-splattered Hessians.

"Bloody hell, Al!" he thundered. "What's happened? Where are the horses?"

"The horses are on their own," the viscount panted. "I've found her. She's at Rood Chapel rectory. . . ."

"Tell me, man!"

"Do you remember when I told you someone was loitering about the town house? That was the night she disappeared. It was James Jessup, old boy. Unless I miss my guess, he took her against her will. He read the third banns on Sunday. She's to wed a man by the name of John Mapes."

"How do you know this?"

"I was there! I heard him with my own ears. The wedding is day after tomorrow."

Mrs. Avery's scream from behind at that news sent chills slithering down Nigel's spine. "Get down off that horse, get into that coach, and see to her, Al. You're drenched. Wait for me at the manor. I don't know how to thank you, my friend."

Alistair had barely slid to the ground when Nigel swung himself up onto the lathered horse's back and spun him around, creating a bit-gouging, forefeet-flying rear that all but pitched him out of the saddle.

"That animal is half dead!" Alistair hollered. "It's the second horse I've nearly killed trying to find you, and it's too late, old boy. You'll never make it in time."

"Don't bet your soul upon it!" Nigel said. *"Heeyaah!"* he yelled at the animal underneath him.

Then, with Alistair's protests ringing in his ears, he dug his knees in, slapped the horse's withers with the ribbons, and rode off at a gallop into the haze.

Saturday dawned dreary with mists creeping up the front steps of Rood Chapel. Watching them weave in and out amongst the crooked gravestones in the churchyard from her broken chamber window, it seemed to Alice as if the wraiths of the dead had risen from their burial places to mourn her wedding day.

All hopes of escape were lost. She had been locked in her room since her brief reprieve with John Mapes. There had been no more social visits. The only person she'd seen since was Mrs. Sills. Mercifully, her father had not come again to her chamber. He'd made it clear that he would house her until Saturday; then John Mapes would bear the responsibility, and he would be glad to see the back of her.

Alice had come to a decision. James Jessup might be able to force her to marry John Mapes, but she would never be his wife. She had to break away from her father's subjugation, to be out from under lock and key. John Mapes couldn't very well lock her in her room, not if he expected meals on the table and chores done. And he couldn't watch her every minute while he was herding sheep. As she saw it, he was the lesser of the two evils facing her.

The first chance she got, she would run. If marrying John Mapes was the only way to be out from under her father's roof, so be it! Once she married, he wouldn't have a say. He could no longer keep his promise to have her before the magistrates or see her shut up in asylum . . . and Nigel would be safe from whatever retaliation her father had planned for him. Jessup couldn't do anything once he'd relinquished his responsibility to another, and wouldn't try, because it would reflect upon his office.

This by no means meant that Alice wasn't terrified. At least she knew her father's mind. John Mapes was a virtual stranger.

There would be no wedding gown. She would wear one of her simple frocks. There would be no wedding breakfast, no honeymoon. After the ceremony, Mapes would drive her to his farm and expect her to perform her duties. Alice tried not to think about that. Her goal was to be free at the first possible opportunity.

What a coil she'd wound, stepping out above her station for one brief blink in the eye of time! She could scarcely believe the nightmare she had wrought, and it wasn't over yet.

James Jessup came to collect her at a quarter to ten. Her heart almost stopped at the sound of his key in the lock. *This must be how a condemned prisoner feels on his way to the gibbet,* she thought. Sweat beaded on her brow, and her hands were clammy and cold despite the sultry summer morning. She didn't speak as he led her down the stairs and out into the ground-creeping mist, so humid and still.

It encircled her feet like ropes as she mounted the chapel steps. There was no sun or breeze to burn it away.

She expected the chapel to be empty. To her surprise, it was nearly filled, and more parish folk were coming up the walk behind and approaching on horseback from the valley below. Of course—her father would want witnesses. There would be no question that his wayward daughter was dutifully wed.

She was so awed by the sea of indignant faces glaring at her that she nearly stumbled as he led her down the aisle to the altar, where John Mapes stood waiting. The ceremony was begun without delay. Her arm was looped through John Mapes's arm, and he had a firm grip upon it.

James Jessup had scarcely climbed into the pulpit and begun speaking when an explosion of foreign sound from behind turned all eyes toward the doors. A prancing horse and rider had crashed through with little regard for the ancient wood. One door sagged on its hinges. The other had split, and it fell to the floor in a cloud of dust motes, giving an earsplitting thud that echoed as the horse plunged headlong toward the altar.

Alice's throat closed over an outcry. She could scarcely believe her eyes. A chorus of screams and shouts rose from the congregation. They were on their feet now, milling about every which way. The din rose above the hollow clopping of the horse's hooves on the bare wood floor as Nigel drove the animal down the aisle straight toward her.

Reaching out, he wrenched Alice free of John

Mapes's grasp, swung her up beside him, and with a thundering "Hayaaah!" wheeled the horse around and galloped out the way he had come.

Pandemonium reigned behind, as James Jessup, fist raised to the heavens and shouting threats, and John Mapes, likewise barking, ran out of the chapel, their indignation amplified by the mist. The congregation poured out after the first two, but Nigel and Alice were well on their way down the hill to the valley.

Nigel's heart was hammering against her face through his waistcoat and superfine topcoat as he cradled Alice against him. Every sinew in him was stretched to its limit of strain, the muscles in his arms rock hard, flexing in a steady rhythm. A turgid hardness lower down forced against Alice's thigh set her heart racing in competition with his own, and she gasped in spite of herself.

"I must know two things," he panted, his voice husky and mellow. "Have I hurt you . . . and was I in time?"

"I am not harmed, my lord," she murmured. "Just winded. And yes, you were in time. *Just.*"

"Thank God!" he said, planting a kiss on her brow. "When I saw him leading you into that chapel from the valley . . . !"

The feel of his rough, dark stubble against her tender skin sent shockwaves of sensation through her body. His scent threaded through her nostrils, that wonderful leather and lime, and his own male essence, heightened by exertion. No wine or brandy sweetened it now. He was as sober as she, though as foxed by her closeness as she was by his. That was physically evident.

She nuzzled against his shoulder. "Where are you taking me?" she asked, though in that one heavenly, enchanted moment, she didn't care.

"To catch the stagecoach for Gretna Green," he said. "This is your wedding day, remember?"

Chapter Twenty-two

They decided against the stagecoach. Fearing pursuit, Nigel hired a comfortable two-seater post chaise. It was lighter and faster than the stage, drawn by four horses, two ridden by post boys for greater haste. A groom rode the dickey in back. Other than stopping for fresh horses, food, and necessities at designated stations along the way, they would drive straight through and cross over the Scottish border, there to be wed. The trip would take four days at best, considering that they weren't taking lodgings each night.

Alice could scarcely believe what was happening. This had to be the most bizarre proposal any woman had ever been offered. Nigel hadn't let go of her since they'd set out. If this was a dream, she begged never to wake from it.

"You're cold," he murmured. The farther north they traveled, the cooler the air became. Now, twilight was approaching, and it had grown cooler still. Stripping off his coat, he wrapped it around her and pulled her close in his arms again. "I shall find a shop at the next station and buy you a proper wrap," he said.

His hooded gaze was intense. Those hypnotic, glacier blue eyes seemed to plumb the very depths of her soul. "You're exhausted," he realized. "You cannot go on like this, with no rest in a proper bed and at least two day's traveling time still before us. We shall just have to chance stopping."

"*No!*" she cried, almost panicked. Ashamed, she lowered her eyes. Recalling Lady Clara's elopement with Lord Chesterton prompted the outburst. It had all happened so quickly she couldn't help but wonder, and she didn't dare to hope. "F-Father is doubtless right behind us, my lord," she said. "You heard his threats. . . ."

She could not meet his eyes. The hurt in them drove hers away. She hadn't fooled him with the last. He'd seen right through her. All at once he let her go. Snatching his walking stick, he thumped it so hard in rapid fire against the chaise roof that it shuddered; for a moment, she thought he'd cracked it. The coach screeched to a shuddering halt with a clatter of jingling tack and outcries from the driver and postilions.

Nigel's stare was misty and dark. Glacier blue had turned to indigo. The muscles along his jaw had begun to tick, and the color had left his lips. She may as well have struck him.

"This coach goes not one hairbreadth farther until we settle this," he said.

"My lord, please," she murmured.

"No. You will hear me out, and then we shall see," he said. "I know exactly what you were thinking just now. That look . . . Do you still imagine that I want you for my mistress? Do you presume to tar me with the same brush as Chesterton? No! Do not answer! Let me finish. You think I suggested that we stop so that I might have my way with you. I could see it in your face—in your eyes—and hear it in your voice. Well, let me tell you, m'dear, if all I wanted was a mistress, there are a number of women who would be eager to accommodate me with far fewer theatrics, I promise you."

"Please, my lord . . ."

"Look at me! I'm unshaven. My togs are covered with mud, and torn besides. I smell of horse. I have just all but killed one, driving him from Cornwall to Wiltshire in a space of time impossible for such a trek on solid ground, let alone through the morass these storms have made of the highways. I have desecrated a church and abducted you before the entire parish of Warminster! No mistress is worth that, and it is a grave insult to me to imagine that I would have to go to such ridiculous lengths to get one!"

Alice wanted to laugh and cry and shout in indignation all at once. Laughter won.

"I fail to see the humor in any of this!" Nigel said. He grabbed his walking stick again, and thumped the roof. "Turn this carriage round!" he thundered.

"No . . . Oh, no, Nigel, don't!" she cried. "Driver, stay!" she called to the coachman.

"Well, make up yer minds!" the man bellowed back.

"Stay!" Nigel called, meanwhile pulling Alice into his arms. "You called me by name," he murmured, searching her face. "Do you know how long I have ached to hear it from those beautiful lips again?" She started to speak, but his gentle finger against her mouth stopped her. "I think I fell in love with you when I first saw you at the masque," he said. "But I didn't realize it until I knew who you really were, because it didn't matter—nothing did, except that I win you for my wife. Well, you've run me a merry chase, my lady, and you *are* my lady, just as soon as we reach Scotland. Let there be no doubt. There will be no more need to pretend. You have bewitched me, Alice Jessup."

Swooping down, he took her lips in a smothering kiss that left her weak in his arms. She tasted him deeply, and he crushed her so close both their hearts beat as one, racing, hammering against each other until she feared she would swoon in a dead faint. He had stirred primeval longings within her, longings she did not understand, but she responded to them nonetheless. Oh, how she responded, melting against him, drawing him closer still.

Something was happening inside her deep at her core, something involuntary. Fire and ice sped through her loins, raced through her blood, pumping wildly in her veins. It transported her out of herself and left her weak and trembling, shuddering with pleasure in his arms.

"N-Nigel," was all she could say when their lips parted.

He buried his hand in her hair and pressed her face against his heaving breast. It was a long moment before he spoke. When he did, there was a tremor in his deep, sensuous voice. "We shan't stop to rest," he said. "We should, but we shan't, because I feel the need to prove myself to you once and for all."

"That isn't necessary," she said, "but we daren't stop. We shouldn't even have paused here. I was right earlier. Father will follow."

"What can he do? You are of age. You no longer need parental consent."

"A license was gotten for another," she reminded him. "The banns were read. He will never bear losing face before the entire congregation. That is why he summoned them there—to prove that I was duly wed to one of my own kind. He already shot you once!" She hesitated. "And there's something more," she said. "Something that you do not know about."

"What?"

"After he shot you and killed Treacle . . . Before I ran away, I stole several notes from the coffer in his study. I had no money of my own. I had learned that he settled a generous amount upon me, to be paid to John Mapes after the wedding. I felt I could put it to better use."

"You have no reason to reproach yourself," Nigel said, tilting her chin up until their eyes met. "That blunt was as much yours as his—your dowry."

"Father does not view it that way. He threatened to turn me over to the magistrates, threatened to ruin you."

"You should have told me at the town house. All this might have been avoided if you'd only confided in me. I'd have taken you to Scotland straightaway, this deuced leg notwithstanding." He gave it a scathing blow. "If I'd known, I would have crawled if needs must. Instead, what did I do? I kept my distance, hoping that would prove my cause, that it would put your mind at ease that I was no Chesterton. Instead, it drove you away. But why? That's what I still cannot understand."

"I was on my terrace the night you dined on yours with Viscount McGovern. I overheard your speech. You were going to have Countess Pembroke broker a match between us. That is how mistresses are gotten. I couldn't have borne that interview, not loving you as I do. . . ."

"Yes, I was about to summon the countess—in fact, I did—but not to broker a contract to make you my mistress. Silly goose, I hoped to have her help me convince you that I wanted you for my *wife*.

"When you went missing, I was like a Bedlamite. I searched for you everywhere—every coaching inn in London and beyond. I prowled the streets and lanes, both day and night, like a stalker. I even went round to Bow Street, for fear that you might have met with foul play. Then there was nowhere else to search. You had vanished without a trace, and I couldn't bear the town house without you in it. I bundled Mrs. Avery into the carriage and was heading for my manor on the coast, when Alistair caught up to me. You have him to thank that we are together at last. He found you out. He recalled seeing a suspicious figure lurking about the town house the night you left. He followed his instincts, and discovered that it was your father. He was in that church when the banns were read, and he rode without stopping through the rain and floodwaters. The poor blighter looked like a drowned gutter rat when he finally reached me. I shall never be able to thank him."

"I thought—"

"I know what you thought," Nigel interrupted. "Do you still think it? Because if you do . . ."

"No, Nigel. But you need to know that even though I thought your intentions weren't honorable . . . I loved you still."

"But not enough to become my mistress."

"No. Not that. Not for you or any man."

He pulled her closer, drawing her to him in those strong, sinewy arms again. "My lady *is* a lady," he whispered against her hair, "and I don't deserve her. But I will have her nonetheless."

"Not if we don't press on," she said. "We're wasting precious time."

Nigel thumped the roof again. "Drive on!" he called. And then to Alice, as he cradled her close, "We have an appointment with a blacksmith, for our anvil wedding."

Gretna Green, a little hamlet just over the Scottish border, was the first changing post after crossing over to accommodate stagecoaches on the main line. They reached it at dusk on the fourth day of their journey and sought out the blacksmith, who would perform the ceremony.

They had stopped longer at the last changing station than was prudent in order to freshen up for the ceremony. There were no accommodations for bathing. That would come later, but Nigel managed to make himself presentable with a shave, and basins of warm water were available to them both for cleaning away the dust of the road. Now they stood in the blacksmith's shop, awaiting the man's wife and daughter, who lived in one of the cottages behind and would serve as witnesses. The smith's son, a lad of ten, who was his apprentice, had gone to fetch them.

The blacksmith—a red-faced, rotund man wearing a leather apron over his breeches—had just taken down their names. All that was required now for the marriage to be legal and binding was that Nigel and Alice declare their wishes to be joined together in matrimony before witnesses.

The rumble of more coaches approaching turned both their heads. Alice gripped Nigel's arm, and he laid a comforting hand over hers.

"Look here, my man," he said to the smith. "There's a bonus in it for you if we can have this done posthaste."

"Somebody after ya, then?"

"It is a distinct possibility."

"Och! Makes no difference ta me," the man said, taking an antiquated blunderbuss from behind the barrel that would serve as an altar of sorts. "We get that a lot hereabouts."

Alice swallowed a gasp, and Nigel pulled her closer.

"Donnae worry, lassie," the blacksmith said. "I donnae usually have ta use 'er. Fearsome sight, though, in'it?"

"Nigel!" Alice cried, looking over her shoulder at the coaches unloading. "*Father!* It is! Oh, Nigel, John Mapes is with him!"

Just then, the blacksmith's wife and daughter came in through the rear door of the blacksmith shop.

"No time!" the blacksmith said, shoving Nigel and Alice toward them. "Take 'em inside and get 'em inta bed—in case these newcomers'll be wantin' proof. Donnae stand there gawkin', woman—move!"

"Into *bed*?" Alice cried.

"Shhh, lassie!" the blacksmith said. "Just run on and do like the missus says. I've got your names down. Whose ta say the deed ain't done already, eh?"

The two women herded Nigel and Alice into an empty cottage at the rear of the shop that Alice suspected had been erected for just such occasions, and then instructed them to undress and get into bed together. The blacksmith's wife touched a worndown candle on the mantel of the unlit hearth with the one she carried. Then both women sketched a curtsy and disappeared.

The room was steeped in shadow. The candle nub gave off no more light than a firefly.

Nigel tore off his topcoat and waistcoat, tossing them down on the floor. His neckcloth and shirt soon followed. Watching wide-eyed from the corner, Alice felt her throat close over a gasp as his boots and pantaloons joined the rest, for he stood before her naked but for his drawers.

The sound spun him toward her. "This is no time

for modesty!" he said. "Get out of that frock and climb into this bed. Don't you know what's happening?"

In truth, Alice did not. She was almost angry. How could he expect her to know? She hardly had knowledge of such things. He reached her in two strides and spun her around, fumbling with the laces at the back of her bodice.

"The blacksmith is going to tell them that the marriage has already taken place," he explained. "They will demand proof, and when they find us in that bed together . . ."

Alice gasped in earnest now. He spun her around, yanking her frock down. It puddled at her feet, leaving her in her thin underwaist. Her arms flew every which way as she tried to cover all her charms at once.

Voices outside captured their attention.

"Get out of my way, you lout!" her father barked. Heavy footfalls were carrying toward them. The thin planking Nigel and Alice stood upon vibrated.

"She's of age. She donnae need yer consent," the blacksmith crowed. "It's too late, anyway, the deed's done, all right and proper. And unless I miss my guess, the furrow's plowed by now."

"The banns were called between her and *me*!" John Mapes chimed in.

"I donnae know nothin' 'bout that," said the blacksmith. "She's *his* wife now. If it's proof ya want, have a look in here. . . ."

Nigel scooped Alice up in his arms, laid her in

the bed, and jumped in beside her. Fumbling with her underwaist, he spread it wide and crushed her close in his arms with a soft, tremulous moan.

Alice was shaking from cold and fright, yet her bare breasts nestled against his naked torso, and the thick pressure of his arousal forced against her thigh made her shudder with something other than the chill in the air. She was on fire for him.

"Steady now, bear up," he whispered against her lips before he smothered them with his own in a kiss that stole her breath.

All at once the door burst open, and James Jessup charged into the room, his cassock sweeping the straw-strewn floorboards. Both Nigel's head and Alice's snapped toward him, the quilt draped low enough about them to suggest that they were naked beneath. Nigel quickly pulled it close about Alice and gathered her against him.

"Just like I told ya," the blacksmith said. "The furrow's plowed, and the seed's been planted." His blunderbuss gleamed in the glow of the lantern in his hand. He slapped the lantern on a small oak table beside the door and aimed his weapon. "Yer business is done here, gentlemen," he said. "I'd be obliged if you'd leave the lad and lassie here in peace."

"What of me?" John Mapes carped to her father. "What of the settlement ya promised me?"

"Be still, you fool!" James Jessup seethed. He turned hard eyes upon his daughter. "You've made your bed, then, have you?" he said. "Well, enjoy it while you can, because when I am through with him, you'll wish you never clapped eyes upon the jackanapes. I will ruin you, sir!" he said to Nigel. "Then I will have satisfaction. I will see you black-listed, never to hold your head up amongst your precious ton again! I will ruin you, I say, just as you have ruined my daughter!"

Nigel raised himself on one elbow. "I have *married* your daughter, Jessup," he said. "I hardly call that ruin, since I am in a far better position to support her than this person here. Do your worst, but do not presume to imagine that your office outranks mine, sir. You overreach yourself. You shot me—an unarmed man! When I've brought charges against you for that, you'll sing a different tune, minister or no. You heard *him*," he went on, nodding toward the blacksmith, who had taken fresh aim in the heat of the conversation. "The seed is planted. Your daughter could at this very moment be carrying your first grandchild. Attempt to ruin me, and you ruin it as well. You are not fit to wear that cassock, sir. Before I've done with *you*, I shall see you stripped of it!"

There was dead silence. But for the thunder of Alice's heartbeat echoing in her ears, there wasn't a sound. James Jessup stared down at them, red faced, his arms rigid at his sides, hands clenched in white-knuckled fists. He looked about to explode.

"All right, Daughter," he said at last, with a brisk nod. "So be it! You've made your choice. Do not think to come crawling back to me. I wash my hands of you!" Spinning on his heel, he elbowed past the blacksmith and John Mapes, who was still protesting, shoving them both aside with heavy hands as he stalked out of the cottage.

The blacksmith took up his lantern and shouldered the blunderbuss with a wink, hitching up his breeches. "Told ya I scarce have cause ta use 'er," he said. "No need ta disturb yourselves. Soon as they've gone, I'll fetch my lassie and the missus and finish the job."

He left them then, and Nigel took Alice in his arms, brushing her temple with his warm, moist lips. Without a word, he let her go and slid the underwaist back up to cover her nakedness.

"You are exquisite," he murmured, folding her in his arms again. "I'm sorry for this. I had to make it appear that we had consummated the marriage in earnest."

Alice could still hear her father's bluster and John Mapes's carping outside. She made a strangled sound, her heart still hammering against him, and Nigel pulled her closer still.

"Don't be afraid," he whispered. "Here we are, half-naked in this bed together, and I am dressing, not undressing, you." He adjusted the shoulders of her chemisette. "If this is not restraint, I do not know what is. If I have not proved myself by now, I never shall. When he comes back, we speak out vows and wed. What happens then, happens at your pace, my ladylove. You are my countess."

The voices faded after a time, and the sound of carriage wheels rolling over gravel was sweet music to Alice's ears. Minutes later, the blacksmith and his wife and daughter knocked and entered. Alice and

Nigel both sat upright in bed, he still naked to the waist—she bundled in the quilt to her neck, the underwaist notwithstanding.

"Ready, then?" asked the blacksmith.

Nigel turned to Alice. "Are you?" he whispered into her ear.

"Oh, yes," said Alice, realizing at last that her dreams had come true. Her father was gone and the future was theirs. No matter what came next, no matter what they had to face with whatever members of the ton chose to visit them, Nigel was the one man she had always loved, and he was hers. She was ready to be his, a counterfeit lady no longer. "More than ready."

"Then give me your hand, Lady Romney," said Nigel, his glacier blue eyes twinkling with mirth and victory, "and make an honest man of me."

JENNIFER ASHLEY
EMILY BRYAN
ALISSA JOHNSON

Invite you to

A Christmas Ball

It is the most anticipated event of the ton: the annual holiday ball at Hartwell House. The music is elegant, the food exquisite, and the guest list absolutely exclusive. Some come looking for love. Some will do almost anything to avoid it. But everyone wants to be there. No matter what their desires, amid the swirling gowns and soft glow of candlelight, magic tends to happen. And one dance, one kiss, one night can shape a new destiny....

ISBN 13: 978-0-8439-6250-5

INTERACT WITH DORCHESTER ONLINE!

Want to learn more about your favorite
books and authors?
Want to talk with other readers that like
to read the same books as you?
Want to see up-to-the-minute Dorchester
news?

VISIT DORCHESTER AT:
DorchesterPub.com
Twitter.com/DorchesterPub
Facebook.com (Search Pages)

DISCUSS DORCHESTER'S NOVELS AT:
Dorchester Forums at DorchesterPub.com
GoodReads.com
LibraryThing.com
Myspace.com/books
Shelfari.com
WeRead.com

☐ YES!

Sign me up for the Historical Romance Book Club and send my FREE BOOKS! If I choose to stay in the club, I will pay only $8.50* each month, a savings of $6.48!

NAME: <u>MARION COUNTY PUBLIC LIBRARY</u>

ADDRESS: <u>321 MONROE STREET</u>

TELEPHONE: <u>FAIRMONT, WV 26554</u>

EMAIL: _____

☐ I want to pay by credit card.

☐   ☐ MasterCard.   ☐ DISCOVER

ACCOUNT #: _____

EXPIRATION DATE: _____

SIGNATURE: _____

Mail this page along with $2.00 shipping and handling to:
Historical Romance Book Club
PO Box 6640
Wayne, PA 19087
Or fax (must include credit card information) to:
610-995-9274
You can also sign up online at **www.dorchesterpub.com**.
*Plus $2.00 for shipping. Offer open to residents of the U.S. and Canada only.
Canadian residents please call 1-800-481-9191 for pricing information.
If under 18, a parent or guardian must sign. Terms, prices and conditions subject to change. Subscription subject to acceptance. Dorchester Publishing reserves the right to reject any order or cancel any subscription.